Arbeenok of the Nunwood

"You say the plague was no accident. Who would knowingly release such devastation?" Arbeenok asked as Vambran turned and began to lead the two of them through the streets of Reth once more. "Why?"

Vambran took a deep breath to steady himself before replying, "Cruel, cruel men, full of ambition and without a shred of compassion within them. Men who would profit from death."

"Such men do not deserve to live," Arbeenok said, the most savage, vehement words Vambran had heard the alaghi utter since he had met the druid.

"Then let's get my armor and weapons," Vambran said just as savagely. "And let's go kill them."

From the deep woods,

to the mean streets,

for the sake of a thousand lives.

Can he save even one?

THE SCIONS of ARRABAR TRILOGY

...

Also by Thomas M. Reid
R.A. SALVATORE'S WAR OF THE SPIDER QUEEN, BOOK II
INSURRECTION

GREYHAWK®
THE TEMPLE OF ELEMENTAL EVIL

STAR*DRIVE®
GRIDRUNNER

THE EMERALD SCEPTER

THE SCIONS of ARRABAR TRILOGY · BOOK III

THOMAS M. REID

Author of *Insurrection*

THE EMERALD SCEPTER

The Scions of Arrabar Trilogy, Book III

©2005 Wizards of the Coast, Inc.

Distributed in the United States by Holtzbrinck Publishing. Distributed in Canada by Fenn Ltd.

Distributed to the hobby, toy, and comic trade in the United States and Canada by regional distributors.

Distributed worldwide by Wizards of the Coast, Inc. and regional distributors.

Cover art by Duane O. Myers
Map by Dennis Kauth
First Printing: August 2005
Library of Congress Catalog Card Number: 2004116930

9 8 7 6 5 4 3 2 1

ISBN-10: 0-7869-3754-8
ISBN-13: 978-0-7869-3754-7
620-96704000-001-EN

U.S., CANADA,
ASIA, PACIFIC, & LATIN AMERICA
Wizards of the Coast, Inc.
P.O. Box 707
Renton, WA 98057-0707
+1-800-324-6496

EUROPEAN HEADQUARTERS
Hasbro UK Ltd
Caswell Way
Newport, Gwent NP9 0YH
GREAT BRITAIN
Save this address for your records.

Visit our web site at **www.wizards.com**

Dedicated to all in the world
touched by the tragedy of the
December 2004 tsunami.

May peace be with you.

PROLOGUE

P lague! It's the plague!"
Those four little words, shouted by
someone running along Tower Street,
made Mardicon Flintelli's heart skip a beat,
made his stomach knot up in momentary
terror.

The plague.

The glassblower turned from his furnace
just as a woman examining some of his new
potion bottles let out a startled gasp and
scurried away, knocking a vase to the floor
to shatter in her wake. She didn't bother to
turn around. Grumbling, Mardicon set his
pipe with its half-finished blob of molten
glass back into the furnace and, picking
his way past the fragments of ruined vase,
stepped out from under his awning and

into the street. In the fading light of dusk, other
merchants on Tower Street were standing in their
own shop doorways, peering about uncertainly.
Mardicon shook his head as he looked up and down
the avenue.

The plague! It couldn't be.

He wondered who would make such a horrific
claim, dredging up childhood fears out of some bed-
time story. But people were running, most of them
away from the center of Reth. Some were alone,
while others held children close to them, or baskets
of goods, or both. Genuine fear flashed in their eyes.
This wasn't just a tasteless jest, the glassblower
realized.

A pair of soldiers, watchmen of Reth, scurried the
opposite direction, toward the source of the commotion. From the way they moved, Mardicon could see
that they were loath to fulfill their duties in the face
of such a terrifying threat.

Controlling his own panic, the glassblower ducked
his head inside his shop, calling for his son. "Luti, go
find your mother," Mardicon told the boy, who had
been busy removing some new goblets from their
molds. "She's at the market buying tinctures. Both of
you hurry back here. Go!" After the boy nodded and
ran out the door, Mardicon gave a quick glance at the
mess the startled woman had made, and at the other
glassware on display under the awning.

No time, he decided, grabbing a burning switch
from his furnace and scurrying inside, leaving his
goods unwatched.

First the man lit a pair of lanterns hanging on
hooks in the walls. Once he could see better, he took
two of his wife's woven baskets and dumped the
dirty clothing from them into a corner. He tossed

some belongings inside, starting with a sack of silver coins, two loaves of bread, a spare tunic, and a bundle of salted fish. He peered about his shop, wondering what else to include.

Ought to be prepared to get out of the city, the man thought. Plague or no plague, something's spooking those people.

Another shout erupted from the street, and when Mardicon turned to look, the two soldiers he had spotted before were running past his doorway again, in the opposite direction. One of them stumbled against one of the posts of his awning, dislodging it. The base of the post kicked out, striking a rack of delicate cups and sending the whole thing crashing to the cobblestones. The fabric of the awning fluttered down, blocking the glassblower's view.

"By Gond!" Mardicon swore, angry at the guard's clumsiness and frightened that something would scare a trained soldier so. He stalked over to the doorway and yanked the ruined awning aside.

Several more folk scrambled past. In their haste and panic, some pushed and shoved those slower than themselves out of the way. A child, a girl of only three or four, was knocked to the ground, teary-eyed. The offender was a tall, lanky merchant from the south, most likely Halruaa, dressed in fine lavender silk, with several rings glittering on his fingers.

"You wretch!" The child's mother yelled at the man as she paused to scoop the little girl up, spilling a bundle of grapes to the street as she did so. She didn't bother to stop and gather the fruit, instead she rushed onward, trying to hold both the girl and their belongings.

The man never broke stride to respond.

Mardicon turned his gaze back in the direction

the people had come from. More were fleeing, though a handful, mostly youthful boys who liked to make trouble in the neighborhood, had begun throwing rocks and other objects at something just out of sight around the bend. Beyond them, along the turn, the walls of the dwellings and storefronts reflected the flickering orange glow of firelight.

There was a fire at the end of Tower Street.

Shadows bounced off those same walls, cast by figures standing in the lane, the targets of the boys' impromptu missiles. As the glassblower watched, the shadows shrank little by little but grew sharper, more distinct. Whatever was casting them was coming closer, moving slowly but steadily.

In the distance, an alarm began to sound, the city-wide signal that Reth was under attack.

"Damn it, Luti," Mardicon muttered under his breath, "quicken your pace, fool boy."

Across the street, a rural laborer and his dog came running out of the building, looking bewildered. As another man tried to run past, Mardicon saw the laborer reach out and grab the fellow by the arm.

"What is it?" the laborer asked as he jerked the fleeing man to a stop. "What's wrong?"

The man yanked his arm free, and even in the growing darkness, Mardicon could see that he was wide-eyed with terror. He shook his head and turned to run again, shouting back over his shoulder, "The plague! The Rotting Plague has returned!"

The glassblower nearly choked when he heard those words. It was the nightmare made real. Must get out of the city! he thought. Got to find Luti and Lyzara and go now!

In his panic, Mardicon didn't know what to do first. Then his attention was drawn to the far side of the avenue. The dog suddenly changed, shifting in form from hound to ... something else. The glassblower had never seen a creature like it before, and for a moment, he could only stare. It was upright like a man, and thick-limbed. Though it was covered in fur from head to toe, it seemed somewhat civilized, dressed in crude clothing and carrying weapons. Still, there was a ferocious, bestial quality to it, something that unnerved Mardicon.

The laborer and the man-beast conversed for a moment, their voices too low for the glassblower to make out, then they dashed off toward the trouble.

At the end of the street, the young toughs had stopped throwing things and were scattering, vanishing into alleys. One lad of about fourteen summers went sprinting past, giving only a cursory glance at the strange creature walking with the laborer as he passed. In his haste to get away, the boy nearly collided with a soldier coming the other direction. The guard, part of a squadron marching in formation, nudged him none too gently to the side with his shield. The sergeant of the unit yelled out, "Make way! Stand to the side, you fools, and let us through!"

Mardicon watched in frozen fear as the soldiers stopped before the building across the street. Several fanned out, positioning themselves so as to protect the entrance, while several more, led by the sergeant, went inside. Two of the guardsmen remaining on the street were the pair Mardicon had seen twice before. Their eyes were wide with terror, and they clutched at their short swords with white knuckles, hunched down behind their shields. The sight made the glassblower shudder.

Lyzara, damn you, come on, the glassblower thought, cursing his wife's name for her slowness.

He started to run back inside one last time, to
grab up the two baskets he had packed, when the
watchmen who had gone inside reappeared, hauling
some large pieces of furniture. They had a bench and
several chairs and they began to stack them in the
middle of the street. Another guard emerged, rolling
a barrel, which he positioned next to the other goods.
They were building a barricade.

"You there," the sergeant called, looking at
Mardicon. "Come help us. We need wood, things that
will burn." Mardicon shook his head, too frightened to think straight. "Now, citizen!" the sergeant
ordered. "We have to stop them from spreading!"

Stop what? Mardicon wondered.

"Sir?" one of the soldiers standing watch in front of
the entrance said, his voice tremulous as he pointed
down the street. The sergeant stopped glaring at the
glassblower and glanced in the direction the watchman indicated.

Mardicon couldn't help but look. He saw a limping, shuffling figure at the end of the street. It was
a man, though Mardicon could not judge much else
about him because he was silhouetted against the
flickering of the brightening fire. His gait was awkward, unnatural.

At a gruff order from the sergeant, two of the
soldiers arrayed themselves in the middle of the
lane to confront the fellow, pulling crossbows off
their backs and cocking the weapons. The rest of
the watchmen resumed their construction efforts,
hurrying to get some sort of barrier spanning the
entire width of the lane. Many gaps still yawned in
the hasty construction.

Two more figures appeared from around the
bend, one a woman in a peasant dress and the other

armed like a guardsman. Each was moving slowly, with no spring in their steps at all. The two soldiers sighted down their weapons and fired at the lead figure.

"By Gond," the glassblower mumbled, rooted to the spot, watching in horrified disbelief. They're just killing them right there in the street! No warning? No attempt to heal them?

The first strikes didn't slow the shuffling man even slightly. As the two soldiers struggled to reload, he continued to advance on them, bolts protruding from his chest.

Horrible realization flooded Mardicon's mind.

The walking dead.

The soldiers, realizing they would not be able to fire again in time, retreated, turning and running toward the rest of their companions, who still rushed to finish building the blockade. The sergeant held a torch and screamed at his soldiers to hurry. Two of his men splashed the contents of the barrel onto the partially finished barricade.

They would not complete it fast enough.

The first zombies reached the barrier and began pushing through it, clambering through the gaps. The other two undead lumbered close behind.

Out of time, the sergeant put torch to tinder and the barricade blazed into a conflagration, immolating the first walking corpse. The whole street instantly glowed orange and the heat that blasted Mardicon's face was almost as hot as his own furnace. The lead undead kept trying to move forward, heedless of the licking flames, though it staggered and fell to one knee. The sergeant ordered his men to fire at will, and the watchmen began to pincushion it with their bolts. Finally it collapsed, but the gap was large enough that the next two creatures could get past the flames and at the watchmen.

Far up the lane, half a dozen more zombies moved down the street toward the soldiers' defensive position.

"Gods preserve us," the glassblower breathed, turning to run, his traveling bundle forgotten.

CHAPTER 1

12 Mirtul, 1373 DR

The holy coin, perhaps the most enduring symbol of Vambran Matrell's unwavering faith, tumbled free of his hand. It dropped against his chest, hanging limply from the leather cord around the mercenary's neck. His intention to call upon that faith, to drive back the advancing zombie visible before him, was forgotten. The lieutenant nearly stumbled and fell as he quavered, stunned by the scene illuminated in the flickering light of several burning fires.

It can't be.

"Uncle Kovrim?" Vambran called, his voice soft. He was almost pleading. His mind refused to accept that the man who had been his family, his mentor, had been reduced to a shuffling undead thing, a mere husk of its former self. But the evidence came on, closer, damning proof that Kovrim Lazelle was no longer a man. "No," Vambran mumbled, feeling devastation wash over him. "No!" he shouted, dropping to one knee, the strength gone from his legs.

The zombie advanced, its gait unnatural, closing the distance between them.

"Vambran, beware!" Arbeenok called from behind the lieutenant. The alaghi's deep voice resonated down the alley, snapping Vambran from his horrified abeyance.

The mercenary officer shuddered, finally tearing his gaze away from the lifeless orbs that had once been his uncle's kind, smiling eyes. He risked a quick glance back at the strange creature who had accompanied him from the Nunwood to Reth earlier that day. The face and upper torso of the druid, something of a cross between a man and an ape, glowed in the light of a small flame held in the palm of his outstretched hand, a magical conjuration. Though outfitted in rough, natural clothing and a hooded cloak, the alaghi's furred arms were thick and muscular, and its expressive face wore a worried frown.

Arbeenok advanced, wary, motioning with his other hand for Vambran to shift to the side.

Vambran turned back to the thing that had once been his uncle, understanding Arbeenok's intentions but unwilling to surrender hope, unable to step aside and allow the alaghi to do what needed to be done. No, he pleaded. Not this. Not Uncle Kovrim.

"Vambran! Back away!" Arbeenok insisted. "It is almost upon you!"

Squeezing his eyes shut as tears began to well up in them, Vambran gave in to the inevitable and dived to the side with a single howl of anguish. He felt cold despair wash through the depths of his gut as he landed on his hands and knees, out of the druid's line of sight and away from the outstretched hands of the shuffling, mottled zombie.

Vambran could only watch as the druid flung the ball of flame, striking the zombie squarely in the chest. The burst from the hit spread across the thing's torso in a matter of seconds, engulfing Uncle Kovrim's remains in an orange blaze. The zombie faltered and twitched, spinning about in apparent confusion as the fire spread, immolating clothing and hair.

The sickening smell of disease and scorched flesh wafted over Vambran, who turned away from the sight of the burning undead form, panting.

Waukeen, I'm sorry! Vambran thought, crawling away from the alley. He turned and slumped to the cobblestones, his back to a wall. I was too slow! I should have been here! I couldn't reach you in time! If only I had—

Arbeenok advanced into the alley, out of sight, leaving the lieutenant in the near-darkness of twilight. Around the corner, Vambran could hear the soft roar of numerous small fiery missiles arcing through the air and colliding with targets. Nothing screamed or cried out in pain. The only victims of the druid's magic were already dead, though they still walked.

The lieutenant drew his knees up to himself and hugged them, silently begging forgiveness from his uncle's spirit for failing the man. For failing all of the members of the Sapphire Crescents.

I should have been here sooner. I'm so sorry.

As his grief washed over him, Vambran dropped his face to his knees and let the torrent of emotion

course through him. He remembered his uncle's
visage, the last time he had seen the man, in the dim
light of a single lantern aboard *Lady's Favor* only
a day previous. To Vambran, it felt like a hundred
days, a thousand. So much had happened since that
last moment together, right before the corsairs had
attacked them. Corsairs, and a kraken, and soldiers
of the Silver Ravens. The list of woes, of troubles,
tumbled through Vambran's mind, reminding him
of each and every obstacle he had endured, had attempted to overcome, to try to reunite his command.
The realization burned the sorrow away and replaced
it with anger.

Lavant.

The name, the face of the fat priest, burned in
the lieutenant's consciousness, searing itself in his
mind's eye.

Vambran rose to his feet then, his back scraping
against the stones of the wall, his fury giving him
the strength to ignore the pain. As he attained his
full six feet, three inches of height, the mercenary
tightened his jaw in determination.

I will see you dead, he vowed to that image. You
will feel the bite of steel in your gut! he swore at
Lavant's leering face, reaching for his sword.

The blade wasn't there.

As Vambran stared down at his hip, remembering
that he was still dressed as a common laborer and not
a mercenary officer, a voice began to whisper in his
head, flooding his thoughts.

Vambran Matrell?

Stunned, unsure he should trust his own senses,
Vambran did not answer.

You do not know me, but I am a friend, the voice
continued. *My name is Schuynir Droloti, employed*

*by House Darrowdryn and charged by Lady Ariskrit
to find and contact you. I am scrying you right now.
Though you cannot see me, I can see you. Your sister
Emriana came to us earlier this evening. Lady Ariskrit wanted you to know that Emriana is safe. You
can answer by whispering back, if you are able.*

"Em?" Vambran replied, his gaze turning upward
to the night sky, trying to discern some sign of the
magical connection. The effort was futile. "She is
with you?"

*No, she and the rest of the Darrowdryns have left
for the Generon, to attend Sammardach tonight. But
she was here earlier.*

"How do I know you speak the truth?" the lieutenant asked. "I have many enemies and few allies
these days."

There was a pause then, *Emriana said you might
not trust us. She said to tell you that you're being a
. . . a meazel-face, and to stop it,* the voice concluded,
projecting a mild sense of embarrassment.

Vambran nearly laughed in relief. Then he remembered where Emriana was headed. "It's not safe for
her at the Generon!" he said, nearly shouting. "She
must stay away!"

They have already departed, the voice replied,
*but I will try to send a message forward. Is there
anything else?*

"I have sent others to aid her, also," Vambran said.
"Soldiers from my company. She knows them—Adyan,
Horial, and Grolo the dwarf, among others. I don't
know when they will arrive, but tell her to let them
protect her."

When she returns I will pass along the message.

"And the plague," Vambran added, "You must get
the word out that the magical plague has returned.

Reth is in danger." Then Vambran's throat grew thick. "Tell Em that Uncle Kovrim died."

There was another pause. *The plague? Are you sure?*

Vambran only nodded, his head bowed. "Yes," he said. "Tell her I'm sorry." There was no answer, and Vambran could sense that Schuynir Droloti's magical scrying had come to an end.

Tell them all I'm so sorry, Vambran thought, wondering if his family would find it in their hearts to forgive him for letting Kovrim die.

Arbeenok appeared from the alley, his stride rapid. "More come," the druid said, no longer holding the flickering flame in his hand. "Too many to keep at bay," he added, giving Vambran a pointed look. Arbeenok's body was silhouetted from behind by dim, flickering light in the alley. Upon seeing Vambran's countenance in that weird light, the alaghi paused. "You knew him," Arbeenok said, sympathy in his tone. "I am sorry."

Vambran nodded, swallowing. His throat felt thick. "My uncle," he replied, his voice wavering a bit. "I didn't get here in time. I should have—" he swallowed again, unable to finish the thought. He turned and glanced back down the alley and spied the still-smoldering remains of the zombie. Several other shambling undead also lay strewn about, burning, but numerous more still approached, shuffling aberrantly in their direction. Still more struggled out of the open sewer beyond.

"Your uncle, all of your companions, would have been proud of your effort," Arbeenok said, grabbing Vambran's arm and pulling him away from the grisly scene. The druid broke into a trot, veering away from the approaching menace. "You never stopped trying, for even a moment. That is all anyone can ask of another." Together, they hurried away from the alley, back down the street in the direction they had first come. "Grieve for your uncle, but do not lose sight of the present dangers. Others still need us. Perhaps, even, your other companions."

"But I failed!" the lieutenant lamented, even as he matched the alaghi's pace, uncaring where they were going. No other people ventured down the avenue. Those who had not already fled had succumbed to the undead horrors walking the streets of Reth. The air was thick with the smell of smoke, though, and Vambran could see the glow of several fires within the neighborhood, perhaps only a street or two over. The incessant clanging of the alarms still rang, unnerving him. "My men counted on me as their leader, and I led them only to death," he said. Then the anger welled up again. "Not even death," he spat. "To die in battle would have been one thing, but undeath . . . that's—" his voice was a whisper by then, and again he couldn't finish the thought.

"It is a blight upon all that lives," Arbeenok finished for the mercenary, "and we must find a way to stop it. Remember that, above all else. For the sake of your uncle, remember everyone else's needs."

The pair turned a corner, destined for Elenthia's home, the woman whom Vambran had come to see upon arriving in the city. As the daughter of one of the seven senators of Reth, he had hoped to meet with her father, find some news on the whereabouts of his men and his uncle. After what he had learned, the visit no longer mattered.

Vambran shuddered once at the image of Uncle Kovrim's bloated, discolored face with its dead, milky-white eyes. Then he shook his head, banishing the

horrible visage and refocusing his thoughts on the
present. "The plague," he breathed, realizing with
horror what he and the druid were up against. "How
can it be? And with everything else that has already
transpired? Does Tymora hate me so that she would
turn my luck so foul for so long? Did I offend her in
some way?" He swallowed hard, feeling despair begin
to overwhelm him once more. "And how could it have
spread so quickly? How could it have gotten to the
Crescents? They only arrived—"

Vambran skidded to a stop on the cobblestoned
street, realization overtaking him. "Not bad luck at
all," he said to no one in particular. "This plague was
no coincidence."

Arbeenok stopped and faced the lieutenant. "I do
not understand," the druid said, his frown deep and
troubled. "What do you see?"

Vambran gave the alaghi a meaningful stare.
"Doesn't it strike you as a bit odd that my men were
brought here on the very same day a plague breaks
out? And that my uncle was apparently one of the
very first to be infected? Once my company and I
left Arrabar, it seemed as though someone had been
trying to kill us. All of us."

As the sequence of thoughts flashed through
Vambran's mind, he felt fury grow all over again.
"The corsairs and the kraken had but one purpose—to
sink our ship and drown us all. And when the Silver
Ravens found us so easily on the beach, I thought
they were a part of it, too, sent to run us down to
a man. But then they simply took prisoners, and it
didn't make sense. Now it does." Vambran realized he
was clenching his fists, digging his nails hard into
his palms. He forced his hands open again. "Now it
does."

"What are you saying?"

"The plague is no accident," Vambran explained, turning and taking Arbeenok by the alaghi's stout shoulders, needing the druid to understand. "Someone wants it here, wants it to spread. And whoever is behind it is working with those same murderous bastards who have been trying to kill me and my men. That's why the Silver Ravens brought them here."

"To spread the plague?"

"Perhaps," Vambran replied. "But definitely to die from it."

"You say it was no accident. Who would knowingly release such devastation?" Arbeenok asked as Vambran turned and began to lead the two of them through the streets of Reth once more. "Why?"

Vambran took a deep breath to steady himself before replying. "Cruel, cruel men, full of ambition and without a shred of compassion within them. Men who would profit from death."

"Such men do not deserve to live," Arbeenok said. Those were the most savage, vehement words Vambran had heard the alaghi utter since he had met the druid.

"Then let's get my armor and weapons," Vambran said just as savagely, "and let's go kill them."

As the two companions turned the final corner before reaching Elenthia's abode, they pulled up short. A great battle raged in the street before the building where she lived. Flames licked out of the windows of the lower story. In the glowing light of the spreading fire, Vambran could see that soldiers battled zombies, and the zombies were winning.

...

Pilos watched, horrified, as Emriana vanished before his eyes. Only a moment before, she had been standing there, watching her dagger sail across the room and into deeper shadows. An instant later, there was a rustle of cloth, a flash of new torchlight from within those shadows, and she was gone. The Abree-ant priest felt a cold sensation grow in his belly as the brash girl simply disappeared, leaving all her clothes and jewelry to form her missing shape for the briefest of heartbeats before crumpling to the floor with a bell-like tinkle of filigreed metal.

From the shadows, a male voice chuckled. "Too easy," he said, and Pilos had to fight the urge to shudder, for he was certain that voice belonged to Junce Roundface, the assassin he and Emriana had followed into the room.

Pilos shrank back, trying to settle into deeper shadows of his own, hoping against hope that Junce had not spotted him. The scroll in his hand, which contained a spell he had intended to use to subdue any guards, was all but forgotten for the moment.

"Don't be shy," Junce said, his voice full of merry cheer. He stepped into better light, looking right at Pilos. "Come out where I can see you." It was indeed the same man, as evidenced by his black doublet and matching trousers, which were tucked into stout boots that flared just below his knees. The man held Emriana's dagger in one hand, and he was smiling, but the intensity of his steel-blue eyes showed no mirth.

Seeing no reason to continue his failed attempt to hide, Pilos took a single, tentative step out into the open. He subtly slipped his free hand into the pocket of his own crimson doublet, fishing for a potion he knew to be there. "What did you do to her?" Pilos demanded, fear giving him false bravado. "Where is Emriana?" The thought of her simply ceasing to exist terrified him.

The assassin laughed. "She's perfectly safe. Come over here and see," he suggested, gesturing with the dagger back toward the spot where Emriana had been standing. "And I'd suggest you quit reaching for whatever you've got in your pocket there," the assassin added, giving the young priest a rather intense look.

Pilos froze, his hand half inside the doublet. "Thank you, no. I think I'll stay well clear of your tricks."

Junce shrugged, glancing away as if disappointed. Or exasperated, Pilos realized, just as the assassin cocked his arm and flung the dagger forward. The blade came hurtling toward the priest, the aim true.

For the rest of his days, Pilos would offer thanks to Tymora for the sudden urge to lunge for cover, even before he saw the impending attack begin. He spun and darted toward a large wooden table just as Junce sent the dagger flying toward him. It was the same table where Xaphira Matrell's belongings had been haphazardly scattered, but Pilos only sought it for its shelter. He crashed to the hard floor of the prison with a grunt just as the spinning blade clattered against the stone wall where he had been standing. The priest struggled to his knees as Junce swore an oath from beyond view.

"You little whelp," the man said, his voice growing louder as he seemed to move closer.

In a panic, Pilos considered his options. Terror made him want to flee, to swallow the potion that would transform him into mere mist and allow him to escape, but he could not abandon Emriana so easily. He had to find a way to stop the assassin and rescue his companion.

The priest realized he still clutched a scroll. Without hesitation, he began to utter the prayer that had been so carefully inscribed upon the parchment, knowing he had only one chance. "The Five Observances of Frugal Spending have many subparts, all of which must be memorized by anyone wishing to gain admittance into the temple clergy," he began in a loud, clear voice, hoping the enchantment was sufficient to enthrall Junce and stop him from attacking. "I will now recite each one, in order, including the various historical footnotes, for completeness's sake," the Abreeant continued, knowing it didn't matter of what he spoke, only that he preach unabated.

As he continued to quote the first-year lessons by rote, Pilos listened for the imminent approach of the assassin, certain that his magic was not powerful enough to stop the man. But he heard no footsteps. Almost not daring to believe, the priest risked a glance over the top of the table and spied Junce merely standing, listening to his words. Amazed, Pilos nearly faltered in his recitations, but he caught himself before the enchantment could dissipate and rose to his feet, still orating.

Cautiously, Pilos walked around the table, observing Junce. He approached the assassin, ready to spring away at the slightest hint of aggression, trying to determine if it was a trick. But Junce's rapture seemed genuine.

Breaking into a slight smile in his relief, the priest skirted past his adversary, toward Emriana's last location, continuing to proselytize. He spied her clothing tumbled into a pile but did not approach it.

He angled in from the side, peering into the shadows, looking for signs of danger. He saw a mirror, large and square, propped against the wall of the cell where Junce had been hiding. From his vantage point, the priest could not see himself in the glass. It was angled to face Emriana's last position.

With mental alarms ringing, Pilos backed away, careful not to look at the glass. He turned back to Junce, who had spun to watch him, though the assassin still stood rooted to the same spot since Pilos had begun his spell. Feeling his mouth going dry, Pilos wished for a cool drink of water, but he ignored his craving and continued orating, lecturing in detail about the meaning behind each of the enormous and elaborate stained-glass windows in the great hall of the Temple of Waukeen. He hoped his voice would hold out long enough.

I need something large and heavy, the Abreeant decided. *Something to shatter that mirror.*

He scanned the room for something—anything— that would suit his purposes, but everything was either firmly anchored to the floor or walls or was much too large. Somewhere in the middle of his description of the third of twenty windows, he remembered the dagger.

Feeling his tongue growing thick and dry, Pilos hurried to where the dagger lay, intending to scoop it up and hurl it at the mirror, hoping that it would be enough to free Emriana. He considered plunging the weapon into Junce's chest, but he feared that he would not deliver a killing blow before the act ruined the spell, and he didn't want to risk such a chance.

No, he insisted. *You've got your plan. Go with it.*

He bent down to pick up the dagger and at that instant noticed the figures standing in the doorway, not three paces from him. In his shock, he nearly yelped in surprise, barely managing to continue his discourse. None of the three men were Generon guards, unalike in every way.

The first was a short, sinewy fellow with long, stringy hair, while the second was large and burly and wore a full beard. Both were filthy. The third was much cleaner, with brown curly hair, and skin weathered as though he had spent many days in the sun. While the first two glared at the priest, the third appeared more pensive than angry.

For a moment, Pilos trembled, expecting the trio to jump at him as soon as they realized he was aware of their presence. None of the three advanced into the chamber, though, instead content to stand in the doorway and listen to the priest's rambling. It took the young Abreeant a moment to remember that his divine magic would affect newcomers as easily as his initial victim. Shaking with relief, he gathered his wits, refocusing his concentration on his spell and trying to steady his breathing. He reached down for the dagger once more.

"That's not going to do you much good," a feminine voice said from the corridor.

As Pilos jerked upright once more, he saw a flash of movement, then three glowing points of light swarmed through a gap between the three men, darting directly toward him. He recognized the dangerous magic, but no lucky evasion could save him a second time. The three glowing points smacked into his chest in rapid succession, sending jolts of fiery pain through his entire body.

Gasping in anguish, Pilos tumbled to the floor, doubled over in abject agony. As he writhed about, trying to soothe the molten wounds he sported across his torso, a shadow darkened above him. When the priest looked up, Junce Roundface was glaring. Pilos's spell was broken and the assassin looked furious. Pilos flinched and tried to roll away, but one quick punch to his midsection took his breath away.

It was all too easy for the newcomers to subdue the Waukeenar. In moments, Pilos sat against a wall, sullen, with his arms and legs locked tightly in shackles taken from the supplies within the prison. The two grubby men had done the heavy work, the big one sitting on him while the other snapped the restraints in place. The female arrival, with short blond hair and a scantily-cut magenta and purple outfit, shoved a wad of sour cloth into his mouth and tied it in place with a strip of fabric that kept him from speaking. He reckoned her for the wizard from Emriana's story earlier that day, which meant the others—or at least two of them—were the thugs aiding her.

I guess she didn't like my speech so much, the priest lamented.

As the trio finished their work binding the prisoner, the other man, the pensive one with the brown curly hair, argued with Junce.

"You said it wouldn't be much longer," the fellow pleaded. "Once their House was wiped out, you said I could see her, take her away. How much longer is this going to take?"

"As long as it takes," Junce snapped, glaring at Pilos. "Now I've got *this* one to contend with, too," he added, pointing at his prisoner. "There's no telling what his family is likely to do. And Vambran is still out there, and he may come hunting for them. Until I know he's dead, it's not over."

"Look," the man continued, "I'll take her far away.

North to Cormyr, or south, to the coast. Somewhere that she won't be a problem for you. But let me take her now. Please."

"I said no!" Junce spat. "Now stop asking." He turned to paw through Emriana's personal belongings, which he had gathered onto the table next to Xaphira's, ignoring the man and signaling that the discussion was at an end.

But the man wouldn't accept such an answer and crossed the distance between them, grabbing at Junce's shoulder, spinning the assassin around. "That's not what we agreed on," he said, his voice insistent. Junce's glare was ice, but the other man didn't back down. "I willingly worked with you, remember? I came to you when I found out Xaphira was trying to sniff you out. I gave her to you, on the condition that I would get her back, unharmed, when you got what you wanted. I held up my end of the bargain, now you—"

The man, whom Pilos just then recognized from Emriana's description to be Xaphira's old companion Quill, crumpled in a heap as the larger of the two thugs smacked him hard in the back of the head with a sap. As Quill sagged into unconsciousness, Junce sighed.

"Thank you, Borth. His whining was detestable, wasn't it?" the assassin said, clapping the large man on the shoulder. "I've really heard enough out of him," Junce finished. He turned back to rummaging through Emriana's belongings, but then he stopped again, turning back to the wizard and her two grimy companions.

"I almost forgot to ask," he said, looking amused. "What are you three doing down here, anyway?"

The woman laughed, her voice clear and rather

pleasant. "With all of this nonsense going on," and she gestured casually toward Pilos, "I almost forgot, too. Lavant wants to see you," she explained, rolling her eyes. " 'Immediately,' " she intoned, trying to sound like the fat priest.

Despite the gag shoved in his mouth, Pilos gasped, drawing a curious stare from everyone except Junce, who sighed in exasperation.

"You know," the assassin said, clearly disgruntled, "if you keep talking about things where our enemies can hear us, they'll know too much."

The woman smirked. "Who, him?" she replied, gesturing toward Pilos. "What's he going to do about it?"

"Nothing," Junce answered, turning to depart from the chamber. "Because you're going to take care of him for me." He paused and glanced down at the still form of Quill. "Both of them. And get it right this time," he finished, jabbing a finger in the air toward the woman. "No more mistakes."

"Whatever you say," the woman replied. "Lak, Borth—I guess we're making another trip down to the docks tonight."

CHAPTER 2

I sn't that the ridiculous little House mage that Talricci employs?" Lobra Mestel asked, her mouth full of pastry. Falagh glanced in the direction his wife was pointing. The figure she indicated was scurrying through a doorway on the far side of the chamber, but even through the crowd of dancing guests, the spectacles, graying head of hair, and frumpy robes were unmistakable. It was Bartimus.

"What in the Nine Hells is *he* doing here?" the man wondered aloud.

"It's Sammardach at the Generon," Lobra said, her mouth filled with food, dismissing the wizard with a wave. "Everyone who is anyone in Arrabar is here. I'm sure he's toadying with Talricci."

"Yes, but Talricci is still a wanted man," Falagh replied, frowning and absently stroking his black moustache. "I would have thought he was smarter than to show his face in this crowd."

Lobra shrugged and reached out to snatch up another miniature custard pastry from the table before her, which stretched from one end of the great chamber to the other and was filled with all manner of sweet confections. The couple had covered perhaps a third of the table's length, but already Lobra's flimsy paper cone was filled to overflowing.

"I do hope you're not planning to consume all of that yourself," Falagh commented, eyeing the cone of sweets. "You'll be pacing the bedroom for half the night clutching your bowels if you do." At his sour tone, Lobra's eyes grew wide with hurt, and Falagh knew a few tears were imminent.

Exasperated, the man attempted to smooth his features and give the woman an apologetic smile. "I'm sorry, my dear," he said, patting her arm and trying to sound more pleasant. "I did not mean to snap at you. Sammardach only comes once a year. You should enjoy yourself," he added. He was relieved to see Lobra sniff once and regain her composure. "I'm going to go see what he's up to," Falagh said once he was certain his wife would not make a scene. He turned and strode across the large room before she could protest. He was only mildly surprised when she fell into step beside him.

Falagh dared not hurry, for if he appeared distraught or on edge, tongues would begin to wag. In a matter of minutes, everyone at the Generon would presume something of interest had upset the man, and it would affect business for tendays to come. Rivals would attempt to learn what had so disturbed the Mestels, hoping to use the information against him in negotiations. Even if they learned nothing, they would bluff that they had inside knowledge, and transactions would inevitably take a downward turn, all based on the hint of a rumor. No, it would not do at all to seem anything other than at ease, enjoying the celebration of Sammardach.

It did not take long to spot Bartimus, who wandered through the various public halls of the Generon, his head swiveling back and forth, looking for someone. The wizard was perhaps forty paces ahead, passing through the crowds, unaware of his own social disgraces. More than a few scowls turned his way after he jostled elbows and caused drinks to slosh, but he never noticed.

Falagh groaned as the wizard spotted his quarry and made a direct line for the man. Grand Syndar Lavant was standing near a wall, engaged in polite conversation with the Lord of Arrabar himself, Eles Wianar. A small crowd had gathered, perhaps to congratulate Lavant on his appointment as Grand Syndar of the entire Temple of Waukeen, or just to bask in the presence of either the Grand Syndar or the Lord of Arrabar. Grozier Talricci stood next to the high priest, making a point of showing his close association with Lavant, while his sister, Marga Matrell, stood off to one side, looking disinterested in the maneuverings. Bartimus headed for the tall, graying man.

Why is he here? Falagh wondered in dismay, pulling up short and pretending to retrieve a pair of delicate crystal goblets of spiced wine. With House Talricci in disfavor, why would he risk arrest to-night of all nights? He casually watched the group as he handed one of the goblets to Lobra, who sipped at it while continuing to nibble at her snacks.

Heedless of the others gathered around the pair of luminaries, Bartimus shoved his way to the front of the crowd and approached closely enough to whisper something in Grozier's ear. When the patriarch of House Talricci heard the wizard's words, he jerked his head around to stare at the diminutive fellow, then turned to Lavant and said something in *his* ear.

Whatever was said, it was serious enough to force Lavant to excuse himself. Eles Wianar nodded and clapped Lavant on the shoulder before he allowed the newly ordained high priest to move off, then the Shining Lord of Arrabar turned his attention to the rest of the group. Lavant and Grozier left the chamber in a hurry, the high priest stalking in obvious ire, followed by Marga and Bartimus. The high priest's waddling gait caused the innumerable gems adorning his cream-colored robes to scintillate in the light of dozens of lanterns. At one point, he paused and made a deliberate gesture to someone on the opposite side of the room, and when Falagh glanced that way, he spotted a blur of magenta and purple vanishing through a distant doorway.

What the blazes is going on? he wondered again.

"Come on," Falagh said, grabbing Lobra's arm once more and heading off after the high priest. "Keep up," he added when his wife nearly stumbled in her rush to turn and accompany him. Falagh felt the woman stiffen in displeasure at his gruff tone, but he did not care. Something was transpiring, and he did not wish to miss any of the conversation.

Falagh and Lobra caught up to Lavant, Grozier, and the other two partway down a wide, alcoved hallway filled with planted greenery. The foursome was just passing through a doorway near a copse of trees

potted in large half-barrels. Lavant was frowning as
Grozier seemed to lecture him, one finger waggling
under the priest's nose as they stepped through the
doorway and into a private parlor.

" . . . looks very suspicious from where I stand,"
Grozier was saying as Falagh arrived. "Highly suspicious. And you won't give me a straight answer!"

Lavant spotted Falagh and his wife and sighed,
then motioned for them to enter the parlor before he
shut the door behind them all. Then the high priest
raised his hands and gestured for calm. "I assure you
that there is nothing to be concerned about. Whatever Emriana Matrell is doing here, there's no reason
to be alarmed. She knows nothing important."

"Emriana Matrell is here?" Falagh asked, pushing
his way beside Grozier, leaving Lobra to fend for herself with the other two bystanders. "I thought Junce
was going to deal with her last night," he added,
giving the priest a pointed stare. "Why is she still
alive? And why are you showing your face around
here?" he demanded, turning to look at Grozier just
as pointedly.

"She showed up this afternoon," Grozier explained.
"Just walked right into the house, looking like a half-
drowned wharf rat, as we were paying our respects
to Hetta's remains."

Falagh started at the bit of news concerning the
matriarch, though he was very pleased to hear it.

Gozier continued. "Apparently, Junce's associates
didn't make sure the job was finished, because Emriana's still very much alive. And right here, in the
Generon, and not just visiting, either. She's sneaking
down into the dungeons. What is she looking for?" he
finished, turning back to Lavant.

Again Lavant tried to motion for calm. "Nothing.

Everything is going exactly according to plan." Then he turned toward Falagh, folding his hands together and resting them upon his rotund stomach as he asked, "Do I speak falsely? You know as well as I the state of things in Reth."

Falagh shrugged. "My messengers report that our mercenary army is doing an effective job, and the prices of lumber are steadily climbing," he conceded, not wanting to allow the high priest to turn the discussion away from his concerns. "But you have become terribly friendly with our Lord Wianar of late, and that concerns me. And you," he said, turning back to Grozier, "didn't answer my question before. Why are you showing your face at this party?"

"Because, my dear Falagh, I am no longer a wanted man. With Hetta dead, my dear sister Marga, here," and Grozier sent a warm smile over to the far side of the room, where the woman was standing, looking positively bored, "is now the ward for the heirs to the entire House."

Falagh glanced toward Marga, widow to Evester Matrell and up until that night, firmly ensconced in the Matrell household. He had been somewhat surprised to see her also at the Sammardach celebration, considering the actions Grozier had admitted in enforcing her cooperation in his plans to gain control of the Matrell estate.

In a very officious tone, Grozier continued. "I have been absolved of all previous accusations and been invited to serve as co-ward over the Matrell estate until the twins come of age."

She doesn't seem too bitter about it, Falagh thought. On the contrary, the woman's face was calm and content. Falagh shrugged it off as a change of heart. Or pragmatism, he mused.

"Only Emriana could be a potential thorn in our sides now, and she had nothing to her name this afternoon when she departed House Matrell," Grozier said. "I made sure of that," he added, looking smug. "With no home, no allies, and no funds to use to fend for herself, it should have been easy for Roundface's, ah, 'associates' to finish her once and for all. And yet Bartimus here tells me that less than an hour ago, he spied her creeping about with a priest of Waukeen, the two of them making their way down into the depths of the Generon. If she is not here to cause trouble for us, what could Lord Wianar possibly have in his palace that might interest her?"

Falagh absorbed all of Grozier's explanation, then turned to Lavant once more. "Yes, I'm very curious to hear your explanation. Is Lord Wianar involved in our little business venture in a way we don't know?"

Lavant opened his mouth again, no doubt to protest his innocence, but he was interrupted by the opening of the door.

"You are too astute, as always, Falagh," Junce Roundface said, sounding jovial as he entered from the hallway. "Emriana Matrell is here because I lured her here."

"You *what?*" Grozier blurted, apparently just as stunned as Falagh felt. "Why in Waukeen's name would you do that?" he added in a softer tone.

Falagh winced at his compatriot's noise, but he felt similar incredulity. "Yes, pray tell, why here?"

"Because," Junce said, still grinning, "it was the best place to capture her."

At that moment, everyone began talking at once. It was clear to Falagh that Junce had just executed some elaborate plan that he had not been privy to, and it disturbed him. He began to wonder how much else Junce—and Lavant, too, it appeared—were doing that they weren't admitting.

"Enough!" Lavant hissed, glaring at everyone. It was the first time Falagh could remember seeing the high priest lose his composure, even the slightest. "This chamber may be private, but it is not warded against sound. If you don't all lower your voices, the entire Generon will know of what we speak." With an elaborate sigh, he then turned to Junce. "So, it is done?" he asked.

"Indeed," the assassin replied, that grin spreading wider. "I have both of them in the mirror even as we speak."

"Mirror?" Grozier asked, again seeming to echo Falagh's puzzlement. "What mirror? Both of whom?"

"Let's just say that someone owed me a large favor and loaned me the use of a very special mirror," Junce explained. "It has a way of safely storing certain individuals who tend to get in the way of things otherwise. Certain Matrell women who make an unpleasant habit of skulking about at night."

"Brilliant!" Grozier exclaimed. "But why is the mirror here? Oh, it must belong to—" and he snapped his mouth shut at the realization of just how Eles Wianar was involved. Then he looked back and forth between Junce and Lavant, a frown appearing on his face.

Falagh felt uneasiness descend upon him. If Lord Wianar is involved, no matter how peripherally, things could become complicated, he thought. He may begin to inquire after our activities, and he might wish to become more involved in them.

Falagh was on the verge of voicing his concerns to the priest and the assassin, but Lobra chose that moment to cut into the conversation. "You say you have captured Emriana Matrell?" she asked coldly, staring at Junce.

"Indeed," the assassin repeated, looking smug. "I have them safely locked away right at this moment."

Falagh turned to suggest that Lobra return to the party and let him finish his business with his associates unhindered, but she continued on, ignoring her husband's stare. "I want her," the woman demanded. "I want to see her, to let her feel a little of the pain and misery she and her family have brought upon me and mine." She spoke the words with absolute conviction, the chill in her voice a sure sign to Falagh that she would brook no argument. She did not often adopt such a tone, but whenever she did, her husband understood all too well that she would not be denied.

Lobra turned to Falagh and added, "Make them give her to me, darling. You must."

Falagh looked at the three other men, wondering how difficult it was going to be to convince them. "You heard her," he said. "What arrangements need to be made?"

"I don't think it would be such a good idea to free the girl," Junce began, his smile wiped from his face. "Where she is now, she cannot be easily located with magical scrying. But should we free her, even to imprison her in a more conventional fashion, others might come looking for her."

"I have House wizards who can deal with that," Falagh said, waving his hand in dismissal. "That won't be an issue." Then an idea hit him. "Or," he said, watching his counterparts to gauge their reactions, "you could simply loan us this wondrous mirror for a while." Junce stole a glance at Lavant, who frowned. Falagh continued. "That way, you wouldn't have to worry about others using magic to locate her. And I'm sure that, after a few days, a tenday or so at most, Lobra would grow tired of taunting the girl, and you could have the whole thing back, prisoners included."

"Absolutely not," Junce declared, shaking his head. "The mirror is much too rare and valuable to be loaned out. It is out of the question."

Falagh smiled, for he had expected just such an answer. Now we can see just how close your relationship is with our Shining Lord, he mused, congratulating himself. He cleared his throat. "My wife is very insistent. If she doesn't get what she wants, I'm afraid no more Pharaboldi funds will be available for this venture. Mestel funds, either, for that matter," he added.

Junce grimaced and glared at Falagh for a long moment. Out of the corner of his eye, Falagh saw Lavant give the barest hint of a nod, and Junce sighed as though caving to Falagh's demand. "Very well," he said, his tone almost too contrite. "I will speak to our host and see if he is willing to agree to your terms. But I promise you, his acquiescence won't come cheaply."

"Oh, I fully expect Lord Wianar will want to get his hands deeply into our pie after this," Falagh said, knowing he sounded smug. "I just wanted you two to finally admit it." When Junce's glare deepened, Falagh laughed. "I am not a fool, and I have warned you not to underestimate me before. Perhaps now, Lord Wianar will be willing to show his intentions more openly."

"I have a question," Grozier asked, interrupting the staring contest. "You said you managed to capture Emriana. But what happened to her companion? A Waukeenar priest, I believe?"

Junce nodded. "Yes, some young whelp from the Darowdryn household, I believe. He really wasn't much more trouble than Emriana. My 'associates,' as you referred to them, are disposing of him now. Both he and the other mercenary, Miquillon, in fact. Fool man wouldn't stop begging me to release Xaphira into his hands. I grew tired of his pleading."

Lavant grunted. "Pilos Darowdryn? I'm not sure killing him is such a good idea," he grumbled. "I couldn't care less what happens to the mercenary, but if Pilos doesn't return to his family or the temple at the end of the evening, the entire Darowdryn clan may begin asking some very pointed questions. We just got House Matrell out of the way. We don't want more of the same trouble from Ariskrit and Steelfists."

Junce shrugged. "He'll be found floating in the bay tomorrow, I'm sure," he said. "Inquiries will be made, but I'm certain no one in the Darowdryn House will openly point out that their whelp was poking around in Wianar's dungeons, now will they?"

"Nonetheless, they will investigate," Lavant countered. "That's attention we just can't have right now. We need a better solution."

"Why don't we replace him?" Grozier suggested.

Falagh turned to look at the man. "How do you mean?" he asked.

For an answer, Grozier motioned to his sister. "Marga, darling, come over here for a moment and give these gentlemen a quick glimpse of your more interesting talents."

The woman nodded, gave them all a rather conniving smile, and began to change like clay molded by an artist.

Falagh wasn't sure he believed what he was seeing

at first, for Marga Matrell became somewhat gray and blurry for a moment. In the next instant, she was someone else, a young man dressed in the garb of the Temple of Waukeen, with a white billowy shirt, matching trousers, and a doublet of rich crimson.

"I encountered Pilos earlier this evening, at the punch bowl, shortly after the Darowdryns first arrived," the image of the lad said in a youthful male voice quite unlike Marga's. "It won't be hard at all to convince his family that I am still alive," he added with a wicked grin.

Falagh nearly choked. "That's brilliant," he said, though he was also uneasy at having been so cleverly fooled. Well, at least that explains why Marga was so agreeable, he thought. "What . . . *are* you?" he asked.

The copy of Pilos seemed affronted by the question, but Grozier interposed himself between the two of them. "Suffice it to say that I pay them well for their services, and let's leave it at that," he said. "They are rather sensitive about their privacy."

Falagh nodded and made a gesture of apology. "Of course," he said, though he was still fascinated. "And you said 'them?' So you have employed more than one?"

Grozier nodded. "For a time, it was necessary to have them pose as Marga's twin children, so no one else in the family would know that I had taken them to House Talricci for safekeeping," he chuckled. It was a cold, mirthless laugh. "Now that no one is left to oppose me within the House, I see no need to continue the ruse. The children can return to their mother, and we can employ my special friends here for other things."

"Such as posing as Pilos," Falagh finished. "Brilliant," he repeated.

"Or for spying on other Houses," Grozier said with a smug grin. "The other one is still at the party, mingling with the other guests in the guise of a distant cousin."

"How interesting," Lobra said, insinuating herself into the conversation once again. She looked at the duplicate of Pilos and said, "Perhaps you or your companion might be interested in working for me for a short time. I have an idea that might just be delightful."

The mimicking creature nodded, though Falagh noticed that Grozier frowned.

Doesn't like to share, does he? the Mestel scion thought.

"I'd love to stay and chat about all the possibilities of imitating our enemies," Junce interrupted, "but I have places I need to be tonight. Events in Reth still require my attention. So I assume we've settled all the issues that concerned you two gentlemen about tonight's activities?"

Grozier nodded, but Falagh had one last point. "The mirror," he reminded them all. "How do I get the mirror?"

"Ah, that," Junce said, grimacing. "Come with me, then. And bring your wizard, Grozier. We'll need his talents to get the thing safely to House Pharaboldi."

As the group dispersed, Falagh followed the assassin down into the deeper parts of the palace. He was still concerned about Eles Wianar's meddling.

But there are ways to get around that, he thought, a plan already beginning to form in his mind.

...

Marga hadn't realized she had dozed off until a light from the hallway beyond her room awakened her. She squinted in the brightness of it, realizing somewhere in the back of her mind that it had grown dark outside, and that no lanterns had yet been lit in her chambers. Whoever had opened the door was speaking to her, but Marga was too groggy to under-stand any of it at first. She just wanted them to pull the door shut again and let her go back to sleep.

Then all the horrible memories came rushing back to her, and she sat bolt upright on the bed.

It was Mirolyn Skolotti, and she had brought a tray of food. "Lady Marga, are you hungry?" she asked as she moved to set the meal on a side table. She carried a taper candle she had brought with her and began to light the various lanterns hanging from hooks on the walls and ceilings. The entire chamber was soon bathed in warm amber light.

"No, not really," Marga heard herself say. "Just leave the tray and I'll try it a bit later. I really want to rest." Don't listen to my words! she thought, silently struggling to say something else. Help me!

Mirolyn looked at her, hands on her hips. "Lady Marga, I know it's been a hard few tendays for you, with all that's gone on around here, and today was particularly difficult, with the passing of Lady Hetta and all. But wouldn't you feel better if you came out into the sitting room to be with everyone else? Don't you think that would make you feel a little better?"

"No," Marga lied. "I just want to rest, by myself, in here." No, I don't! she silently screamed, unable even to contort her face to make her frantic feelings obvious to the other woman. Damn you, Bartimus, what did you do to me?

Mirolyn started to shake her head and say something else, but then she seemed to think better of it and snapped her mouth shut again. She took one last glance around the room and her frown deepened. "Where are the children? I just realized I haven't seen them all day."

Marga wanted to sob. My babies, she thought. Please help me save my precious babies. Instead, she simply said, "They went to stay at House Talricci for a couple of days. I thought it better for them, with the gloom that has settled here."

Mirolyn scowled at the mention of Marga's brother, but she was too polite to voice her dislike. "Very well," she said at last. "I'll leave you alone, then." And she turned to depart. Then she turned back at the door and said, "If you need anything, you come find me, all right?"

"I'm sure I'll be fine, but thank you, Mirolyn." Don't leave! I don't want to be alone! Please come back! Please figure it out!

But Mirolyn did leave, pulling the door shut behind her, never noticing the single tear that ran down the woman's face.

After she was gone, Marga couldn't even force herself to walk across the floor and pull the door open again. She wanted to—with all of her will she wanted to dash out into the sitting room and beg them all to help her. But the enchantment that Bartimus had laid upon her—at Grozier's direction, of course—prevented her from acting on her wishes. Being imprisoned in her chamber was even worse than the time Bartimus had turned her into a living statue so she couldn't move.

The wizard's instructions had been simple, direct. "You are to remain in this room at all times, and you may not tell anyone that anything is wrong, or that you have been magically hindered, or that your children are in any way threatened or in danger. If anyone asks about you, you are to claim that you are simply tired and wish to rest."

And it had worked.

After Grozier and those two fiendish changelings had departed, Marga had spent the better part of the afternoon trying to leave her chambers, but Bartimus's spell was quite effective. She could no more approach the door than she could walk on the ceiling. She spent the next part of the day crying herself to sleep, until Mirolyn had appeared.

But the young woman was gone again, and Marga was alone once more to uselessly fight against the magic that restrained her.

Then it hit her. Why am I such a fool? she thought, so angry with herself. I cannot fight the enchantment, but perhaps I can find a way around it, a loophole. Something that slipped that worm's mind when he set the conditions. What could it be?

Marga spent a few moments wracking her brain, trying to remember the wizard's words exactly. On impulse, she moved to her writing desk and took up a piece of parchment. She grabbed a quill and tried to write the truth of the matter.

The ink, and the words, flowed freely.

For the first time in several days, Marga Matrell smiled.

CHAPTER 3

Vambran reached for his holy coin, ready to charge into the fray and aid the soldiers. His sword and crossbow were still inside the burning building, but more importantly, so was Elenthia.

The mercenary took two steps before Arbeenok grabbed him by the arm. "Wait," the druid said, clutching a strange urnlike object made of pottery decorated with colorful beads and etched with complicated mosaics. Arbeenok held the object over the lieutenant's head, and with an indecipherable chant, the alaghi smacked his hands together, shattering the tiny urn and showering Vambran with a fine white dust. "Something to protect you from the plague," he added, nodding in the direction of the fighting.

Vambran gave his companion an answering nod of thanks and turned back to the battle.

The four soldiers had formed a defensive line across the side of the building, guarding the stairs leading up to Elenthia's abode. Their training and equipment should have been more than enough to keep the half-dozen or so shambling undead at bay, Vambran thought, but the Reth watchmen seemed sluggish to him. Even as he ran across the street to drive away the nearest zombie, he saw one of the soldiers crumple to the paving stones, clutching at his belly. The zombie staggered toward the man and kicked at him, causing the watchman to cry out in pain and alarm. The soldier next to the wounded man shifted slightly to try to keep the zombies away from his downed companion, but that only served to open a hole in the line, and the zombies, slow as they were, pressed the attack.

Vambran wanted to wallop one of the stumbling, staggering horrors with his sword or perhaps a mace, but without weapons, he dared not get too close. That left him with the tools of his faith, but he knew he would have to get in with the soldiers, on the other side of the zombies, to be effective.

Perhaps I should just jump past them, the mercenary thought, looking for a way to slip through the conflict.

Beside Vambran, Arbeenok approached one of the zombies and, locking both fists together like a huge cudgel, swung his arms fiercely, slamming them into the shoulder of the undead thing. The druid's blow crushed bone, sending the zombie tumbling to the side fully three paces away. Without hesitating to see if the living corpse rose again, the alaghi moved to the next one on the line, swinging his thick bulging arms and clamped fists a second time.

The lieutenant watched Arbeenok in awe. What incredible strength, he thought. Shaking himself out of his amazement, Vambran came in behind the druid, weaving his way through the gap that Arbeenok had created. He reached the closest of the soldiers, who was down on one knee, coughing and clutching at his chest.

"Can't breathe," the man said. "Help me," he pleaded. Vambran gave the soldier a reassuring pat on the shoulder and turned to face a pair of zombies that were coming toward the two of them. Grasping his holy coin tightly, the mercenary thrust the symbol forward in defiance and called on Waukeen's favor to drive them back. "Begone, you stinking things!" he shouted as he poured his own holy energy through the coin.

The zombies hesitated and flinched, groaning. Vambran shoved the coin farther in their direction. "You must get away! Waukeen will not permit you to foul this place any longer! Begone!"

The two zombies turned and lurched down the street, groaning and shielding their eyes from the coin Vambran presented. Once he was certain they were truly fleeing, he turned back to the soldier, ready to draw upon his healing magic to aid the man.

The watchman lay unmoving on the paving stones, his eyes glassy and staring up at the night sky. His skin was strangely hued, with blotches and blisters forming right before Vambran's eyes.

Swearing softly, Vambran resisted the urge to back away from the sick man and instead knelt down, placing his hand upon the ill soldier's forehead. He

closed his eyes in prayer, but even as he felt the healing energy pour through his arm and into the man,
he heard the death rattle of a last breath escaping.
He opened his eyes to see those eyes, lifeless, staring
at nothing.

Shuddering, Vambran rose up and turned away,
horrified and afraid of the swiftness of the disease.
He took several quick steps to put some distance between himself and the new corpse, desperate to wipe
his hand on something, to bathe, to run.

A scream from overhead made the lieutenant
pause in his retreat. Craning his neck, Vambran
peered up, seeing that the flames from the first-floor
fire had spread to encompass the second story, too.
Smoke billowed thick in the air, and the mercenary
could just make out a silhouetted image in one of
the upper windows. He turned to dash up the stairs,
but Arbeenok was in the way, still battling two of
the walking undead. The druid was holding his own,
pummeling the zombies with gusto, but outnum-
bered, he would not last too long in the fight.

No time, Vambran decided, spinning away and
trying to find another route up to the second floor.
The conflagration had spread to the roof. There was
another scream, and he could see a frantic hand
waving from one of the windows.

Remembering his other magic, Vambran wished
suddenly for a live spider, but there was no way he
would be able to locate one before the entire building
was an inferno. He started to curse his ill luck when
the urge hit him to try to activate the magic without
the spider. Frowning at such preposterous notions but
sensing something genuine about it, he darted toward
the wall, muttering the arcane phrases to grant him
the magical climbing skill.

Vambran began scampering up the wall with no trouble at all.

Not wasting time trying to figure out why he no longer needed the spider, Vambran reached the window, shielding his face from the heat with one arm as he tried to peer inside. "Elenthia!" he shouted, coughing from the hot smoke that poured out of the room. "Elenthia, come to the window!"

"Vambran!" the woman screamed, and she was there, her face black with soot, coughing and crying. "Help me!" she pleaded. "Get me out!"

Vambran scrambled in through the window. "Stay low," he instructed the woman as he dropped to all fours, his eyes watering as he looked about. He could feel the heat rising up through the floor of Elenthia's apartment, could sense that it would erupt in flame soon. But he had to reach his belongings, had to recover his weapons and breastplate.

"What are you doing?" Elenthia screamed, grabbing at Vambran as he tried to crawl deeper into the apartment. "We can't go back in!"

Vambran ignored her and scrambled across the floor, searing hot and beginning to smolder, toward the place he had left his satchel. He coughed and gasped as he maneuvered through the room, having to fight the urge to stop and wipe the soot from his burning eyes. He spied the bulky, elongated bundle still leaning against a wall where he had left it, though the cloth was beginning to smoke because of its proximity to the spreading flames. Grabbing the satchel, Vambran slung it across his back and turned to navigate back the way he had come.

Flames blocked his path.

Vambran considered rising up and making a run for it, but at that moment, the majority of the floor fell away with a thunderous crash, and more flames roared up from below. Elenthia screamed from beside the window, already half outside, trying to escape a fiery death.

It appeared that the mercenary was trapped.

Undaunted, Vambran scampered to the closest wall and began to crawl up it, still feeling the effects of the spell. The maneuver took him higher into the smoke and heat of the fire, but he squinted and held his breath as he hurried up the wall, almost to the ceiling, and darted past the licking flames to the other side. He kept moving at that point, feeling his skin blistering on the scorching walls of the structure. He reached the end of the wall and turned the corner, scrambling as fast as he could toward the window, where Elenthia was preparing to jump.

"Wait!" Vambran called, reaching the opening just as Elenthia swung herself fully out to hang by her hands. Vambran darted through the window and out onto the wall, maneuvering past Elenthia, who watched him wide-eyed with fear and amazement. "Let me get below you," Vambran said, pressing his mouth close to her ear to make certain she could hear him, "and you can use me like a ladder. Do you understand?"

Elenthia nodded, and Vambran wasted no time positioning himself below the woman. As soon as she saw him below her, she began to scramble down the wall, stepping on Vambran's fingers and ear. The mercenary officer grimaced in pain as he felt her boots scraping his backside. She half-climbed, half-slid down him until she could drop the remaining distance to the street below.

Once Elenthia was away, Vambran made a mad

dash down the wall himself. As soon as he reached
the cobblestones, he sprinted as fast as he could from
the building.

Even before he got to the other side of the avenue,
Vambran heard the structure collapse, felt the vibration of tons of material striking the ground and the
rush of heated air that burst out from the conflagration. He winced as that searing heat washed over
him and he turned his ankle and stumbled to the
pavement at Arbeenok's feet. Elenthia stood a little
distance away, trembling and gazing back and forth
between the alaghi and her ruined home.

"I did not think you would make it back out," Arbeenok said, helping Vambran to his feet. "You are
either very brave or very foolish," he added.

Vambran gave the druid a wry grin and held up
his satchel, wincing as he did so because of his painful ankle and the various patches of blistered skin on
his body. "I couldn't let these burn," he said, unrolling
the cloth from his sword and armor. "They're family
heirlooms."

"I don't think your friend knows quite what to
think of me," Arbeenok said, gesturing toward
Elenthia, who eyed the druid, a wary look on her
soot-smudged face.

Vambran limped over to the woman and pulled
her to himself to give her a hug. "Are you all right?"
he asked, looking into her red-rimmed eyes.

Elenthia sagged into the man, grasping him and
weeping for a long moment. When she pulled back
to look at him again, tears glistened on her cheeks,
making tracks through the smudges of black soot.
Her slap to Vambran's face was unexpected and stung.
"What in the hells do you think you were doing,
going back in there for your *things?*" she demanded

as Vambran gingerly rubbed his jaw. "You almost got us both charred!"

"They were important," he said.

"More important than my life? Than *yours?*"

The mercenary officer shrugged. "I did what I did. You're safe." Changing the subject, Vambran turned back to the druid. "This is my companion, Arbeenok, from the Nunwood. You've already met, though you do not know it. He was my canine companion earlier this evening."

Elenthia's eyes grew wide for a moment, and she said, "A druid! I knew it!" The words were not kind. Then she turned to Vambran and asked, in a tone filled with ice, "What are you doing traveling with the likes of *him?*"

"Do not let what you think you know of the Emerald Enclave prejudice you against him," the lieutenant warned. "Arbeenok is both honorable and steadfast. If not for him, we'd be roasting in the fire or hip-deep in zombies—take your pick."

Elenthia sniffed, obviously unconvinced, but she said no more about the alaghi's allegiances. Instead, she turned and stared at the burning remains of her home and the bodies of both soldiers and undead strewn everywhere upon the street. "My father sent those soldiers to protect me," she said. "He must have realized the city was under attack. What is happening?" she asked in a near-whisper, her dismay making her voice crack. "Has the plague truly returned to Reth?"

"It has," Vambran said. "The zombies are spreading it. I fear it's now too late to get to my men." He sighed and added, "I've already found my uncle. It was too late for him." When Elenthia turned to look at the mercenary officer, horrified, he merely nodded. "We've got to get you out of the city."

"No!" Elenthia replied, her eyes wide with animalistic fear. "I must get to my father! Please take me to him!"

Vambran started to protest, but the words died in his throat as a soft groan reached the trio's ears from across the street. As the lieutenant turned to look, one of the watchmen's bodies stirred and began to rise.

...

The tower upon which Darvin Blackcrown arrived with the aid of his magical boots stood well above every other point in the city of Reth. From there, atop the Palace of the Seven, an observer could see well out into the Reach, watch either of the two roads—one that skirted the Nunwood approaching from the south and the other winding its way into the Akanapeaks to the east—or study the woods or low-ridged mountains. A visitor coming to that tower could also see almost every point in the city of Reth itself, though few of the palace's inhabitants ever did. Indeed, few even knew which back passages and stairwells to traverse to attain that high promenade. Nonetheless, when Darvin appeared in the center of the tower, another figure was already there.

Rodolpho Wianar barely gave the newcomer a cursory glance.

Darvin, known to most of Chondath as the assassin Junce Roundface, strode over to where Rodolpho rested against the crenellations of the tower, looking out over the city. Far below, the orange glow of several fires shone in the evening darkness. Darvin realized the fires were burning buildings, and that dismayed him.

"What is happening down there?" he inquired, peering across the landscape and counting conflagrations. "Why is the city burning?"

Rodolpho began to chuckle, but it was not a merry laugh. It sent a shiver up Darvin's spine with the insanity of it. "Yes," the man said, not looking at Darvin. "It burns. It is a beautiful sight, isn't it?"

"No," Darvin rebuked, turning to look at his counterpart. "Eles isn't going to be very happy to see Reth in flames. Why are you allowing this?"

Rodolpho snorted. "Allow? I'm not allowing anything. Events are simply taking their natural course. The plague has begun to spread outward from the sewers. The people are panicking, fleeing into the night, and some among them who most fear the disease have set fires in hopes of containing its spread. But they will fail," he said, finishing with another chuckle.

"How is it possible for them to become so panicked so quickly?" Darvin demanded, grabbing Rodolpho by the shoulders and turning him so they were face to face. "What did you do?"

"I did what my cousin demanded," Rodolpho snapped back. "I created the plague for him, just as he ordered! And now, it's taken on a life of its own! Now my creation will thrive, and you and Wianar can rot with it!" he said, cackling.

"By the gods," Darvin muttered, staring back down on the city. "You've made it too virulent. It'll kill them all."

"And what if it does?" Rodolpho cried out. "What if all of Reth burns to ash? What do I care? I did not choose this course. I did not ask to be here, hiding for

twelve years, just so my dear, beloved cousin could
stake his claim to another piece of land."

"You made your choice back then," Darvin said.
"You agreed to his terms."

"I was given no choice!" Rodolpho screamed, jabbing a single finger into Darvin's chest. "You sent
me to my grave, you craven worm, and I was dead!"
The veins in the man's neck bulged in his fury, and
spittle flecked his lips as he shouted. "Oh, certainly,
my dear cousin called me back from the grave, gave
me a chance at life again, but only if I agreed to his
plans. Only if I took a new identity, came here to
this gods-forsaken city, and did his dirty work for
him. Yes, *there* was a fine choice." He spun away from
Darvin and again stared down at the city.

"That's between you and Eles," Darvin said after
a moment, not wishing to debate with the man any
longer. "We're well beyond that, and it's time to put
the last part of the plan in motion." He waited, but
when Rodolpho did not answer him, he asked, "So,
do you have it?"

Rodolpho didn't answer.

"Rodolpho, do you have the formula?"

Rodolpho Wianar glanced up at Darvin, smirked,
and said, "There is no formula. The plague cannot
be stopped."

Darvin reeled. He suddenly wanted to be far away
from there, to call on his magical boots to take him
away from Reth, away from Chondath, to some distant
corner of Faerûn where the disease could not reach
him. He wanted to throw Rodolpho from the tower.

He dared not, not while there was a chance that
the man was lying.

"You're insane," Darvin said. "Eles will kill you
again."

"Let him try," Rodolpho snarled. "Rodolpho Wianar disappeared a dozen years ago, assumed dead, and no one was the wiser that I became Dwonlar Aphorio, Senator of Defense in the city of Reth. I'll simply die again, disappear again, and Eles will never find me." Then the man turned back to Darvin, and he smiled a cold, chilling smile. "And you can tell him I said so."

Again, Darvin had to fight the urge to shove the figure before him backward, to send him teetering over the edge of the tower to plummet to his death. But he knew Eles would not be happy with that, would not accept Darvin's measure of justice.

"I'm sure I'll be seeing you again," Darvin said at last. "Eles may still have something to say about your betrayal."

"Get off my tower," Rodolpho said.

"Eat horse dung," Darvin countered. Then he muttered an arcane phrase and vanished.

Darvin blinked when he arrived in the camp of Captain Beltrim Havalla, leader of the Silver Raven Company, for the place was alive with activity. In the darkness, numerous cook fires burned, enabling the assassin to see soldiers hustling in every direction. It appeared the mercenaries were preparing to ship out.

A soldier spotted Darvin appearing out of nowhere and leveled a crossbow at the man, challenging him. "Who in Tempus's name are you?" he called out.

For a moment, Darvin just stood there, trembling in rage. He needed to hit something. The assassin drew several long, deep breaths, calming himself. Damn him, he thought. I should have pushed him.

"Answer me, or I'll spit you!" the soldier shouted, taking a single wary step toward the intruder.

"I've come to speak with Captain Havalla," Darvin replied. "Tell him that Junce Roundface is here."

"Tell him yourself," came another voice, older and gruffer than the soldier's. It was the captain, striding through camp with a cluster of aides gathered around him. "What in the Nine Hells are you doing here? I've got a war to fight."

"That's what I've come to talk to you about," Darvin replied, stepping over to fall in with the man. "A few adjustments need to be made."

Beltrim Havalla swore. "I knew it," he muttered as they reached his command tent and ducked inside together. "It never fails. I don't care how much gold you promise, I always end up regretting fighting for you city folk and your wars. What is it *this* time?"

Darvin made a point of peering around the inside of the tent, examining the various tapestries that had been hung up for decoration, in order to hide his grimace at the captain's words. He turned back and pointed at a map on the table in the center of the tent. "Captain Havalla, it's imperative that you take your mercenaries to Reth and establish martial law there. No, wait," he said, correcting himself. "Surround it and establish a quarantine."

"Beltrim eyed Darvin suspiciously. "What for?" he asked. "I thought Reth was your own city. Why do you want me to lay siege to it?"

Darvin sighed. "I can't explain it right now, but please do this now, tonight. I'll give you half again as much gold as we've already agreed upon if you can have the city surrounded and sealed off by sunrise."

Beltrim swore again, but that time, Darvin knew it was greed that overwhelmed him. "You make an offer I shouldn't refuse," he said at last, "but I've already got half my army in the field, keeping the druids at bay while the Rethite regulars hit the Hlathians. Something stirred up the Enclave but good, and they're fighting mad. Just keeping them out of the way of the main battle is going to be a trick, and I can't easily extract my forces without winding up in a nasty pinch when the Enclave counterattacks—and they most certainly will try."

Darvin threw up his hands in exasperation. "There's nothing you can do? What about reserves? Two days ago, you had nothing but time on your hands and lots of antsy troops being held in reserve."

"Aye, I did," Captain Havalla admitted. "And I still have a reserve force, but those men are tired after chasing down your Crescents and hauling them off to Reth. Besides, I need them to plug gaps in my lines for *this* fight."

"I think," Darvin said with an edge to his voice, "you could push them a little harder than usual in exchange for the additional gold I mentioned. It really is necessary."

"If it's so necessary, why don't you tell me what it's all about?"

Darvin grimaced again, not caring if the captain saw him or not. "There's a problem," he began. He then explained that the plague had erupted in Reth and had to be contained, lest the disease spread beyond the city's walls and into the countryside—into the midst of the various armies on the field of battle. When he was finished, he eyed Beltrim Havalla, wondering if the man would be willing to put his forces at risk by getting so near to the disease-ridden city.

After a long and rather uncomfortable silence, Havalla asked, "Do I have permission to cut down any man, woman, or child trying to leave the city?"

Darvin nodded without hesitation.

"What about the Reach? How are you going to keep ship traffic from coming and going?"

Darvin had considered that already. "I know someone who has enough ships at his disposal to keep them hemmed in," he said. He made a note to talk to Falagh about that as soon as he returned to Arrabar. "So what do you say?"

"I say, it doesn't look like we have much of a choice, do we?" Havalla answered. "If we don't hold it back, it'll chew right through my armies, and everyone else's. It'll be the Battle of Nun all over again."

"It really is necessary," Darvin said again, rising. "Remember, by sunrise, if at all possible."

Beltrim sighed. "I'll have to march them all night, and they will be in fine humor by morning, but I think we can do it."

"Excellent," Darvin said. "I'll make sure the gold is on its way immediately."

As he began to put his magical boots to use once more, Darvin heard Beltrim say, "You do that." Then he was gone, teleporting back to the Generon.

...

Everything was nothingness around Emriana.

The girl feared that she was becoming nothingness, too. Only her thoughts seemed to hover there, letting her cling to the notion that she still existed. She had to concentrate to keep everything else.

The sensation of being totally blind, of not having her eyes adjust to even the tiniest bit of light, had at some point begun to terrify the girl. And though she could feel her own body, could touch naked skin in that nothingness, it was horrific not to be able to see her fingers wiggling in front of her face. She had to fight to convince herself that not being able to see them did not make them any less real.

Emriana was neither cold nor hungry, nor could she feel any air move when she breathed. Her buttocks never became numb or sore from sitting. Time did not seem to pass for her, except for her thoughts. Something told her that she could remain like that forever, just thinking. And the longer her thinking went on, the less substantial the rest of her might become. She might altogether cease to exist physically, just floating in the black void, a consciousness trapped.

Emriana fought against that image. She needed to remind her senses to work, needed to keep moving, functioning. She had tried singing—when? how long ago?—thinking that hearing herself would help, but she was unnerved by the way her voice sounded in that place. Instead she reached out around herself.

The walls imprisoning the girl were certainly real enough. She could feel them when she pushed out with her hands. Beyond that sensation, though, they had no substance, no qualities. They were neither hot nor cold, smooth nor rough. They simply held her in the midst of the nothingness. She could follow the surface with her hands, rising to her knees and finding eight corners. She could not quite stand, for the ceiling was too low. And she could not quite lie down, either. It was a box just big enough for her to sit, to draw her knees up to herself protectively, to waste away.

Junce Roundface had not been lying when he had told her she would spend a long, long time in there. That thought nearly made her start screaming again.

"Please," the girl pleaded, her voice resounding in her skull but nowhere else. "I want to get out." She waited, listening, but there was nothing. No sounds, not even the roaring in her ears. "Please!" she screamed.

Nothing.

Emriana curled up into a ball and lay on her side. She would have liked to sleep, but sleep wouldn't come. She was simply left with her thoughts.

Later—an hour? a year?—Emriana became aware of something. It was not clear what she had noticed, but just the fact that she was noticing anything at all snapped her out of a sort of stupor. She rose up onto her knees, turned her head, tried to determine which sense had detected something.

It was light.

Very faint, above her, a pinprick of light had appeared. The light grew, became a window, grew still more, dazzlingly bright, making the girl cringe. It became one whole side of her prison. It burned her eyes with its brightness, but she was oh, so thankful just to feel pain in her eyes.

Emriana blinked repeatedly and managed to focus on the scene beyond her prison, through that window.

She spied a room, one that she vaguely remembered from another time. A large bed stood against a distant wall, with a couch to one side and a dressing table beside that. It was a woman's room, draped with bright, colorful tapestries and illuminated by numerous pierced lanterns hanging from the walls and ceiling. Textures, temperature, length, and form all seemed wonderfully welcome right then, even if a recollection nudging at the edge of her memory was vaguely unsettling. Emriana knew that if she could just think hard enough, it would come to her.

At that moment, a woman dressed in a formal gown stepped into view in front of her precious window, blocking out the rest of the world. The owner of the room, triggering all of those memories.

Lobra Pharaboldi.

Denrick's sister.

Emriana gasped and shrank back. The look on the woman's face told Emriana that she was not being rescued.

"Hello, Emriana Matrell."

"Please let me out," the girl began, crawling right up against the window, pressing her face as close as she could, hoping she looked sufficiently anxious that Lobra would take pity on her and not blame her for what had happened to Denrick. "I don't know how I got in here, but if you could ask someone, or have a wizard perform a divination, I'm sure you could let me out, and—"

"Hush," Lobra said, her voice soft and yet commanding. "Not just yet."

Emriana felt tears on her cheeks. "Please?" she begged, and she thought she sounded rather pitiful, like a child. "Please?" she repeated.

"Oh, I will let you out in a moment," Lobra said, smiling just a bit. "To serve your penance for the crimes you and your family have inflicted upon me."

"I didn't mean to do anything," Emriana began, feeling frantic to convey remorse, anything to win Lobra over. "It was an accident, a big misunderstanding, and I'm sorry for that. It would never, ever happen again," and she went on, babbling anything she could think of to convince Lobra that she should be allowed to get out of the mirror.

"Hush," Lobra repeated. "There is someone here who would like to see you," she said, looking up, past Emriana, to some place out of the girl's field of view.

Denrick Pharaboldi strolled around the side of the window, stepped right up and knelt down, that familiar, terrible, wolfish grin spreading wide. "Hello, Emriana," he said. "It's good to see you again."

CHAPTER 4

L avant knows we're watching him," Falagh said, sounding impatient. "He must. He hasn't said anything of consequence to Lord Wianar since we began."

"Perhaps," Grozier replied, leaning over Bartimus's shoulder and watching the scene displayed on the wizard's mirror.

The glass was smaller than the one in Bartimus's chambers at House Talricci, handy for travel, but it made viewing the images more difficult. Since they were performing the viewing in the sitting room of House Pharaboldi, it was a necessary inconvenience. He would have liked to use the larger one, the exquisite glass he had been ordered to fetch from the dungeons of the Generon, for it was much more suitable for scrying. But the woman Lobra had it in another room, along with one of the shapeshifters, who had taken the form of her dead brother.

Bartimus wondered if she had some ability at magical scrying, too.

"Stop shaking it!" Grozier ordered. "It's hard enough to see what's going on."

The wizard sighed and held the small mirror still, wishing his employer would stop putting so much weight on him. Grozier's breath stank of salted fish roe, a delicacy served at the celebration and something Bartimus knew the man enjoyed.

"He doesn't seem to be paying any attention to our spy, though," Grozier continued. "I think Lavant would have taken action if he suspected something."

"Well, if the two of them try to wander off alone and put some distance between themselves and our planted guard again, that might be a good clue that they sense trouble," Falagh replied. "Maybe he and the Shining Lord just aren't willing to discuss their private matters with guards standing about, and if your doppelganger insinuates himself into their midst one more time, they are bound to realize he's shadowing them."

"Perhaps," Grozier said again, sounding doubtful, still peering into the mirror. "Give it a little more time."

Bartimus thought Falagh's initial plan had seemed promising. After Junce had shown the lot of them where the magic mirror was stored and then vanished to deal with other issues, the scion of House Mestel had suggested that their duplicate Pilos wait a bit before carrying out his ruse with the Darowdryn family. Instead, Falagh had suggested, they should have him transform into the likeness of a Generon guard and get near Lavant. He reasoned that attempting to use Bartimus's magic to scry directly on either Lavant or Lord Wianar might trigger some magical defenses one of the men had in place, but focusing the magic on another figure who could get close to them might let them overhear a conversation with little chance of getting noticed.

Thus far, the high priest and the ruler of Chondath had done nothing but make small talk, and frankly, the wizard was growing bored. He didn't much care to return to the party, not so much because he would rather be somewhere else, but because he so often got lost in the middle of conversations. He always found himself mulling problems in his head, letting his mind wander over spells he was developing. Being drawn back into a discussion in which someone was waiting for him to reply to a missed question made him uncomfortable, so he tended to keep to himself at public events, standing off in the corner and avoiding groups. That wasn't much fun, either.

"Bartimus!" Grozier snapped, drawing the wizard out of his thoughts.

"Um, yes?" he stammered, realizing that he had actually managed to daydream about daydreaming and thus missed his employer's question.

"I said, let's forget this for a moment and try something else. Can we peek in on someone else's situation?"

"Why, yes," Bartimus answered, mentally ticking off the number of applications of the scrying spell in his head. "I planned ahead and scribed the requisite spell several times, just in case you would desire me to perform several viewings at once."

"Excellent," Grozier said. "Let's take a look at what

our good friend Vambran Matrell is up to. I wonder if he's dead yet?"

Bartimus nodded and withdrew a small rolled parchment from a hidden pocket in his robes. Unfurling the thing, he began to call on the magic embedded in the script he had placed there, drawing on the arcane energies locked away in the phrases. He felt the swirl of magic surround him and pour from his hands into the mirror. As the spell took effect, a new image formed in the glass. At first, Bartimus could make out little more than a shifting, swarming light from some flame, with black figures silhouetted against the blaze. With a mental command, the wizard adjusted the point of view, drawing back from the image to get a more panoramic orientation.

Behind Bartimus, Grozier gasped. "What is that?" he asked, leaning down to better scrutinize the mirror. "Are you sure you found Vambran? Where is he?"

The diminutive wizard pushed his spectacles farther up his nose and stared for a moment at the scene before answering. "Yes, I'm sure I've focused in on him. That looks like a city street. I don't know what's burning, though."

"Look," Falagh said, pointing. "There he is, fighting." Then the man leaned in closer, right next to Grozier, crowding Bartimus out. "What is that thing next to him? And what in the Nine Hells are they battling?"

"By Waukeen, that's a zombie!" Grozier said, jerking back. "Bartimus, pull the image back some more. Get the whole street, if you can."

When the wizard complied, the three men could see that a multitude of hunched and limping forms shambled around the periphery of three figures fighting back to back. One of the three was a man, clearly Vambran Matrell, another was a woman, and the third was inhuman.

For a long moment, the three of them sat and stared at the grim battle taking place within the mirror. Finally, Falagh asked in a quiet tone, "Bartimus, can you draw back even more? I'd like to see as much of the city as we can. That has to be Reth."

Bartimus sent a mental command to the mirror and the image panned back, encompassing several blocks of stone buildings. A multitude of fires burned in the scene. Everywhere the three men stared, houses and shops were engulfed in fire.

"Our logging," Grozier rasped, his eyes wide. "It's all going to burn! We'll lose everything!"

...

Horial Rhoden attempted to stifle numerous yawns as he trudged along a poorly lit path, following one of the druids leading him through the damp and misty Nunwood. On the third such mouth-splitting gape, he stumbled over a tree root and nearly fell on his face. Disgusted, the sergeant rubbed his eyes and smacked his cheeks a few times to force himself fully awake again.

Pay attention! he ordered himself.

"Contemplating a nap?" Adyan Mercatio asked in his distinctive drawl, hiking along beside Horial in the near-darkness, his breathing somewhat labored in the muggy night. Selune's light barely penetrated the canopy overhead, making it difficult to spot the many branches, roots, and bushes that slapped and clawed at the five mercenaries along their journey.

The half-dozen or so druids accompanying them did not have the same problem navigating the woods.

"I've forgotten what sleep feels like," Horial replied, yawning again. "Other than a brief nap when we were imprisoned in that cave, I don't think I've slept since we were on board *Lady's Favor.*"

"That sounds about right," Adyan agreed. "I'll tell you one thing," he added with a chuckle, "I've had about enough of traipsing through dripping forests in the dark of night. I'm soaked."

Edilus, the druid leading the expedition, appeared out of the darkness beside the two sergeants. "Shhh!" he hissed, motioning with his hand for the two mercenaries to be silent. "Stop speaking, or you will bring the enemy down on us!" he snapped in a whisper. "And can't you walk more quietly?" he asked before turning back. "You move like a herd of rothé," he called over his shoulder.

Horial opened his mouth to retort, then thought better of the idea and instead covered his mouth with his hand, fighting yet another yawn. Edilus disappeared once more, drifting off under the cover of night without a sound, presumably to scout ahead.

"I thought we *were* the enemy," Adyan remarked with just enough volume that Horial was certain the druid had heard.

Horial grunted at his companion's humor. Behind the pair, the other three members of the Order of the Sapphire Crescent followed along, making considerably more noise as they crashed and stumbled through the undergrowth. The racket made the druid's scathing remarks seem more apt than the sergeant wanted to admit. The dwarf Grolo, in particular, stomped along, cursing every so often as vines and saplings slapped at him.

I guess he's got a point, Horial thought in grudging appreciation. We sound just like a herd of rothé.

It was not easy to acknowledge the druid's skills. Edilus had taken every opportunity to express his dislike, both in word and manner, since the Crescents' capture and subsequent release by the Emerald Enclave nearly a full day earlier. Whether he used a sour look or a cross word, the man was determined to make clear just how much he disliked having to cooperate with soldiers from beyond the borders of his forest. Horial had no doubts that Edilus would just as soon run them through as help them.

The feeling is mutual, Horial thought. Thank Waukeen that Shinthala is the one making decisions.

"It's sure a good thing Vambran has a way with the ladies," Adyan drawled in a near-whisper. "Otherwise, Shinthala probably would have already let that fellow work off his frustrations on us."

Horial chuckled at how Adyan was echoing his own thoughts. "He might still do it," he replied with a grin, though he knew his friend could not see the expression in the dimness. "Shinthala isn't here to rein him in."

Adyan grunted but did not reply otherwise, for at that moment, the signal came from up ahead for the procession to halt.

Horial slowed to a stop and gave a soft "hold," over his shoulder to the other soldiers coming up behind him. He crouched down and peered ahead, trying to see the reason for their pause. Adyan dropped low beside him. In the darkness, it was difficult to tell what was beyond, but it appeared that a clearing lay not much farther along the path. Moments later, Edilus appeared next to the two sergeants once again.

"We are almost there," the druid said as he dropped down beside them. "But we must be cautious now, for we leave the safety of the forest and will be out in the open and more easily seen. Ahead of us, the road from the city passes. On the far side, among some ruins, is the magical way."

"What's your plan, then?" Horial asked.

"I have scouts ahead," Edilus replied, "making sure the road is clear. Once we are certain we are alone, I will take you to the portal. It won't be long, and I can be rid of you once and for all," he finished.

Horial rolled his eyes, knowing that in the dark, the other man could not see his expression. "We're just as ready," he replied.

"You have the key I gave you?" Edilus asked, ignoring the sergeant's comment.

Horial felt in his pocket for the gem the druid had given to him back at the encampment. The shard of quartz was still there. "Yes," he answered. "And you're sure it will get us all through the portal? Just the one piece?"

"As long as you do not delay," Edilus answered. "The one with the key must go first, and all others who wish to pass through must follow quickly behind, while the magic is active. It should be accomplished easily."

"All right then," Horial said. "Let's go."

"As soon as I receive the signal," the druid said, "we will cross the road and enter the ruins."

At that moment, a low, cooing call of a morning bird sounded from the distance. Edilus snapped his head around in the darkness. "There," he said, rising to his feet. "That's the signal. It's time to cross."

The group rose up and began moving forward again, and after only a few paces, passed out of the forest and through the scrub brush along its fringe. Out in the open, Selune—although a mere sliver right before her new phase—cast welcome illumination to light the journey. Wading through damp, waist-high grass, the five mercenaries and their escort of woodfolk crossed the open ground toward the place where the road from Reth circumnavigated the Nunwood toward Hlath. Although it was the only overland route between the two cities, the avenue was nothing more than hard-packed soil, but it was wide enough for three wagons to pass.

As the entourage reached the road and crossed to the far side, Horial noticed the outline of a structure in the distance. It seemed all leaning angles and jagged edges, and Edilus was leading them toward it. They closed the distance, the mercenaries following Edilus while the rest of the druids fanned out on every side, staring into the night, sniffing the air or listening. Horial thought they seemed on edge.

"That must be it," Adyan whispered beside Horial. "It'll be nice to sleep in a soft, dry bed in Arrabar tonight. It seems like it's been a month since we left."

Horial started to reply, but the whinnying of a horse cut him off. It sounded close. At almost the same instant, Edilus went to ground, dropping low enough into the grass so as to vanish.

What the—? Horial thought as he looked in the direction from which the sound had seemed to come. Nothing was visible—merely the open road under the night sky. There were no horses and no place to hide within several hundred paces. But the mercenary had not imagined the sound, for everyone around him was reacting as well.

"Back into the trees," Edilus hissed, rising up into

a low crouch and beginning to jog toward the safety of the forest.

Before the druid had even gone three steps, an arrow hissed out of the night, sinking into the ground near his feet. A shout rose up from nearby. "To arms, to arms!" someone cried, and light suddenly illuminated the area from several locations about the group as more arrows fell among its members.

Horial spun about in place, trying to discern where the shouts had originated, but the sudden glow of lights in the sky forced him to squint and shield his eyes. He recognized the magical effect.

Just like Vambran's signal flares, the sergeant realized.

By that point the pounding of hooves sounded nearby, and the mercenary could see a cadre of cavalrymen rushing toward the group. They seemed to have appeared out of thin air, for there was no place close by where they could have hidden beforehand. From another direction, more soldiers charged toward them on foot, again much too near to have been hiding anywhere but in the tall grasses. Then Horial noticed a group of infantry, and yet another of cavalry. In all, nearly half a dozen small units of troops were bearing down on them, easily forty soldiers or more.

Silver Ravens.

"Ambush!" the sergeant cried out, realizing that the group was almost surrounded. The only direction that remained open for retreat was away from the forest. "To the ruins!" he shouted, grabbing at Burtis, who had dropped to one knee and was loading his crossbow. "Don't waste your ammunition!" he told the Crescent as he shoved the man in the direction of the portal.

A crossbow bolt zipped past Horial's head as he spun and found Filana looking about, dazed. Horial tried to take hold of the woman and show her the direction he wished her to go, but she sagged down at his feet then, and he saw the arrow jutting from the small of her back.

"Damn it to the Nine Hells," Horial swore as he bent down and scooped the soldier up. Hefting Filana over his shoulder, he began to charge across the field as fast as his burden would allow. He spotted Edilus nearby, twirling a sling over his head and aiming at an oncoming mounted soldier. The druid released the sling and fired the stone just as Horial reached him. "Help me!" Horial said, trying to grab at the woodsman and pull him along. "I can't carry her by myself!"

Edilus spun to stare at the sergeant, hatred plain in his expression. "Betrayer!" he shouted in fury. "You warned them that we were coming! You planned this ambush!"

Horial nearly punched the druid in the face. "So they could run down my own soldiers? You're crazed!" Then he shook his head. "Suit yourself," he said, trying to quell his anger. He turned to run.

Ahead, Adyan, Burtis, and Grolo had reached the base of the outer wall of the ruined structure. The had formed a line and were firing back toward Horial and the wounded Filana, aiming at targets that must have been just behind the two of them. To Horial's amazement, two druids—one a wild elf and one a halfling, both with leaves and twigs tangled in their hair—had joined the mercenaries, working together to try to hold the ambush at bay long enough to allow their companions to catch up.

In the next instant, Horial felt the jolt of impact

twice in succession, and Filana jerked on his shoulder with a scream of agony. The mercenary felt two more strikes, but the woman did not react at all.

Then an arrow sank into the flesh of Horial's leg, just above the knee, and he went down in a tumble.

This is it, the sergeant thought, groaning as he waited for the mounted troops to ride him down. May Waukeen deem me worthy to be received in Brightwater, he prayed.

Just beyond Horial's sight, he heard the scream of men and mount, and the clash of weapon on weapon. Then, without warning, Edilus was there beside him, trying to help him up. Horial reached for Filana, trying to find a way to lift her while pushing on one good leg.

"Leave her," the druid snapped, grabbing at the sergeant and dragging him to his feet. "She's already left this world."

Indeed, Horial could see by then the multitude of arrows protruding from her back, one at the base of her skull. He closed his eyes for a heartbeat in sorrow, then grunted as Edilus forced him to move. Together, the mercenary and the druid limped toward the others. But they could not move fast enough to evade the first group of horsemen bearing down on them.

Edilus let Horial slide down to the ground as the druid yanked his scimitar free of a scabbard across his back and slashed at the closest cavalryman. Horial managed to get to one knee and bring his crossbow up, aiming at the next mounted foe coming in, a mace held high and ready to deliver a crushing blow. The sergeant fired his weapon and saw the horseman twitch then pitch off the far side of his saddle as the horse thundered by.

A hail of arrows and bolts swished through the air near Horial, and one caught him in the shoulder. The force of the missile wrenched him around and he groaned, letting the crossbow slide free of his grip as he sagged forward, his face pressing into the cool damp earth beneath him. For the second time that night, the mercenary was certain he would die.

But the riders did not come.

"Come on!" Edilus rasped, trying to lift Horial once more and cross the few remaining paces to the ruins. The sergeant looked around and saw that the cavalry had retreated under a hail of bolts and missiles from the group at the base of the ruins. They were reforming, though, and the infantry was moving in, coming straight at the tiny band of defenders with bows and swords brandished.

Horial limped beside the druid, who had the sergeant's good arm wrapped around his shoulders. Dizzy with pain, Horial could barely tell how close they were to the safety of the crumbling walls, and he expected at any moment to feel the sharp pain of more arrows piercing his flesh from behind.

After what seemed like an eternity, the pair reached the wall. Adyan took Horial's other arm and helped Edilus bear him into the structure while the remaining defenders continued to fire their weapons at the onrushing foes.

"Where's the portal?" Horial asked, fumbling in his pocket for the shard of quartz. He drew the fractured stone out and tried to hand it to Adyan. "Lead the way," he told his companion. "Go without me," he added.

Adyan shook his head. "We're all going back together," the man drawled, the scar along his chin shining faintly in the light of Selune. "Not leaving you here for those bastards to tear apart."

A cry of pain arose just on the other side of the wall, and when Horial turned to look, Grolo came dashing in through the gap in the stonework amidst a shower of projectiles. The dwarf looked Edilus squarely in the eye and said, "One of your mates is down, and the other, the wee fellow, went scampering through the grass in a blood fury. I don't think we'll see him again."

Edilus nodded but said nothing.

"Where's the thrice-damned portal?" Horial asked again. "We're out of time!"

"This way," Edilus said, turning and guiding Horial toward a partially collapsed flight of stairs. "The archway at the top," the druid said, pointing as they moved.

Horial eyed the top of the steps, for it looked as though the stairway was hanging by will alone and would fall over at the slightest push. "You're crazed," the sergeant breathed. "That will never hold us," he told the druid.

"It will," Edilus replied, "if you go one at a time."

"That doesn't help me," Horial said wryly, still leaning against the druid. "I don't think I can climb fast enough." He grabbed hold of Adyan's hand and slipped the shard of quartz into the man's palm. "Get up there," he said. "Get through the portal." Adyan started to protest, but Horial talked right over him. "If I make it, I make it, and if I don't ... Vambran is counting on us."

Adyan gave his friend one measured look, then he nodded and spun around. "Let's go," he said to Grolo.

The dwarf turned and followed Adyan at a distance,

waiting until the sergeant was at the top before proceeding.

Beside Horial, Edilus had drawn forth a totem, a bundle of twigs, leaves, and beads all tied together with strands of vine, and was chanting something indecipherable, his face turned heavenward and his eyes closed. Horial snuck a quick look toward the gap in the stone. The first shadows of moving figures were there, risking glances into the ruins, wary of attack from the defenders within. A lone swordsman stepped inside and rushed to the base of another crumbling wall, using it for cover. The figure gave a whistle and motioned for others to follow.

When Horial turned back to see what Edilus had planned, he saw that the druid had opened his eyes and was surveying the new arrivals. "Wait here," the woodsman said, then sprang up and launched himself forward, sprinting straight toward the wall behind which their enemies crouched.

If Horial hadn't heard the druid's command, he would have assumed that Edilus meant to throw himself among his enemies, going down fighting and buying the mercenaries the time they needed to escape. But the sergeant knew he would never reach the top of the stairs in time. Already, he was feeling light-headed from the wounds he bore. He watched, stunned, as Edilus rushed straight at the wall.

With a primal grunt of exertion, the druid slammed into the wall full on, driving his shoulder against it and making it shiver. The wall, already canted from time and neglect, shuddered. Edilus continued to push, snorting with the strain, even as the first of the enemy soldiers came around the end of the cover to confront him.

Horial managed to draw the line tight on his

crossbow and cock it in place with his good hand. He pulled his last bolt from the quiver at his hip, slotted it, and took aim, balancing the weapon on his knee and holding it with one arm. The enemy soldier stepped closer to Edilus, drawing back his blade. The druid, involved in his own efforts, hadn't yet seen the man. Horial steadied the crossbow as best as he could and squeezed the trigger lever, sending the bolt flying.

The sergeant's aim was not true, but the shot managed to graze the soldier across the buttock. He yelped in pain and staggered as his intended strike was ruined. The blade slammed down against the stone wall with a clamor, inches from Edilus's head. The druid jerked away in surprise, and the resulting extra force seemed to overbalance the wall just enough. It began to sag away from the druid, rumbling as it teetered over.

The soldier standing next to Edilus gave a warning shout to his men, but the wall was already on its way down, crashing to the earth with a bone-jarring roar. Horial had no idea how many soldiers were caught beneath that deadfall, but he knew they had little chance to survive. Those who were lucky enough not to be inside the ruin yet would have to find a new entrance, for Edilus's efforts had sealed off the opening with rubble and dust.

The enemy soldier, limping, tried to retreat from Edilus, but he was not quick enough to jump out of the way of a ferocious kick from the druid. The man's head snapped sideways and he dropped like a stone. Edilus wasted no time checking whether his enemy had fallen unconscious or not. He raced back to Horial, who was trying to drag himself up the stairs.

"At the top," Edilus said as he bent and scooped Horial up like a bundle of laundry, "you must go through the portal on your own. I cannot touch you to help you through."

Horial grunted as the druid began to ascend the leaning, groaning staircase, taking the steps two at a time even with the burden of the wounded sergeant. "You're coming, too," the wounded man said, spying Grolo just beginning to step through the archway. "If you stay behind, you'll die."

"Then so be it," Edilus replied, not even breathing hard as he climbed. The staircase was beginning to twist and lean more, and Horial could feel the druid shifting his weight, trying to maintain his balance and reach the top before the whole thing gave way. "This is where I belong. I will stay."

"Don't be a fool!" Horial said. "If the fall from up here doesn't kill you, the soldiers will! Come through with us, and return to fight them another day!"

Edilus didn't say anything, for all of his energy, all of his concentration seemed to be devoted to making the last few steps. The stairs were dissolving , bits and pieces crumbling away as the main part of the staircase began leaning, falling. At the top, on a tiny ledge that had remained intact, Edilus set Horial down so the man could put his weight on his good leg. He tried to step back, give the sergeant some room, but Horial shook his head.

"Come on!" he shouted, just as a swarm of Silver Ravens poured into the open space below. Edilus shook his head in denial, but Horial wasn't having any of it. Grabbing the druid, he jerked the man toward him. At the same time, he reached out to fall through the portal, intending to drag Edilus with him.

Horial was stunned to discover that his companion seemed rooted to the spot like a rock, but it made no difference. As the first swarm of arrows flew toward the two men from below, all the world shifted, and the sergeant and the druid vanished from sight just as the stones of the staircase crashed to the ground below.

CHAPTER 5

"Come on, you, move it," the small, wiry man known as Lak said, jabbing at Pilos's back with the butt end of his dagger. The priest grunted from the poke and tried to step faster, but descending the narrow, steep spiral staircase with his hands manacled behind his back was tricky work. The task was made even more difficult because of the limited light. The wizard in the magenta vest carried a single torch with her, but she was in the front of the procession. The other prisoner, Quill, walked behind the woman, with the big thug, Borth, keeping an eye on him. That left Pilos and Lak to bring up the rear, and in the narrow, crowded confines of the stairwell, not much illumination was reaching them.

Still, Pilos did the best he could, figuring if he did stumble and fall, he would land on Borth rather than tumble down the stairs. For a moment, he considered doing that anyway, wondering what the chances were of inflicting a few broken necks on his captors as they went sprawling. Those odds seemed better to the young priest than meekly being led to his death, but just when he was working up his courage to try the stunt, the stairwell began to give clues to their location.

The young Abreeant priest had noticed during the descent that the air was growing more humid and carried the odor of the harbor, and he suspected that they were nearing sea level. His suspicions were confirmed when he noticed that the steps and walls had abruptly turned slimy with moisture. The stairs also ceased then, leveling out into a straight and narrow passage. The entourage stopped as the wizard reached some sort of gate that barred their way.

The woman fumbled with it for a moment, presumably manipulating a lock, though Pilos couldn't see to know for sure. She shifted a huge bar, allowing the gate to swing open, away from herself. She passed through the barrier and the rest of the group followed behind. After perhaps half a dozen more steps, the route emerged into a much larger passage. Pilos was wary, wondering where the thugs had brought him.

The open space was actually a low-ceilinged tunnel, perhaps ten paces wide, that vanished into the distance, well beyond the light of the torch. It stank of waste and sea salt. Runnels of liquid poured down the walls or directly from small holes in the ceiling in various places, and the sounds of drips and splashes echoed in the distance.

The group stood at the end of the tunnel. At the

time, only brown sludge covered the bottom of the passage, but Pilos understood that the water level sometimes rose up past the roof when—

When the tide comes in, the priest realized, his fears growing. This is the sewer, and it connects to the harbor!

As if sensing Pilos's desperate recognition, the wizard chuckled. "Lak, Borth, get them ready," she said, sitting down on one side of the gate and opening a bag she carried. "We don't have much time," she urged.

Lak grabbed Pilos's arm and shoved him forward, sending him sprawling into the nasty muck. Without his hands free to stop himself, the young priest landed hard against the floor of the tunnel with a splat, striking his chin and coating his face with filth. Spots swam in his vision. When he regained his senses enough to realize what had happened, Lak was sitting on top of him, locking the second cuff of a pair of leg irons around his ankle.

No! Pilos thought, grunting and thrashing, trying to shake the little man off and free himself. No!

Lak jumped up once he had finished, and Pilos turned to see that Borth had similarly secured Quill, who was mumphing through his own gag and jerking at the manacles still restraining his wrists behind his back.

"Consider yourself ready," the small man said, his tone smug.

"If you could swim fast enough," the wizard said with a smirk in her tone as she pawed through the contents of the bag, "you might reach the end of the tunnel before you drown." She laughed and looked at Lak and Borth, who stood chuckling. Pilos saw that she was examining Xaphira's and Emriana's belongings. "It's a shame to lose these fine things," she commented, examining the various blades and jewelry, "but we can't take the risk that someone will come looking for them. So I guess we'll tie the bag around your neck so it can disappear with you. The current usually washes the bodies out in a day or two, doesn't it?"

The two thugs nodded. "Yeah, sometimes the fishermen find them floating near the boats," Borth said with glee in his voice, "but sometimes they head out to the open water and no one ever finds them."

Pilos watched as Quill suddenly tried to rise to his feet and rush at the three of them, desperation perhaps lending him strength, but Lak saw what was happening and kicked him with one boot, sending the bound man sprawling into the slimy muck again. The mercenary landed on his side with a grunt and lay there for a moment, gasping for breath.

Pilos turned to stare at the three thugs, wanting to give them one last defiant speech, but he held off when he saw the wizard. She had a very strange, almost pained look upon her face. He watched her as she stared at nothing for a moment. Then she stood suddenly and turned her attention down the tunnel. "What's that?" she said.

"What?" Lak asked, looking where she did. "What do you see?"

"I thought I saw something shiny," she said, pointing. "Way down there."

"Shiny like what?" Borth asked, craning his neck to get a better view.

"Maybe a bit of jewelry, glittering in the light of the torch. Go see," she ordered.

"Aw, there's nothing down there," Lak fussed, turning back to gloat over Pilos. "You're imagining it."

"What if there is something? What if it's a tiara covered in rubies? Part of the lost treasure of Narneth Elor, washed out of some secret hidey hole for us to find? Don't you want to make certain? Here," she said, holding out the torch for Lak. "Go check."

Lak looked at the wizard for a moment, his expression doubtful, then he sighed and grabbed the torch. "Come on," the small man grumbled at his larger companion, trudging down the tunnel. "Let's go see what she's talking about."

The two men took the light with them, leaving the wizard and her two prisoners in the ever-deepening darkness, and splashed through the slime. Pilos noticed it had risen slightly and had become shallow water.

Now, the young priest thought as he struggled to his feet, my only chance.

Pilos was up on one knee, trying to decide whether to slam himself into the wizard first to incapacitate her and stop her from using magic, or if doing so would give the two men too much time to return and catch up to him. Then the woman was beside him, her mouth close to his ear. Pilos wanted to bash his forehead into hers, possibly stunning her, but her words stopped him.

"Don't move," she whispered. "Let them get a little farther away first, or they will hear us."

The Abreeant gaped at her, though all he could see was the silhouette of her head. He opened his mouth to ask her what in the Nine Hells she was talking about, but she placed a finger on his lips, shushing him.

"Trust me," she said.

"Where is this thing?" Lak called from the distance. "We don't see any treasure!"

"I don't think you've gone far enough yet," the wizard called. "It was really a ways down there."

Pilos wasn't sure, but he thought he caught the sound of some disgruntled swearing. He waited, though, his heart pounding, wondering what the woman intended.

Finally, after another interminable moment, his captor said, "Now. Head for the stairs, as quietly as you can. No matter what happens, don't stop, don't turn around."

Pilos still didn't understand, but he didn't object as she helped him to his feet. He began to walk in the direction of the stairs, feet shuffling. His blind movements made splashing sounds like a roaring torrent in his ears.

In the distance, Pilos heard Lak shout, "Hey!" and he made the mistake of turning to peer over his shoulder. He could make out the silhouette of both Maquillon and the woman directly behind him, their outlines illuminated by the glow of the distant torch, which was growing stronger. "What are you doing back there?" the small man shouted.

"Damn," the wizard said from right behind Pilos. "Move it, you two," she muttered. "Get up those steps."

Pilos turned back to the task at hand, his heart threatening to leap out of his chest. He tried to take a few more steps, then slammed face-first into solid stone. He sat down with a grunt of pain, tasting blood on his lip and realizing that he had missed the smaller opening at the end of the tunnel. Right behind him, Quill nearly toppled over him, and the wizard collided with both of them.

"Don't stop!" she said, scrabbling around in the dark, trying to help them to their feet. "Get through the gate!"

Pilos could hear running footsteps behind them, but he was too afraid to turn around to see how close their pursuers were. Instead, he felt his way along the stone wall, sensing Quill frantically shoving him from behind. When he suddenly felt space in front of him, he darted forward, fighting against the water, which was nearly up to his knees. Three or four paces beyond the barrier, he crashed against the partially open gate, badly bruising his shoulder. He grunted in pain again as the gate creaked and swung almost completely shut. Quill bumped into him again from behind, and the man gave an urgent, almost frantic grunt, urging Pilos to keep moving.

Blessed Brightwater! Pilos thought, trying to wedge his shoulder between the gate and its frame so he could slip past it. Hold your ever-loving horses!

Finally he shifted enough to nudge the gate open and stumbled past the barrier, Quill right on his tail. Blind, Pilos continued forward until he struck the first submerged step with his toe and lost his balance, careening forward and slamming himself against the rough edges of the stairs.

Gods! the priest swore as he wailed in pain, for Quill tumbled on top of him once more, multiplying the injury. Next time, he thought miserably, you can go first.

The priest heard the harsh clang of the gate closing behind him, and he struggled to sit up and look back. Lak and Borth were perhaps thirty paces away, charging as fast as they could toward the three of them, fighting against the deepening water. The wizard was fumbling with the lock, trying to seal the barrier shut against the two men.

"Damn it, Laithe, what are you doing?" Lak demanded as he splashed along, closing the gap.

"Open that gate!" he yelled. "This isn't funny!"

Just as the wizard managed to snap the lock shut, Lak reached for her, Borth a few steps behind. The small man grabbed for the wizard but just missed her as she leaped back, out of reach. His face wedged between two of the bars of the gate, Lak stared at her, looking demonic in his rage. "I don't know what you think you're doing, but open it, now!" he snarled.

Borth reached past his companion and grabbed the bars of the gate, rattling them furiously. "Laithe," the bigger man said, a different edge to his voice. "Laithe, please unlock this gate. Whatever game you're playing, it's time to stop and let us through."

Pilos felt the water rising against him where he was still sprawled out on the steps. He felt a twinge of guilt at the thought of leaving the men locked behind that gate, but he banished it. They were ready to leave us there, he reminded himself.

Laithe moved to help Pilos and Quill to their feet, removing their gags as she did so.

As soon as the wad of cloth was out of his mouth, Quill began demanding an explanation. "What's going on? Why are you helping us? Unlock these manacles!"

"Hush, Maquillon!" Laithe scolded. "Be thankful I let you come along at all," the woman said, nodding her head toward the two men, who were frantically trying to yank the gate free. "After what you did to Xaphira, I had half a mind to leave you back there with them."

"Laithe!" Lak screamed, shaking the gate with his entire body. "Laithe, please!"

The wizard studiously ignored the two men and said, "I don't think they brought the keys for those manacles, I'm sorry to say. I guess they didn't expect to need to unlock them ever again. You'll have to manage as best as you can on the stairs until we find a way to get them off." Then she turned to Pilos and said, "Can you conjure up one of those magical lights Vambran and Kovrim are so fond of? Otherwise, we'll be climbing the stairs in the dark."

Pilos gaped at the woman, realizing at last. "Hetta?" he said softly, suddenly overjoyed.

The wizard smiled. "Yes, child. It's me." And she held up her hand, showing the ruby ring on her finger. "She started playing with the ring, and I took a chance. She's trapped in the stone, mad as a hornet, but she doesn't get her body back until I say so."

"Laithe or whoever you are, please!" Lak begged.

"Hetta!" Quill gasped. "It's actually you?"

The woman turned and glared at Quill. "Yes. Now hush. I don't want to speak to you for a good long time. Now," she said, turning back to Pilos, "how about that light? Time's wasting."

"I need my coin," Pilos said, relief flooding through him and making his voice waver. "It should be in the bag with the rest of Em's and Xaphira's things."

Hetta, in Laithe's body, fetched the holy symbol from within the bag and quickly enough, Pilos enchanted it to glow with soft, pearlescent light. She hung it around his neck and they turned to climb the stairs by its illumination, leaving Lak and Borth pleading in terror not to be left behind.

Their voices echoed up the spiral stairwell for a long time after Pilos, Quill, and Hetta left them, then without warning, the echoes were gone.

The climb was awkward and painful with the chains locked about their ankles, but the threesome made steady progress to the top. The route back to the prison was not far, and the trio returned to the chamber where Pilos and Emriana had first been captured.

The mirror was gone.

. . .

"There are too many of them!" Vambran yelled, yanking his sword free from yet another twitching, quivering zombie. The undead thing dropped in a heap at his feet, but two more shuffled closer to take its place, pressing the mercenary officer back. Even more of them, visible in the glare of the magical flare he had launched to help his tiny group see and fight, swarmed around the periphery of the battle. He slashed at the nearest one and lopped its arm off, but with every swing of his sword, the blade felt heavier. "We can't keep this up!"

"We should fall back," Arbeenok said, fighting on Vambran's left. "But the path is cut off in both directions."

Behind him and to the other side, the lieutenant heard Elenthia gasp, and he risked a quick glance in her direction to see what had upset her. Though she continued to swing the light mace they had found for her to use, pounding with both hands on anything that got close, her eyes were wide with unsuppressed horror, staring at something in the gloom. He shoved his blade out, skewering the nearest zombie, and stole another quick glance away from his fight, in the direction she had been staring.

Four more of the creatures were ambling out of a building on the far side of the street, distinct enough in the glow of the flare that Vambran recognized the identical cut and color of their clothing.

The Order of the Sapphire Crescent.

By the Bitch Queen, Vambran silently swore, recognizing them, naming their names in his head automatically: Hort Blogermun, Blangarl and Tholis, and the lad Velati. He wanted to retch.

Vambran stared for only a moment, but it was long enough for one of the nearest zombies to swing a fist near his head. He barely ducked in time, then anger and grief made his next swing vehement. The two halves of the zombie tumbled apart as they flopped to a street already slick with blood.

I kept hoping, the mercenary realized, that maybe they were still alive, imprisoned but safe. Damn! Damn them!

The lieutenant tightened his grip on his sword and slashed at the next zombie to stray near, and the next, and the next. His swings were vicious, driven by fury and grief. Chunks of bruised and decaying flesh flew in all directions, accompanied by spatters of cold, congealed blood. Undead bodies fell to the street, shorn apart by the mercenary's bitter rage. He waded in among the nightmare creatures, relentless. With every one he destroyed, he prayed to Waukeen, and to every other god he could think of who might care.

He prayed for the spirits of the people he was freeing from their already-dead bodies. Prayed for their families and loved ones.

He tried not to see their faces, not to see them as actual people. Some of them, sadly, were short and slight, after all. He kept cutting and slashing, trying to destroy the taint of the plague, driving forward, clearing a swath through the undead as tears rolled down his cheeks.

He didn't even let up when his blade sliced through the white and blue of a soldier he once knew.

What seemed like a long time later, exhausted, Vambran Matrell could find no more zombies to destroy. All around him, the tattered and broken remains of undead lay sprawled on the blood-slick cobblestones. None moved. Somewhere along the way, the magical light of his flare had vanished, and he had continued to battle by the light of Selune's sliver. The night was unnaturally still.

The mercenary let his blade drop then felt the overwhelming weariness in his arms, his legs, and his broken heart. He almost sat down right there, in the middle of the street. He didn't want to look at the bodies. If he looked at the bodies, he would see people—merchants, midwives, and children who were both horrific and all-too-human and fragile at the same time. So he stared at nothing for a while. Stared and panted and felt nothing but numbness.

Finally, Vambran remembered that he was not alone. Two people, alive, had been with him. He looked around.

Arbeenok was near the garden wall where they had started fighting. He watched the mercenary—a grim look was fixed on the alaghi's face. Elenthia was beside the druid, kneeling, her arms folded and resting across her raised knee. She also watched him, her eyes wide, staring. She seemed aghast.

The lieutenant began to walk toward the pair, and he thought Elenthia recoiled the tiniest bit. He held up his hand to show her that he was all right, and what he saw nearly made him stumble. He halted in mid step.

The mercenary's entire arm was sheathed in thick, black blood.

Vambran stared down and saw that he was drenched in gore from head to foot. The realization chilled him despite the warm, humid evening. Blood clung to him and ran in rivulets down his arms. It was matted in his hair. Somewhere, he knew, the blood of his soldiers was mingled in that mess.

"Water," Vambran said, filled with the urge to wash it away. "I need water," he repeated. He came closer, his arms spread out, unable to abide touching the slick wetness all over himself.

Elenthia said nothing, merely stared. But Arbeenok nodded. "On the other side of this wall," the alaghi said, "I can hear water running. Let's find a way inside."

Vambran nodded and stumbled after the druid. Elenthia rose and followed the two of them, but she kept her distance from the mercenary.

Vambran glanced over at Elenthia once and caught her staring at him. In her eyes he saw sorrow and repulsion. "It will wash away," he told her. He wondered if he meant it for himself, too.

"You—" she said, faltering. "I watched you—" Elenthia shook her head, unable to continue. She sped ahead, running to catch up to Arbeenok.

Vambran started to call to her, but he understood that words could not undo what he had become in her eyes. He recognized that haunted look all too well.

The druid led them to the side of the garden wall and discovered a gate set into it near the corner. It was locked, but the alaghi threw his shoulder into it a couple of times and broke through. Beyond the portal, the garden was filled with thick, flowering vines and meandering paths. Lush greenery rustled in the gentle sea breezes, blending the scent of their blossoms, and the trickle of running water came from near the middle of the enclosure. Arbeenok pushed through the dripping foliage and headed in that direction. Elenthia followed right behind the druid, leaving Vambran to bring up the rear.

When Vambran caught up to his two companions, he found them standing very still. They were at the edge of an open courtyard partially lit by a few lanterns hanging from poles around the perimeter. A fountain had once stood in the midst of the tiny plaza, a sculpture of a deific being bearing a shield and a horn and posing regally. But it was knocked over, and water flowed out of its basin and spilled onto the paving stones. There, a pair of great battles had been fought.

The first was all in miniature, an elaborate set-up of children's blocks made to look like a city, all walls and towers. Tiny toy soldiers were scattered through the city, many of them fallen, as though a great and terrible dragon had arrived and blasted them all from their defenses. The water from the ruined fountain spilled into the miniature city and flowed along its streets before draining away into the grass beyond.

The second battle was far more real. A contingent of what appeared to be House guards lay dead, scattered about the plaza. Intermingled with them were others, citizens, their skin pasty and blistered in the pale moonlight. It was clear to Vambran that the plague had visited that house, and no one had survived.

"Will any of them rise?" he asked Arbeenok as he stepped around Elenthia. "Perhaps we should not tarry here."

Arbeenok said nothing, though, so Vambran moved to the fountain, stepping among the toy blocks as he did so. He knelt down next to the basin and began to wash himself, rinsing away the film of blood as best as he could. He dunked his head in the water, swishing his hair about, trying to cleanse both his body and his mind of the terrible crimson taint that covered him. He didn't even care that the three blue dots inked on his forehead, his symbol of his education, were little more than pale turquoise smudges by the time he finished.

"I don't understand," Arbeenok said.

Vambran wiped water from his eyes and looked at the druid. "What?" he asked.

"My vision," Arbeenok said. "I see you there, as it was in my vision, but I still do not understand what it means."

"Your vision? What vision?"

"In the days before this journey, I foresaw this image. A man of blue and red, standing over a drowned city, a city surrounded by twelve swords. But I did not understand it."

Vambran looked around at himself, at his position. All the elements of the druid's description were there. He was in the middle of it all, partially washed clean so that his blue tunic showed through, and partially still tainted red by countless people's blood. And the soldiers' swords that lay scattered about the periphery completed the scene. It was not a pleasant image.

"Twelve swords?" Elenthia asked, seeming at last to come out of her stupor. "I don't count twelve. There are only nine dead guards."

Arbeenok nodded and pointed at the fountain. "There is a pair upon that shield," he said, and Vambran saw that the symbol engraved on the stone was indeed a set of crossed swords.

Then he looked down. "And my own blade makes twelve," he breathed. "But what does it mean?"

"It is the means of stopping the plague," Arbeenok said. "It is salvation for this city."

"What? Me, here? In this garden?"

"I don't know," Arbeenok replied, looking doubtful. "I don't think so. I—I don't know," he finished, shaking his head.

Elenthia bent down then, staring at the tiny city. "You said it was a drowned city?" she asked. "As in, covered in water?"

Arbeenok nodded. "Yes," the alaghi said. "But I do not know what that means."

"I think I do," the woman replied. "The Cities of the Twelve Swords."

"What?" Vambran asked, standing and shaking water from himself. He felt cleaner but still tainted.

"Ancient Jhaamdath," Elenthia replied. "The cities of Jhaamdath were called the Cities of the Twelve Swords."

"But Jhaamdath is at the bottom of the Reach," the mercenary said, doubtful of her interpretation.

"Exactly," Elenthia said, nodding. "Washed away by the wrath of the elves over fifteen hundred years ago."

Arbeenok nodded eagerly. "We must go there. Now. The secret of stopping the plague can be found there."

Vambran turned to look at the druid askance. "That's an awful lot of water to swim through," he said. "Do you have any idea where we should start?"

"No," the alaghi answered, smiling, "but you do."

"Me?" Vambran said, shaking his head in denial. "I don't have the smallest notion," he insisted.

"You are the man in my vision," Arbeenok said.

"Just because I had a little blood on me does not make me the figure in your portent," Vambran argued.

"It does," Arbeenok insisted. "I thought at first it symbolized a man who was at odds with himself, struggling between two paths—the blue and the red—and would find himself somewhere in between. But I was not taking it literally enough."

Vambran sighed. "Blue and red at odds, you say?" he asked. "As in my struggle between my duty to the Crescents and to my House?"

"Your house is red?" Arbeenok asked, puzzled.

"No, but the insignia is. A red four-pointed star, and all the guards wear that as a patch on their uniforms."

Arbeenok smiled again. "There, you see? You do believe it."

Vambran grimaced and nodded. "I still don't know how I'm supposed to find whatever it is we're looking for," he said.

"Let that take care of itself," the druid said. "The visions will guide us true."

"Vambran," Elenthia said, coughing.

"What?" the mercenary asked, turning to look at his counterpart.

Elenthia was holding her arm up in the air, staring at it. It was discolored, turning purplish blue. She coughed again, harder. "The plague," she said. "I think I've gotten it."

...

Being drawn back out of the mirror was just as unnerving as having been sucked into it. Emriana felt turned inside out, but just as soon as it washed over her, the feeling was gone again. She found herself huddled naked on the thick throw rug in the middle of Lobra's bedroom. Denrick stood beside her, leering down. The hunger in his eyes made her shiver.

On the far side of the chamber, Lobra sat upon a small couch, one leg drawn up beneath her. She regarded Emriana with what appeared to be mild amusement. "Well? Aren't you going to thank me?" she asked.

"For what?" she asked, disoriented.

"Why, for letting you out, of course," the woman replied. "Or did you forget your manners while you were tucked away in there?"

Emriana wasn't sure there was a correct answer to that question, but she didn't want to anger the woman before she even had a chance to get her bearings. "Thank you," she mumbled, huddling tighter. "Can I have my clothes, please?"

"Oh, I'm sorry," Lobra said with mock dismay in her voice. "I don't think they got delivered along with the mirror. But you don't really need them, anyway," she added with a sneer. "I think my brother prefers you without them."

Emriana didn't want to look up at Denrick, but she did anyway, regretting it. He looked ravenous. You're dead, she insisted, jerking her gaze away again sharply. You aren't really here. I watched you fall!

"It's not really him," Emriana muttered. "I watched him die. Your tricks aren't going to work."

"Did you, now?" Lobra said coldly. "Are you certain? Denrick, did she watch you die?"

By way of an answer, Denrick frowned at Emriana and said, "That wasn't very nice, what you did to me, kicking me over a balcony like that. It really hurt."

Emriana gaped at Denrick. She wanted to attribute the dead man's presence to a trick, an act of illusory magic, one of the twisted perversions of Lobra's House wizards. But no one in House Pharaboldi knew what had happened that night, when the young man had tumbled over the side of the third-story railing.

He was too real.

"No," she mumbled, "They said you died."

Denrick took up a small wooden chair, one that matched the writing desk near the mirror, and placed it right in front of her so that it was facing backward. He straddled the chair and sat, staring at the girl, letting that wolfish grin that had haunted her nightmares in recent tendays return. "I think they made a mistake," he answered.

Emriana retreated from him, backing herself into a corner of the room. She drew her knees up and watched him, remembering exactly how he had cornered her once before, in her bedroom. "You tried to rape me," she said, hatred mixing with her fear. "I'm glad I kicked you over! You deserved it!" She shrank away, turned her head, tried to blot the boy out of her consciousness.

"I knew it!" Lobra crowed, standing and pointing an accusing finger at the girl. "It *is* all your fault!"

Emriana looked at the other woman, incredulous. "Didn't you hear me?" she said, nearly shouting. "I said 'rape.' He tried to rape me. He even had that nasty wizard Bartimus ready to help him! Charm me and make me like it!" She felt tears running down her cheeks. She wiped them away defiantly, but Lobra only chuckled.

"And now he's going to finish the job," the woman said, the ice in her voice making the girl shiver. She crossed the room to stand right before the girl, bending

down to sneer at her. "You and your wretched family
ruined me, ruined my House," she said, her lips drawn
back in a rictus of hatred, showing her teeth. "Took
away my family from me. So now I'm returning the
favor. They'll always wonder what became of you. But
they will still be the lucky ones, because they'll never
know. You, however, *will* know. You'll sit in that mirror
and remember it forever." With those chilling words,
she moved back to the couch. As she passed Denrick,
she added, "She's all yours. Whatever you do, don't go
easy on her," she added, her voice dripping with hatred
as she sat down again, adjusting her skirts while she
watched.

Emriana couldn't help but look up at Denrick as
he stood, slid the chair out of the way, and came at
her. She balled her hands into fists, ready to make
him pay dearly for what he sought.

CHAPTER 6

The celebration of Sammardach was winding down in the small hours of the night, but a few guests still seemed reluctant to depart the Generon. As Bartimus followed Grozier, Falagh, and Lavant through the halls of the great palace, the wizard began to wonder if those last few stragglers might not be changing their minds. He certainly wished he were somewhere else right then. He cringed as Falagh Mestel swore again.

"Stop avoiding me," Falagh ordered Lavant, nearly shouting as he followed the Grand Syndar. "I asked you a question!"

The high priest moved rapidly for such a hefty man, and the other three with him had to scurry to keep up. He neither spoke nor turned back toward Falagh. What had

surprised Bartimus the most, however, was the
strange smile Lavant had adopted once he heard the
news from Grozier and Falagh.

Reth was swarming with zombies.

"You knew this was going to happen," Grozier
accused in the direction of Lavant's elbow. "You've
been waiting for it. Why?"

Finally, Lavant stopped and turned to face his
pursuers. "Gentlemen, please. The activities taking
place in Reth at this very moment have nothing
whatsoever to do with our venture. It may turn out
to be an unforeseen complication, but I do not think
it will limit our profits in any way. Now, you must
excuse me. I need to speak with Lord Wianar immediately. There is much to do." And with that, the
ample man turned and hurried down the passage,
leaving Falagh and Grozier staring after him in
bewilderment.

"This isn't over!" Falagh called after Lavant,
drawing a few uncomfortable looks from nearby
guests. "House Mestel will have its due!"

Lavant ignored the man.

"Tar and trollops!" Falagh cursed, smacking a fist
into his other palm. "He's practically gloating!"

"I don't understand," Grozier said, pacing. "Why
would he want Reth to burn? You saw the look on his
face. He's positively gleeful! It's as though he wasn't
just expecting it, but actually planning—" Bartimus's
employer stopped in mid-sentence, frozen in place, his
jaw hanging open. "He planned it," the man finished
in hushed tones. "He's been waiting for it because he
planned it."

Falagh gave Grozier a measured look. "I think
you may be right," the Mestel scion said. "But your
first question remains. Why would he want such a

thing?" Then, as if he were realizing for the very first time that they were not alone, Falagh glanced around. "We can't discuss this any further in here," he announced, turning to Grozier as he gestured all about. "We need to go somewhere more private. Bartimus, open one of your doorways and take us back to House Pharaboldi."

The wizard nodded and started to comply, but Grozier grabbed his arm and held it. "Now wait a minute, Mestel," Talricci said, waggling a finger at Falagh. "Bartimus works for me, not you. *I* tell him when and where to take us."

Falagh threw his hands in the air in exasperation. "Don't be ridiculous," he said. "It doesn't matter who—" Then he stopped and sighed. "Very well," he said with mocking patience. "Please instruct your wizard to whisk us somewhere more secure so that we might discuss this further in private. I would suggest the sitting room at the Pharaboldi estate, but it is entirely your call."

Grozier nodded. "I think that's a fine idea," he said, then turned and nodded to Bartimus as he released the wizard's arm. Though his employer didn't notice it, Bartimus saw Falagh glower and shake his head.

For the briefest of moments, Bartimus contemplated just whisking himself back to his own chambers, leaving the other two men behind to sort their conflict without him. He did not much care for their company when they bickered, which was happening more and more frequently. Then he dismissed the thought and conjured the magical doorway, concentrating to anchor the opposite end in the sitting room, as Grozier—and Falagh—had instructed.

One by one, the three men stepped through.

Bartimus sought his favorite corner and waited to be of some use. Grozier began to pace and Falagh sent a servant scurrying for glasses and a decanter of something to drink.

"Make it something strong," the man ordered, then sat down on one of several sofas to wait. "Unbelievable," he muttered, and Bartimus wasn't certain whether he was speaking about Grozier's behavior or Lavant's.

"All right," Grozier began, oblivious to Falagh's continued disapproval. "Let's work through this and figure out what that fat toad is up to." He began ticking points off one at a time on his fingers. "First, he puts together a business deal between my House, the Pharaboldis, and the Matrells."

Falagh grimaced but nodded. "A reasonable, if ambitious, effort. Lots of investment up front, very little return early on. Something that few other Houses in Arrabar would agree to, given the risks and outlay of coin." He shook his head. "Looking at it from that perspective, it begins to sound like a real confidence job. Notice that the temple has nothing invested in the venture, Grozier."

"Right," Grozier answered. "The temple's gains would be through favorable contracts. We need an army, the temple can supply one. I always assumed that he was just generating business for the glory of Waukeen."

"Perhaps," Falagh said, stroking his moustache as he thought. "Heavy skirmishing was a key part of the plan, that's for certain."

At that moment, the servant returned bearing a tray with crystal ware and a decanter with a fiery red liquid inside. Bartimus noted that another figure followed the servant. It was Lobra. She crossed to a chair in a corner of the room and sat down, ignoring Falagh's brief frown as he stared at her.

"What are you doing here?" he asked, sounding somewhat put out. "I thought you were tormenting the Matrell girl."

"I got bored," was all she would say in response. "My 'brother' is still with her, though," she added, adopting a rather unpleasant smile.

Falagh grunted and turned back to the discussion. "So, why did Lavant's plan hinge on skirmishes to drive up the cost of lumber?" he asked, stroking his moustache again. He stood up as a revelation seemed to strike him. "Not just a little skirmishing, but out and out war," he said. "Lavant wanted to see full-scale war in the region. The lumber scheme was just an excuse to stir up hardship in the area. We improve lumber prices by controlling supply militarily. And if it gets out of hand, so what? The temple benefits regardless. He played us perfectly," Mestel snarled.

Grozier shook his head, seeming uncertain. "Why go to all that trouble just to generate conflict? There's enough war in all of Faerûn to keep the temple armies steadily employed without our help."

Falagh shrugged. "Maybe to justify it to the Waukeenar. Their motive is profit, not war. It probably wouldn't set well with the rest of the clergy to start a war for war's sake alone. So he fabricated our ill-fated lumber empire to cover it all up."

Grozier nodded, looking grave. "But that just seems to come full circle without accomplishing anything. And it doesn't explain the zombies."

Falagh shrugged again. "What difference does it make? We gave him what he wanted, and now we're left holding the empty coin purse while he feeds the flames of war. Nine Hells, maybe he needed the undead to underscore just how valuable a mercenary army of priests would be, where other forces fall short."

"But they had to come from somewhere else, right?" Grozier said, his expression full of doubt. "None of the plans we developed involved necromancy. If he was behind the zombies, then he had to get someone else involved, someone we don't know about."

Bartimus realized the answer was on the tip of his tongue, so he spoke it aloud before anyone else did. "Lord Wianar."

Falagh turned to look at the wizard as Grozier stopped pacing, realization making them both gape. "Ah, yes," Falagh said, pursing his lips. "Our dear Shining Lord. Zombies would be just his touch. But why?"

"He is always fostering war," Grozier said, shrugging. "Why is this any different?"

"He's always fostering war among the great Houses of Arrabar," Falagh corrected. "He likes to see us squabbling, to be sure—it leaves us little time to challenge him directly. But this is in Reth. He doesn't even have a claim to—"

Bartimus saw Falagh sit up straighter then, a look of profound understanding mixed with something ... horrific ... upon his face. He imagined his own expression must have been similar, for a most unsettling thought had crossed his mind at about that same moment.

"He's letting Lavant destabilize the region so he can conquer it," Falagh uttered, an incredulous look upon his face. "He wants to bring Reth back into the fold."

"That's preposterous," Grozier said, shaking his

head as if he doubted his own thoughts. "He would have to react so quickly, be ready to pounce at a moment's notice to take advantage of the chaos. He would need major armed forces in the field right now to do such a thing."

"Such as, perhaps, the kinds of mercenary forces that could be put together with sizeable contributions from three Houses?" Falagh suggested, giving Grozier a knowing stare. "Talricci, we've been played, but good."

Grozier sank down onto the sofa and placed his head in his hands. "We have," he agreed. "We let Roundface and Lavant handle so many of the details, let them serve as go-betweens and deal with our armies in the field. We are fools!" he shouted, his voice echoing through the room.

None of the men spoke. Each was absorbed in his own thoughts, his own painful realizations. Finally, Grozier raised his head again. "So, what do we do now? How do we regain control and get something out of this?"

Falagh shook his head. "No, no. I'm not going to put a twist on this whole mess and place my House between Lord Wianar and his objectives. If he wants to expand Chondath's borders, the two of us can't hope to stop him. That's a fool's errand."

"But we can't just let it all slip through our fingers," Grozier argued, sounding on the verge of wailing. "I've invested far too much into this enterprise! House Talricci will be ruined!"

"As will House Pharaboldi," Falagh said, shrugging. "Fortunately, Lobra will have House Mestel to fall back on. In fact, my family will most likely just absorb her assets, to recoup our own investments, of course," he added, turning to look at his wife.

She seemed completely unfazed by her husband's words.

"Don't you dare back out of this now," Grozier growled, standing and squaring himself to Falagh. "Don't you leave me hanging in the midst of this. I'll kill you."

Falagh raised his eyebrows, giving Grozier a disapproving look. "Oh, do you think so?" he said sardonically. "Big words from someone standing in a house filled with another man's guards."

"You forget," Grozier said smugly, "that my wizard there can deal with your House guards quite effectively."

No! Bartimus thought, groaning. Don't bring me into the middle of this!

"Get out," Falagh said, his voice cold. "Out of this house right now."

Grozier sniffed. "I think not," he said, and Bartimus wondered why his employer would choose to make a stand right then, with the odds arrayed against them.

At that moment, all went to chaos. Falagh flung his glassful of beverage at Grozier's face. As the man threw up his hands to ward off the attack, Falagh grabbed a dagger from inside his tunic and raised it high, ready to plunge it into Grozier's back. Grozier, stunned by the sudden attack, shouted in pain and staggered away, pawing at his eyes.

Bartimus opened his mouth to shout a warning, then changed his mind and decided on a quick spell to hurl at Falagh, then changed his mind once more and began reaching for a wand he had hidden away, but he was not fast enough. The Mestel scion leaped forward and plunged the blade squarely into his foe's back. Grozier grunted and arched his back, but instead of penetrating the man's flesh, the dagger glanced off to the side with an audible clank.

Falagh stared at the dagger in surprise as Grozier whirled on him, pulling a dagger of his own. "Fool," Talricci sneered, waving his blade in front of himself, threatening his opponent. "You're not the first coward who's tried to plunge a blade into my spine."

Ah, Bartimus remembered, the ring I crafted for him. I forgot about that.

The two men crouched, both their expressions grim, but before the skirmish could truly begin, Lobra pounced. Bartimus thought she would go for Grozier, expecting that she was attempting to aid her husband, but instead, she grabbed Falagh by the arm and flung him sideways, twisting his wrist as she did so and forcing him to drop the weapon. The woman's strength was remarkable, and Falagh smacked into a tapestry-covered wall head-first, then slumped to the ground with a groan.

Bartimus stared in amazement, wondering why the woman would turn on her own husband. Lobra began to shift, becoming the changling in its natural form. The wizard smiled, feeling the fool. "Very clever," he said.

At that moment, a Pharaboldi House guard entered the room, perhaps to see what the commotion was about. Upon witnessing the violence taking place, he yanked his sword free and began screaming for reinforcements as he took a step forward.

Avoiding his previous hesitation, Bartimus withdrew a small crystal rod from a pocket inside his robes. The hollow rod was filled with glowing moss that gave off a very faint greenish light. Bartimus gestured rapidly at the guard with the crystalline object. A swirling, undulating curtain of colors sprang up, catching the man in its midst when he put one foot in the room. The shimmering coalescence writhed in place, filling the doorway. The guard stopped and stood still, staring dumbfounded at the colors surrounding him.

Bartimus slipped the rod back into its protective pocket and turned toward Grozier, who was wiping his eyes with the hem of his doublet. The wizard moved to the man and muttered, "We must leave right now," hoping the shapeshifter would help him convince Grozier of the prudence of departure.

A gasp and a cry of dismay sounded out in the hall, and Bartimus turned his attention that way once more. Two more guards stood mesmerized in the middle of the swirling curtain of color, enraptured with the shifting veil all around them. On the far side of it, unable to circumvent the enchantment, three others watched in dismay. One of them spun and ran in the opposite direction.

"Wizard!" the guard yelled at the top of his lungs as he disappeared. "I need a wizard right now!"

Bartimus, knowing they were running out of time, turned back just in time to spy his employer plunging Falagh's own dagger into the downed man's back. Mestel jerked and cried out, shuddering. Grozier stood over the man, a sneer on his mien, and raised the blade high for another blow.

"No time!" Bartimus shouted, already preparing the last of the magical doorways at his disposal. "The whole House is coming!" And with that, he conjured the blue, shimmering portal.

Out in the hall someone shouted, and Bartimus glanced over long enough to see that his swirling halo of magical light had vanished. The guards who had been ensnared in its effects were regaining their bearings, and the rest pushed past them, trying to get into the room and at the perpetrators. The wizard scurried to his blue doorway.

Not waiting, he thought, as he launched himself at the portal.

Grozier gave a quick kick at Falagh, snapping the man's head sideways, just as the shapeshifter grabbed him and hustled him toward the magical exit. All three of them reached it at the same time. They plunged as one through the passage, which vanished just as three guards closed in on it.

· · ·

When Darvin arrived at the Generon, it took him a few minutes to track down Eles. Though the Sammardach celebration had dwindled to small groups of partygoers gathered in nooks and crannies of the palace, talking earnestly, it still took the assassin some time to wander through the halls, searching. Periodically he would stop and ask guards if they had seen their lord about. He finally caught up with the man standing on a balcony on a high level of the palace, looking out over the gardens and into the warm, humid night.

Lavant was there already, and the look on the high priest's face told Darvin that they already knew at least part of the situation in Reth.

Darvin strolled up to the two men and cleared his throat. Lavant looked up with annoyance clear on his face, but when he saw who it was, his frown changed to a gleeful smile. "Have you heard?" the Grand Syndar asked, almost chortling. "It's begun."

"Yes," Darvin said, nodding. "I just came from there. But all is not shiny and wonderful in dear Reth," he said. "We have a problem."

"What problem?" Eles Wianar said, turning and scowling. "Now is not the time for problems."

Darvin took a deep breath. He did not relish bringing such unpleasant news to the most powerful man in Arrabar. "Rodolpho is not being as cooperative as we would like." Then he shook his head. With others, he could deliver bad news in a roundabout way, smooth the edges, sugarcoat the nuggets. But with Eles, it was better just to speak plainly. He had a way of seeing exactly what others did not want him to see. "He made the plague too virulent," Darvin explained, "and refused to create a cure. He apparently still harbors some resentment over his forced involvement with your plans."

Lavant clucked his tongue. "Not surprising," the high priest said. "There are ways around that. I can formulate a cure in a matter of hours. I'm sure of it."

Darvin shook his head, not so sure. "It may be too late in a matter of hours," he replied. "Half the city is engulfed in flames, and bodies are rising on the streets before they're even cold."

That description wiped the largest portion of Lavant's smile from his face. "Truly?" he said, his voice less exuberant than it had been before.

Darvin nodded. "As I said, I was just there moments ago. I saw it myself. And Rodolpho was painfully clear about his intentions."

"I'm sure he was," Eles said, though the tone of his voice was not terribly humorous. "He was the one biggest wrinkle in my plan," the Shining Lord mused. "I thought he might be reticent about cooperating. Twelve years is a long time."

Darvin started to ask Eles why he had chosen his cousin if he had had misgivings, but he thought better of it. Instead, he said, "In the interests of preventing a total disaster, I took the liberty of redirecting some of our forces a little earlier than we had planned. I had Havalla turn some of his troops around and lay siege to Reth. Maybe that way, we can contain the plague as long as necessary to devise a solution."

Lavant made a slightly strangled sound. "Why do you keep taking it upon yourself to change things without consulting us?" he demanded. "You may have just ruined our chances of swooping in at the right time."

Darvin shook his head again. "Trust me, there will be plenty for you and your temple troops to clean up. Even with that change, it may not be enough to keep the disease localized. All of Reth may be a graveyard or worse by morning."

"You exaggerate," Lavant said, his eyes wide.

It's about time you understood the true magnitude here, Darvin thought. "I don't," he said. "Half the city was in chaos, burning. This was a calculated acceleration on Rodolpho's part. He intended for it to get out of hand. I don't think he even expects to survive."

Lavant's loss of composure was brief. "Nonsense," he said, drawing himself up. "I will still arrive at the head of Lord Wianar's army, prepared to deliver defeat to Arrabar's enemies and blessed healing to the ravaged people of Reth. You will have your city back, my lord."

Eles shook his head. "Don't be cocksure," he told the priest. "I trust Darvin's judgment as much as I trust anyone with anything, and if he's concerned, then I am too."

Lavant looked wounded, but he recovered. "Then I am at your disposal to handle this however you see fit," he said, bowing slightly. "Though I still assert that I can generate an effective cure for the plague rapidly enough to prevent disaster."

Eles waved a hand, dismissing Lavant. "Then go and do so," he ordered, "and let me know as soon as you have something definitive."

Lavant bowed again and departed.

Once the Grand Syndar was out of earshot, Darvin turned to Eles and said, "He is too sure of himself, my lord. This plague that Rodolpho cooked up is horrific. I don't think you should place all of your trust in the Waukeenar. You need a second option."

"Of course I do," Eles answered, smiling that smile that always made Darvin's skin crawl. "You're going back to Reth to wring a solution out of Rodolpho."

Darvin sighed. "I don't know if that's possible. When he said he hadn't created one, I got the impression he was sincere. I think he somehow knew this was the last great thing he was going to do with his life, and he took great delight in thwarting you."

Eles's scowl became a glower. "Lesser opponents do not thwart me," he said. "Deal with this."

Darvin nodded in resignation. Somehow, he had known all along that it would come down to that. "All right," he said at last. "But I can't get back there on my own. Laithe will have to help me."

"Fine," Eles said. "Take your sister along."

"Half-sister," Darvin corrected, then immediately regretted it.

"Darvin," Eles said, his face a mask. "Don't think that just because you are my flesh and blood that you can fail me in this. I will have Reth."

Darvin nodded. "I know, Father. I'm on my way."

...

"Can you heal her?" Vambran asked.

Arbeenok shrugged, trying to imitate the human gesture. It still felt strange to him to do so, even after several years among humans. "I do not know," he said, "I can try."

"Do it," Vambran said, forcefully, but Arbeenok understood that he was asking, pleading, not ordering. The alaghi understood, and he did not object, but the man's intense drive was remarkable. There was a fire in his eyes, a fierceness to act, to succeed, burning inside him at all times.

And there was conflict.

Arbeenok could see that Vambran questioned himself with every decision he made. The soldier scrutinized all his choices, never satisfied that he had selected wisely or had done enough. Arbeenok wondered where in his life he had failed. He wondered what had convinced the man that he was not capable of choosing the wise course.

His passion is admirable, the alaghi thought, but he will burn himself up if he cannot find balance.

Arbeenok turned from the soldier and examined the woman, Elenthia. She stared back at him with wide, frightened eyes. He understood her fear, too. Hers was far more defined. She was dying, and she knew it. "Try to relax," he told her.

Then Arbeenok began to sing.

The druid sang to the wind and the stars, to the earth somewhere below, calling to the natural soil that lay beneath the carefully aligned stones, down past the unnatural layer of the garden. He sang to the ocean that he could smell but could not see. He sang to them all, asking them to restore the balance in Elenthia, to cleanse her of the perverse disease that infested her.

They could not aid him.

Arbeenok's song turned inward, seeking some energy that he could harness within himself, from the spirits of the animals that resided in harmony in him, hoping perhaps to drain away the woman's sickness into himself and dissipate it.

The sickness was too strong.

Arbeenok opened his eyes and looked at his companions. Both were watching him intently. He had seen such looks before by those who had never heard him use his magic. He paid their stares no mind. "It cannot be cleansed by my magic alone," he said. "It is too unnatural for my healing skills." Arbeenok watched Vambran's face turn stony, as though bracing for the inevitable. "I can arrest it, though," the druid said, hoping that the two of them would understand. Sometimes, finding the words to explain things to outsiders was difficult. "Slow it," he added.

"Do it," Vambran said again, once more in that forceful, demanding tone. For him, failure was a fate too horrible to contemplate. Arbeenok could see that.

"It will not cure her," Arbeenok warned, wanting the soldier to understand that it was a temporary solution and would hold for a day at most. "She will still be ill, but the sickness will not ... progress."

Vambran began nodding even before Arbeenok finished speaking. "Buy us time, that's good enough," he said. "And we'll go to the bottom of the Reach, burrow into the rock if we must in order to find whatever it is we're supposed to find."

Arbeenok smiled, glad that Vambran was ready to accept the alaghi's vision, to follow their entwined fates to their logical conclusions. "Yes," he said. Then he closed his eyes and began to sing once more, a different song, one to slow the poisons in Elenthia's body rather than drive them out. He felt the contagion begin to slumber, fall dormant. Satisfied, he finished the song, locking the magic in place for as long as he was able.

When it was done, Arbeenok opened his eyes and nodded to tell his companions so. The relief on both their faces was clear. "We must rest," he said.

"There's no time," Vambran argued, his intense eyes looking away to some distant place, not just in space but also in time. He was peering toward the future, always toward the future, trying to catch up to it and yet never seeing it as it went by. "We have to go, get out of the city. People are dying."

"No," Arbeenok said. He stood, then, pulling Vambran away from the woman, off to the side where they could talk alone. "We must rest. *She* must rest." Vambran stared hard at the alaghi for a long moment, his eyes glittering dangerously. "I have seen you yawn many times just since we arrived in this garden," the alaghi added. "When was the last time you slept?"

Vambran looked away. "I don't remember," he said, avoiding the question. "A lifetime ago."

"You have not slept since I met you, when you were dangling from a pole by your tied hands and feet, hardly a good bed. And that was in the small hours of this morning. How long before that?"

Vambran sighed. "Not since the ship," he said. "Not since two nights ago."

"You cannot save the city if you wear yourself to exhaustion," Arbeenok said. "And she will not last long without rest. The harder you push her, the more quickly my magic will ... vanish. No, fade.

The more quickly it will fade. Do you understand? It can weaken if her body is not strong enough to maintain it."

Vambran sighed then, letting his shoulders slump. "All right," he agreed at last. "If she needs the rest, I could do with some as well. But we've got to find some place safe. Some place where we can defend her, you and I, without her needing to fight. Better yet, someplace where damnable zombies won't bother us at all."

Arbeenok looked toward the house. "Up there?" he asked, pointing to a second floor window that overlooked the garden. "I do not think the former owners will mind," he said.

Vambran nodded. "I'll take a look inside, just to make sure nothing is hiding in there. You stay here with her."

When the soldier was gone, Arbeenok sat beside Elenthia. She leaned against a tree, her breathing eased somewhat by the effects of Arbeenok's song, but it was still raspy. The alaghi thought it best not to discuss the sickness. "Do you love him?" he asked, thinking to begin a nice conversation.

"Vambran?" Elenthia replied, looking aghast. "Ilmater's mercy, no. He's . . . he's just a friend."

"But you are mates," Arbeenok said, puzzled. "I can sense it in the way you look at one another. You have shared a bed."

Elenthia blushed slightly. "Yes, we have," she admitted. "But only as friends. Our lives are much too different. He visits me from time to time, and I enjoy his company when he comes to Reth. That's all."

Arbeenok considered the woman's words for a few moments. "It must be that way between Vambran and Shinthala, too."

"Pardon me?" Elenthia said, looking sharply at the alaghi. "Who in the Nine Hells is Shinthala?"

"Shinthala Deepcrest, Grand Cabal of the Emerald Enclave. They, too, are friends."

"I see," Elenthia said, but her tone was strangely flat. "So, he's bedding a druid, is he?"

Arbeenok looked at the woman strangely, not understanding the question, but at that moment, Vambran returned.

"The house is empty, save for a few unfortunate souls in one downstairs room. I checked to make sure they were really dead." His eyes flickered away for a moment, gazing into that invisible distance. "It was the rest of the family," he concluded, his voice thick.

Together, Vambran and Arbeenok carried Elenthia up to a bedroom and laid her on a thick, soft mattress. Vambran settled onto a divan against the wall, facing Elenthia as though to watch over her. The alaghi saw her give him one curiously unpleasant stare, and she turned her back on him, wrapped the silk sheet about herself, and closed her eyes.

Vambran was breathing slowly and softly a moment later.

So they rested, with the alaghi keeping watch, listening for the approach of enemies, of undead, of anything that would disturb them. Outside, beyond the garden wall, fires still burned everywhere in the city. Occasionally, shouts rose from down in the streets, though Arbeenok could not see what transpired there. Nothing came to disturb them.

Arbeenok felt a small amount of gladness in watching his companions sleep, for their faces were peaceful. He was thankful that he had done something, some small thing, to thwart the terrible sickness, to thwart the strange men of the cities who had brought it.

The three of them remained in sheltered quiet for several hours. At last, Arbeenok spied the sun beginning to peek over the tops of the closest buildings, the first rays coming to warm the land, to bring bountiful life-giving essence to all the birds and beasts and fishes. He closed his eyes and sighed, enjoying for a brief moment the joy that came to him with the dawning of each new day.

CHAPTER 7

Pilos peered through the cracked doorway
out into the hall beyond, but no one
stood near. Sighing with relief, he shut
the portal again and made certain that it
latched properly.

"Must have been some stray draft, blow-
ing the door open," he said as he returned to
the far end of the room, well away from the
door. "There was nothing out there."

Pilos and Quill, along with Hetta—still
hosted inside Laithe the wizard's body—
had retreated to the library where the
young priest and Emriana had hidden
before, when they had been searching
the Generon for Xaphira. After failing to
locate the mirror in which Emriana was
trapped, they had decided to hide out for a

while and plan their next move.

Hetta had located a set of keys in the prison chamber that freed the two men from their manacles, for which Pilos was truly thankful. His wrists and ankles were sore and bruised from being jerked and banged about by the metal. Once they had the restraints off, they wasted no time departing the dungeon, retracing the path the Abreeant and the girl had originally taken to get down there.

"Why don't you tell me exactly what has happened here?" Hetta demanded, standing over Quill, who sat leaning against one of the bookshelves, looking forlorn. "Start from last evening, when you met with my daughter and granddaughter, and don't you dare leave anything out."

Sighing in resignation, the mercenary began. "After Xaphira came to see me the first time, I knew she was asking for trouble hunting for a man like Junce Roundface. But I was so glad she was still alive, so happy that I had found her after all these years, that I wanted to try. For her. Somehow, Junce knew before I did that I was going to come looking for him. He arranged it so that when I started asking around, the information I got led right to him—and about five thugs.

"The long and short of it is that the meeting went exactly the way he wanted. He made it vividly clear that I could either help him, or Xaphira would die. I decided to help him, because he assured me that once he was done with her, I could take her away, slip out of Arrabar, and the two of us would never look back. That was his promise."

"And you trusted him?" Pilos asked, his words harsh, clearly both incredulous and resentful. "You know what kind of vile serpent he is, and you actually agreed to get him what he wanted," the priest added, shaking his head and turning away.

"That's precisely why I did it," Quill argued. "I knew that he could make good on his threats, and I didn't see much choice. I didn't want to see Xaphira disappear again after . . . after so long."

"Did Roundface manage to let slip exactly what he intended to do?" Hetta asked, her words no less harsh than Pilos's. "Did he mention how he has been trying to destroy my entire family? Did you really think Xaphira would want anything to do with you once she found out your role in such a thing?"

Quill shrugged, his expression sullen. "I wasn't thinking beyond just trying to save her life," he muttered, looking down. "I just wanted to protect her. I'm just one man. I can't save your entire House."

Hetta snorted. "You certainly can't if you don't even try. I'm glad you're not one of my children. I'm sure your mother would be very proud right now, if she'd heard your little explanation."

Quill didn't say anything, but he continued to avoid his companions' gazes.

"So what happened?" Pilos prodded. "You obviously set it up for her to be caught."

Quill nodded and continued. "He told me that all I had to do was meet her as I had originally agreed, then take her to 'meet a man who knew where he was.' He said he would take care of the rest. We set everything up in a shed in the alley behind the Silver Fish—that's the *rathrur* where I was to meet her. All he told me was, once I had entered the shed, I had better close my eyes. So I did."

"And just like Emriana, he got Xaphira to gaze into a mirror," Pilos said. "She never had a chance."

"Yes," Quill said. "Then he kept promising me that

he would free her once he had dealt with the other members of the family who were troubling him. After he caught Emriana, I thought he'd be finished, but it was pretty clear that he never intended to let her out."

"And now you know, too late, that you never should have trusted him," Hetta said. "So you learned your lesson. Now you have to live with what you've done."

Quill looked up at the woman, sorrow and desperation clear in his mien. "I'll help you find her," he said. "Let me do that."

"Oh, absolutely," Hetta replied. "I would expect no less from you. I think you owe her that, at the very least."

Pilos began to pace. "But we have no idea where the mirror has gone. How are we going to find it now?"

Hetta looked at him. "Isn't your magic strong enough to track it down, as you did before, with Emriana?"

Pilos shook his head. "There are ways I could do it, but I have nothing prepared. By the time I do, it'll be too late."

"Then we'll consider that a fallback idea," Hetta said in a businesslike tone, "and come up with other, more immediate solutions."

"Laithe probably knows something," Quill ventured. "Can you ask her?"

"Yes," Hetta replied. "I could release her from the ring and let her back into her body," she said. "But it's doubtful I could overwhelm her a second time. She'd be ready for it, and her will is strong."

"Then we need to make sure we have the upper hand," Pilos said, grabbing the manacles he had worn. "We'll bind and gag you before you release her, then we'll persuade her that it's in her best interests to aid us."

Hetta considered Pilos for a moment, then she nodded. "It's the best choice we have," she agreed. "Let's do it."

It did not take them long to secure the wizard. Pilos and Quill locked her legs together and chained her arms behind her back, as theirs had been. After they stuffed a large wad of cloth in her mouth and tied it in place, they sat her down in a corner and took up positions on either side of her.

"We're ready," Pilos said, and Hetta nodded.

For a moment, the woman's eyes glazed over, then her head snapped back and her eyes flared in anger. Immediately, she began to grunt and struggle, but Pilos and Quill held her down.

"Stop it," Pilos ordered, grabbing her by the hair and jerking her face up toward his. "You can't get out of them, so give it up."

Slowly, with a sullenness in her visage, Laithe relaxed.

"Good," the young priest said, releasing her. He reached behind her and slipped Hetta's ring from her finger, then pocketed it. "Now, we have some questions, and you'd do well to answer them. Because if we don't find out what we want to know, we'll let our good friend take over your body again, and she might never give it back. Am I clear?"

Laithe's eyes widened, and she nodded.

"Excellent," Pilos said. "I'm going to remove your gag, but only if you agree not to call out. If you lie to us, I'll make sure you don't have any teeth left to talk to whomever comes to rescue you. Again, do I make myself clear?"

Once more, Laithe nodded.

Pilos reached out and began to untie the gag while Quill stood next to him, his fist drawn back menacingly.

When the Abreeant had removed the binding, Laithe spit the wad of material out of her mouth and made a sour face. "You two fools ought to run while you have the chance," she said.

"Shut your hole," Quill said, drawing his fist back farther. "We ask questions, you answer. Otherwise, no words better come out of your mouth."

Laithe glared at the man, but she nodded.

"Fine," Pilos said. "Now, this is very easy. Where is the mirror?"

"What mirror?" Laithe asked.

Quill's slap echoed off the bookshelves, and the wizard grunted. When she turned back to face them, her lip was bloody.

"You know what mirror," Pilos said. "Where did Junce take it?"

"I don't know," Laithe answered. She tensed, as though ready for another slap. Quill seemed to think about it, but he didn't strike her again.

"Are you sure you don't know?" Pilos asked. "Because if I have to let my friend invade your body again to find out for sure, we can do that."

"I told you, I don't know. I don't ask the man what he does when I'm not around."

"Where did he likely take the mirror?" Pilos asked. "Possible places?"

Laithe shrugged. "I don't know anything about his mirror. Only that he uses it to catch people. I don't know where he got it or where he keeps it."

"Liar," Quill snarled, and he smacked her again.

"That's enough," Pilos said. "She's telling the truth."

Quill turned to look at the young priest, a hurt look on his face. "How do you know?" he asked.

"I just do," Pilos remarked. "She may not be volunteering information, but what's she's telling us is accurate."

"So what do we—" Quill's words died on his tongue as the door to the library slammed open.

The three of them had chosen their hiding place wisely—the doors were not visible to them—but Pilos knew beyond a doubt that whoever had entered the chamber knew they were there, and had come to hunt them down.

Laithe apparently knew also, for she began to yell. "Junce! I'm here! Hurry! They're both here!"

Quill moved to punch the wizard in the face, but Pilos grabbed him by the arm and stopped him. "No time," he said, handing the man a small vial. "Drink this and follow me," he ordered.

Without waiting for Quill to comply with his instructions, the young priest downed his own magical elixir, feeling the moisture vanish from his mouth and noting the familiar smoky taste. He felt himself become insubstantial, a cloud of misty vapors drifting off the floor. There was no weight to his body, no sense of push or pull in his legs. He just floated there, able to see in every direction at once, an ability his mind had a difficult time accepting.

Pilos willed himself toward the ceiling just as Junce came charging around the last of the bookshelves, a blade drawn. As Pilos wafted up into the rafters where Emriana had hidden earlier that evening, he noted that the assassin had brought a number of Generon guards with him.

Laithe was yelling at Junce that they were escaping, jerking her head up toward the ceiling, but Pilos didn't wait around to see if the assassin figured out what she meant. He saw that Quill was not standing there, and instead had transformed into a mist himself, so he led the way out of the library. At the door, which was closed and was now guarded on both sides by two soldiers each, he simply imagined flowing through the crack at the top. As quickly as he considered it, it happened, and he slipped through the gap. None of the guards thought to look up as Pilos and Quill drifted along the ceiling of the corridor outside, though Laithe was yelling orders and curses back in the library.

Hetta, are you with me? Pilos asked as he wafted along.

Yes, child, I am still here. That was quick thinking, drinking those elixirs.

Pilos wanted to nod, but the sensation to do so was simply not there. *Don't know why I thought of it, but I'm glad,* he projected. *Now we have to hope that we can stay this way long enough to get out of here. If we're still down in the bowels of the Generon when the potions wear off, we're in trouble.*

Chimneys, Hetta thought. *Go up.*

Of course, Pilos realized. *Good idea.*

The priest sought out the next room along the corridor, and inside, he drifted toward a fireplace. From there it was a simple matter to follow the flue up, ignoring any connections that did not continue vertically. It was a long ascent, but as he neared the top, Pilos was helped by updrafts rushing along, carrying him ever faster toward the chimney top.

Soon enough, Pilos and Quill stood on a roof of the Generon, looking out over the city.

"That was an adventure," the mercenary said, looking around. "But how do we get down?"

Pilos shrugged. "One thing at a time," he said. "Be glad we're not still down there."

Quill nodded in agreement. "It looks like we can drop over that side and climb down to a balcony," he said, pointing.

Pilos followed the man to the edge of the section of roof where they had just exited. Directly under them was a colonnaded walkway, and beyond that, there were gardens. "I guess I'm going to be climbing around the Generon after all," he muttered, thinking of Emriana. It seemed like an eternity ago that she had tried to convince him that they would need to climb over a wall to sneak inside. He almost laughed at the irony that he was climbing down to sneak out, but thoughts of her quelled any mirth he might have felt.

Don't worry, child, we'll find her, Hetta said, her presence soothing him. *She's a strong girl. She'll be all right.*

I hope so, Pilos replied. Then he dropped down and swung his legs out over the edge of the roof, hoping he would find a safer way of getting down than falling.

...

Emriana's strength eventually gave out, and sometime after she had stopped fighting him, Denrick turned to Lobra and said, "I grow weary of this. Torment her yourself, if you must, but I am done." And he stood up and left the room, drawing the door shut behind him. Emriana turned her head and watched the man go, beyond caring any longer. She glanced over to where Lobra still sat, having watched from a sofa. The woman was brooding.

After a moment, Lobra stirred, rising from her seat. "I guess it's time to put you back into the mirror," she said, false cheer in her voice.

Bitch, Emriana thought, turning away again.

She heard Lobra cross the room toward her, and Emriana considered punching at her, pummeling her face and stomach and fighting her way out of the house, but she didn't have either the strength or the will.

Denrick had been so strong. Stronger than she ever remembered.

"Are you going to cooperate, or do I need to call him back to help me?" Lobra asked, her voice too sweet.

Mocking.

"Rot in the ninth layer," Emriana muttered, turning at last and staring balefully at her captor. "Try and make me go back."

Lobra clucked her tongue in disapproval and was just turning toward the door, ostensibly to summon Denrick back to assist her, when a shout erupted from down the hall. "Guards!" a man cried out. "To the parlor!" Lobra froze, her back tensed with fear, and Emriana saw her chance.

Clambering from the bed, her aching body protesting, the girl stumbled toward Lobra and grabbed her by the shoulder. Lobra jerked at the sensation, but Emriana managed to spin the woman around. Bracing herself, Emriana swung her fist with all her might, popping her foe right in the cheek.

Lobra stumbled back, eyes wide in shock, clutching at her face and grunting in abject pain.

Emriana didn't give her a chance to recover. Summoning some reserve of energy she didn't know she had, the girl leaped on Lobra and knocked her to floor. She pelted the other woman with a flurry of punches, pummeling her just as she had imagined.

It felt so good to hit her.

Lobra writhed and squirmed as she was struck over and over, crying out and trying to protect her face and head. Emriana didn't let up, but finally, Lobra got hold of some bare flesh and clawed at Emriana. The girl yelped in pain and jerked away, and Lobra managed to buck Emriana off her. As Emriana landed in a heap, Lobra began to scream.

"Guards! To me! Help!" She was staggering to her feet as she called out, weaving unsteadily, her face already swollen and bloody.

Emriana lunged up and grabbed at Lobra, jerking her away from the door. "Shut up, you nasty wench!" In her pent-up fury, Emriana found one last well of strength and slung Lobra across the room. The woman stumbled and staggered, trying to maintain her balance, but she lost the battle and went sprawling—right at the great mirror.

With a horrendous crash that was far more than the sound of glass breaking, the mirror shattered. Emriana could feel a powerful emanation burst forth from the ruined object, a wall of arcane force that had been bound in the reflecting glass however long before. It rushed over and past the girl, leaving her feeling breathless.

Lobra dropped like a stone, settling among the shards and fragments that skittered across the floor, finally coming to rest in a heap in the midst of the wreckage.

Beside the woman, Xaphira flopped to the floor, as naked as Emriana. Her body was covered in purplish bruises.

"Aunt Xaphira!" Emriana yelled in delight, rushing across the space toward her. Barely mindful of the jagged glass strewn everywhere, Emriana reached the woman and clenched her gingerly in a hug, feeling tears begin to well up in her eyes. She hadn't realized how alone she had felt until then.

Xaphira gave a soft, muffled groan at the girl's touch and stirred. "Em?" she said softly, her voice dazed. "Is that you?"

Emriana was crying in delight when she answered, "Yes, it's me." Then she hugged the woman even tighter, unwilling to let go.

Xaphira groaned in pain and the girl released her, realizing she was hurting her aunt. She scanned the marks all over the older woman's body, horrified.

"What happened?" she mumbled, feeling more tears welling up. "What did they do to you?"

Xaphira rolled to her knees and tried to sit up. "I'm all right," she said, looking around, her dark hair damp and plastered to her face. "Where are we?"

Emriana scowled over at Lobra's still form. "House Pharaboldi," she said. "That's Lobra there. She had Denrick—Denrick, he—" and Emriana shuddered.

"Denrick's dead," Xaphira said, looking at Emriana with concern in her eyes. "It couldn't have been real."

"It was," Emriana insisted. I did not just imagine what happened, she silently added. She wasn't sure if she wanted to explain or not. Blinking back a few tears that she hoped Xaphira didn't see, she held up her hand. "Later," she said. "We have to get out of here." As if to punctuate the girl's words, the muted sounds of someone shouting erupted beyond the door.

"How did we get here? I thought we were in the Generon." Xaphira's voice sounded weak, dazed.

"I don't know," Emriana replied, standing and

looking about for anything she could use to cover herself. "Lobra had something to do—"

The girl's sentence was interrupted as the door leading into the hall slammed open. "Lady Lobra, come quick. It's your—" It was a woman, a servant, and as she dashed into the bedroom and spotted her mistress lying on the floor, along with two unclad intruders, she froze, her words dying in her throat.

"Grab her!" Xaphira hissed, trying to rise on wobbly legs in the midst of the broken glass. "Don't let her get away!"

The servant let out a startled squeak and tried to flee, but Emriana managed to bound across the room and seize her by one wrist. Using the woman's own momentum against her, Emriana managed to sling the servant around and back into the room, flinging her across the floor in the direction of the bed. As the woman lost her balance and sprawled across the mattress, Emriana shut the door, careful not to slam it, and turned to face the woman.

By that time, Xaphira had managed to get to her feet and tiptoe her way out of the multitude of glass shards. As the servant flopped on the bed, Emriana's aunt half fell and half pounced, landing on top of the woman and pinning her arms to her sides. She clamped a hand over the servant's mouth. "Find something to tie her with," Xaphira commanded, looking unsteady. "Hurry, before I pass out."

Instead of complying with her aunt's instructions, Emriana moved around to face the bucking, struggling woman. "Patimi," she said, believing she recognized her. She got down close to the servant's face to be certain. At the sound of her own name, the servant stopped struggling and eyed Emriana, her expression wary. "It's Emriana Matrell. Do you remember me?" she asked.

Patimi's eyes took on a puzzled expression, then they widened and she nodded.

"Good," Emriana replied. "I know this seems suspicious, but you need to hear what we have to say."

"You know her?" Xaphira asked her niece. "Can we trust her?"

"Yes to the first question," Emriana answered, "and I don't know to the second. We'll see." She got down in Patimi's face again and said, "I'm sure that Lady Lobra has said all sorts of terrible things about me and my entire House, but I suspect most of them are not true. Now," she warned, "you can either sit quietly and listen to us, or we can tie you up as my aunt suggested and lock you in a closet. Which do you prefer?" The woman grunted and nodded again, and Emriana took that for acquiescence. She looked up at her aunt. "Let her up."

"Em," Xaphira started to argue, "one sound from her and we're caught all over again."

"I know, but if we're asking her to trust us, don't you think we should return the favor?" Emriana asked.

Sighing, Xaphira fell off the woman, who quickly sat up and rubbed her arms where her captor had pinned them down. Emriana grabbed the chair Denrick had used and slid it in front of the bed. She pointed to it. "Sit," she commanded, and Patimi moved to comply. "Good," the girl said. "Now, I really would like to put some clothes on. Will you sit there quietly while we make ourselves decent?"

"Yes, ma'am," Patimi answered, looking at the floor as though she were embarrassed at the women's naked condition.

"All right, then," Emriana said, looking around. "Since our own clothes don't seem to be here . . ." she said, leaving the thought hanging. She walked over to a wardrobe in the corner, the same one from which Patimi had helped her find a riding outfit months before.

Before I found out what a fiend Denrick was, Emriana thought.

The girl rummaged through the clothing in the closet and pulled out two dark outfits that would aid them in hiding, if necessary. "Here," she said, turning to toss the garments to her aunt.

Xaphira was bent over Lobra, checking on the woman. "She's still alive," she said. "No major cuts, just a lot of scratches. She was lucky," the woman added, looking down at all the broken glass.

"Too bad," Emriana snapped, wishing Lobra had been impaled on a particularly long and nasty shard. "She doesn't deserve to be lucky." She saw Patimi flinch at her comment, and she almost wished she hadn't said it aloud. Grabbing up two pairs of riding boots from the closet, Emriana turned back.

Xaphira was giving her niece a single concerned look, but Emriana simply handed the boots she had chosen to her aunt and they dressed silently and quickly.

Donning clothes seemed to aid Emriana's courage, and once she was finished, she went to the doorway and opened it a crack, peering into the hall. No one stood near, and no sounds arose from elsewhere in the house. "It's clear," she whispered to Xaphira, who had come up behind the girl.

"We can't go out that way," her aunt replied. "Too many people will see us. Whatever you want to say to this one, do it quickly. We've got to leave before someone starts missing them."

Emriana nodded and turned back to Patimi. "Do you remember what we talked about the last time I was here?"

"Yes, ma'am," the servant answered, looking sorrowful. "You were one of Denrick's lady friends. But I told you that Jithele was carrying his baby when the city watch killed her, and you got pretty upset. Did you really murder him, Lady Emriana? Over a serving girl?" She sounded horrified at the prospect.

Emriana had to clench her fists to keep from shuddering. "No. He fell from a balcony fighting my brother. *He* wanted to kill *me*, though." She took a deep breath. The next question was the hardest. "Are you saying he's truly dead?" When Patimi only stared at her, Emriana shook her head. "Never mind. It's too complicated to explain right now. But the reason you found the two of us here tonight is because we were brought here as Lobra's prisoners. She wanted revenge. You saw the bruises on my aunt, didn't you?"

Patimi only nodded, her eyes big.

"That was her doing," Emriana lied. Well, Lobra might have done it, she told herself. I wouldn't put it past her. "Now we just want to get out, to escape and get home. Will you help us?"

"Me?" the servant said meekly. "What can I do?"

"All we need to know is how to get out without getting caught," Xaphira said. "Which way should we go? That's all. No one will catch on, we promise."

"I'm afraid," the woman said, shaking her head. "Lady Lobra's husband, Lord Mestell, was wounded in a fight tonight, and the guards are very alert. It will be very hard to get out unnoticed. And Lady

Lobra will be terribly angry if she finds out I assisted you."

"Falagh Mestell was hurt?" Xaphira said. "What happened?"

"I don't know, ma'am," Patimi replied. "I was sent to fetch Lady Lobra so she could go to him, and I found you two in here with her. At first, I thought you might have had something to do with it," she trailed off, obviously not comfortable voicing her accusation.

"If she was supposed to find Lobra, someone will come looking for her—and Patimi—very soon," Emriana said, concerned. "We can't wait any longer."

Xaphira nodded. "Here's what you do, Patimi," she said. "First, tell us the best route to get out unnoticed. Then you go back out there and act like you're searching other parts of the estate for Lobra. If anyone wants to know what you're doing, you simply tell them she wasn't here. No one will know you had anything to do with our escape."

"All right," the servant said, not sounding very sure of the plan. "But what about Lady Lobra? And all the glass? If someone else comes looking for her, they'll know I was lying."

"Don't worry about that," Xaphira said, reassuring the woman with a pat on her arm. "We'll take care of it."

"All right," Patimi said again. "There's an arbor not far from Lady Lobra's balcony that's little used and overgrown. On the back side, there are several trees close enough to the outer wall that the boys used to climb up and slip out at night. But the guards may think to watch there—some of them have been with the family for a long time and might remember that route from chasing Jerephin and Denrick for so many years."

"Good," Xaphira said, nodding. "That's perfect. Now go, and act like you're still looking for Lobra."

They let Patimi out of the room after making certain no one was in the hall. The servant gave them one last panicked look before scurrying off.

When she was gone, Xaphira said, "I've been thinking. If Lobra acquired the mirror from Junce, then she must know some of what's going on. We should take her with us."

Emriana looked at Lobra. "Fine with me," she said. Give me a chance to figure out a proper payback, she thought.

"Em," Xaphira said, moving to stand before her niece. "What happened tonight?"

Emriana shook her head. "Later," she insisted. "When we have time." When I can talk about it, she silently added.

Xaphira gazed at the girl a moment, then nodded. She walked over to the still-unconscious woman. "Help me," she said, and Emriana moved to the older woman's side, ready to aid her.

Under Xaphira's direction, the two of them bound Lobra Pharaboldi hand and foot using shredded clothing, and stuffed a hunk of cloth into her mouth to silence her once she regained consciousness. Then they stepped back.

"It's going to be a lot harder to sneak out of here dragging her along," Emriana commented. "Just the two of us, we can sprint and hide, but carrying a trussed up Lobra is really going to slow us down, especially since you must be sore and weak. Why don't you heal some of those bruises?"

Xaphira shook her head. "I did that as much as I could already."

Emriana's eyes widened at the implication of her

aunt's words. She started to ask what happened,
despite her own admonition earlier that they should
wait until later.

"We'll go through the arbor and hope for the best,"
Xaphira replied, cutting the girl off and changing
the subject. "If we get caught, we leave her behind
and fend for ourselves. Ready?"

Though she felt immense sorrow for what Xaphira
must have endured, Emriana nodded, thankful to
have her aunt beside her once more. It's so much easier
with someone else by my— "Pilos!" she gasped. "What
happened to Pilos?"

Xaphira paused in her attempt to try to hoist up
Lobra. "Who? What?"

"Pilos Darowdryn," Emriana explained as they
got the unconscious woman between them and began
shuffling their way toward the doorway leading out
onto the balcony. "He came with me to the Generon to
save you. I don't know what happened to him."

"And how did you manage to enlist the aid of a
Darowdryn?" Xaphira asked as they maneuvered
out into the dark of night.

"After Hetta died, and Grozier took over the house,
I went to the Darowdryns for help."

Xaphira nearly dropped Lobra. "Mother's dead?"
she asked, her voice meek, and Emriana could see the
woman shivering.

You're an idiot! Emriana screamed at herself.
"Not exactly," she said hastily, "but she's in a ring,
which—oh, no! The ring!" The girl nearly dropped
Lobra then, realizing she had been separated from
her grandmother. "Oh, no," she said again, feeling
despair wash over her once more. "I lost her, Xaphira.
I lost Hetta."

"Shh," Xaphira said, and Emriana thought she was

trying to comfort her, to tell her it was all right. In the next moment, though, the woman crouched down into the shadows, and Emriana did likewise just as a patrol of House guards stalked past below the balcony. It was not the casual sauntering Emriana was accustomed to seeing in House Matrell guards.

"They don't look happy," Emriana said once the soldiers had passed.

"I guess not, after everything that happened tonight," Xaphira said. "If I say run, you let go of Lobra and go as fast as you can. Do you understand me? Don't look back, just run for safety."

"All right," Emriana said, knowing her aunt was suggesting that they might get separated. Not on your life, she thought silently. Never again.

Once they were certain the guards had moved out of earshot, they started down the steps of the balcony, hauling their still-unconscious prisoner between them.

CHAPTER 8

Horial landed hard on his back, and
though the ground was soft and spongy
beneath him, the sudden appearance
of Edilus directly above him made the
mercenary's journey through the magical
portal a painful one. As the druid collapsed on top of the sergeant, the weight of
both of them together drove Horial down
hard against the earth, and the arrow still
rammed in his shoulder sank deeper into
his flesh. The sergeant gasped and barely
refrained from crying out fully.

"By the gods," he groaned, panting. "Get
off me," he pleaded, pushing at Edilus with
his good arm.

The druid scrambled off Horial and stood,
muttering in that language the sergeant

had heard the Enclave use back in the Nunwood. It sounded like Edilus was cursing.

"You two be quiet!" Adyan hissed from nearby, his drawl exaggerated with his insistence. "You want to draw the entire Generon down on us?"

Horial groaned again and tried to sit up, but Edilus was there in front of him, grabbing him by the collar of his tunic. "Why, you traitorous wolf? Why did you bring me through the portal with you?"

Horial stared at the man, his mouth agape. "Why? Because those soldiers were going to kill you!" he hissed. "If you want to die so badly, then go back!"

Edilus swore again softly. "I would if it were possible, but it is not! The passage conveys those who use it in one direction only! I cannot return!"

"You hate us so much you'd rather die than come with us?" Horial demanded, controlling his voice only a little more than before. "I saved your life. Maybe some day, you'll get back to your precious forest and do something worthwhile with what's left of it." And with that, he grabbed Edilus's hand, the one still clutching at his tunic, and slung it off.

"I'm not kidding!" Adyan said, his voice also a whisper. "We're smack in the middle of the Generon grounds, and they will hear you if you don't quiet down!"

Horial could see the scar along Adyan's chin glowing faintly in the moonlight. It was twitching from the other man's agitation.

Grolo, sitting nearby, said, "He's right. You two are making enough noise to draw the whole city watch here."

Horial glared at his companions, disliking the rebukes while he was in the middle of a good fight, but he realized the wisdom of their words. Finally, he said to Edilus in a whisper, "Like it or not, you're here with us, and unless you want to ruin what all of your brethren—and my other soldiers—just died to help make happen, let's save this argument for later."

Edilus stood very still, staring at Horial for a long moment as if thinking. Finally, the druid nodded. "I will help you as I can," he said, "because Shinthala believed you had a purpose that did not cross us. But my aid will not include anything that would harm my people in some way."

Horial spread his hands in acceptance and said, "None of us would expect any less of you. And so you understand, I grieve for your brethren as much as I do for my own soldiers." He tried to roll over onto his side, but the arrow embedded in his knee would not allow it. Wincing as he jarred it, Horial sank back to the ground in pain.

"Let me see your injuries," Edilus said, kneeling next to his counterpart. "I may be able to tend them."

Horial nodded and tried to sit still while the druid worked on him, several times stifling cries of pain as Edilus's touch became too ambitious. As he waited, the sergeant tried to get his bearings.

The group had arrived in a lush garden, and in fact, the portal that had delivered them there seemed be anchored to an overgrown archway that formed a lopsided arbor. It looked very old and neglected, and thick vines and shrubs had completely enclosed it on every side, providing a welcome screen of camouflage for the four of them. Though he could not distinctly remember seeing the location before, something about the place convinced Horial that Adyan was correct. They were on the grounds of the Generon.

"Why does this look familiar?" he asked, looking

over at Adyan, who was just returning from a quick
foray into the underbrush to scout. "Have you been
here before?"

"You don't remember?" the other man asked softly,
squatting down beside Horial.

Horial shook his head. "It reminds me of something, but ..." Whatever memories were hidden away
were giving him an uneasy feeling.

"It was a long time ago," Adyan drawled, sounding
pensive. "Vambran was with us."

Horial looked at his friend, remembering it all.
"That night," he breathed. "The plantains."

Adyan nodded. "Yes. The plantain trees are just
that way," and he pointed in the near-darkness, "and
the pond where we found—" he stopped himself then,
pointing but not finishing the thought.

"Of all the ridiculous luck," Horial said, bracing
himself as Edilus took hold of the first arrow, the one
in his knee. When the druid jerked the missile out,
Horial had to clench his teeth to keep from yelling.
"How did Tymora see fit to drop us right here?" he
asked after he got his breath back.

Edilus handed the sergeant a little leather pouch.
"Eat it," he said, moving around to Horial's shoulder.

Opening the pouch, the sergeant could see something gray and moist inside. It did not look tasty. As
Edilus took hold of the second arrow, Horial tipped
the pouch back and let the contents slide down his
throat. The mixture tasted sour, but he did not have
long to reflect on it, for Edilus yanked hard.

Horial squeezed his eyes shut to deal with the
burning pain, but whatever Edilus had given him
warmed his body and eased the discomfort. He suspected it might have been some druidic variation of
a temple-issue healing potion. Soon, his wounds had

closed and he felt good enough to walk. He climbed to his feet and peered around.

"So," Horial asked of no one in particular, "which is the fastest way out of here?"

"Through the front gates," Adyan said.

"Yes, I'm sure that the guards won't bat an eye as three members of the Sapphire Crescents and a fellow from the distant woods go strolling past with no explanation of how they came to be on the grounds," Horial said wryly. "That's not one of your better plans."

"I'm serious," Adyan replied. "We might look a little odd, but tonight's Sammardach. Next to Spheres and the Night of Ghosts, it's one of the biggest parties of the season. Why shouldn't we be visiting the Generon tonight?"

"Sammardach," Horial said, musing. "That just might work," he agreed. "Though it's pretty late to still be here."

Adyan shrugged. "We got to drinking with some stable hands," he offered, "or we got lost in the gardens and had to find our way out. Sounds reasonable to me. The palace is huge, after all."

Horial shrugged, too. "Let's do it," he said.

Grolo snorted. "What was that you were saying about Tymora?" he muttered as the four of them began to push through the bushes, forcing their way out from the forgotten arbor.

"I was saying," Horial answered, shoving aside a low-hanging branch dripping with moisture, "that we ought to remember to drop a coin in her fountain next time we pass by. And I thought we were done tromping through wet bushes in the middle of the night," he added, drawing a soft, if brief, chuckle from the rest of the Crescents.

It did not take them long to break through onto open ground. Once they were visible, the group began to stroll casually, trying to look as if they had just been meandering through the grounds of the palace, minding their own business at the party. A couple of times, Horial suggested to Edilus that it wasn't necessary to prowl, but the druid couldn't quite grasp the concept of acting natural.

Or rather, Horial realized, he's acting as naturally as he knows how. He's probably never been to a city before.

Indeed, as Horial watched, Edilus stared about in wonder and amazement at the grand edifice known as the Generon. More than once, the sergeant thought he saw the druid shake his head in dismay or heard him mutter some unintelligible expletive, but otherwise, Edilus seemed able to keep calm.

The foursome made its way across the grounds and along the paths toward the front of the palace, where the gates stood, and Adyan began to whistle a cheerful tune as they walked. They spotted a guard or two along the way, and both times they were given careful scrutiny, but no one challenged them.

Before long, the gates came into view at the end of a long path that wound its way toward the bottom of the hill, and it seemed that the group was in the clear. Horial actually sighed in mild relief, thankful for the small favors of both Waukeen and Tymora, when Edilus suddenly stopped and cocked his head as if listening.

"What is it?" Grolo asked, stopping beside the druid. "What's wrong with you?"

In answer, Edilus darted off the pathway and into the nearby bushes, disappearing into the undergrowth.

"What the—?" Horial groaned, and he dashed after the druid. "Edilus, no! We can't go that way!" As he neared the spot where Edilus had vanished, though, he heard a grunt and a sudden rustling, and someone gave a muffled shout.

Eternal damnation, Horial thought, grabbing for his blade as he carefully shoved through the outer layer of foliage. What's he unearthed in there?

There was another muted shout, and someone cursed, a string of expletives favored among mercenaries. Horial swore in return and pushed deeper into the greenery, aware that Adyan was right behind him. He spotted a break in the growth ahead of him and detected movement, so he forced a path that way, stumbling through just as Edilus popped up on the other side, yanking another figure along with him. The druid shoved the figure forward and Horial was startled to see a second form down on the ground, a man who was rubbing his head gingerly. As the first one dropped down beside the second, Horial noted that he was dressed as a Waukeenar, an Abreeant, in fact.

"Ow!" the figure cried as he landed on his hands and knees. "By Brightwater, you're strong!" he said, rubbing his wrist where Edilus had gripped him. Then the Abreeant looked up at Horial with a look of both recognition and concern upon his face. "Who are you?" the priest asked, a fellow a few years younger than the sergeant. He sounded fearful.

Instead of answering the priest, Horial turned on Edilus. "What the blazes are you doing?" he demanded. "We were almost to the gate!"

"I could smell these two hiding in here," the druid replied. "And I suspected they were doing something untoward."

Horial had to clench his hands together to keep from reaching up to grab the druid by his collar. "First of all, it's none of our business why they are hiding in here. We were hiding in the bushes a few moments ago, too, remember?" When the druid merely scowled, Horial continued. "And second of all, even if they are up to no good, it's not our fight tonight. We have more important things to deal with."

"Horial?" the young priest asked, startling the sergeant out of his admonition.

The mercenary looked down, surprised. "Do I know you?"

The Abreeant shook his head. "No, but I'm in contact with someone who knows you, and she's very glad to see you. You know Hetta Matrell?"

Horial nearly choked, then he sank down and pressed his finger against his mouth, signaling for the younger man to speak quietly. "Gods and demons, boy! How in the Nine Hells do you know Hetta Matrell?" he asked in a near-whisper.

The young man might have smiled, though it was hard for Horial to be sure in the dim light. "That's a very long story, but suffice it to say that we're on the same side tonight."

Horial's eyes narrowed. "How do I know you're speaking straight with me?" he demanded.

The Abreeant didn't reply for a long moment, and he said, "Hetta tells me to remind you of all the times she had to swat your fanny for crushing her hoplilies when you, Adyan, and Vambran would use her garden wall as a shortcut."

Horial stood there for a long moment, stunned. No one but Hetta, Adyan, and Vambran himself would have remembered something from his childhood.

He threw his head back then and just laughed, and Adyan was chortling too, right beside him. He tried to keep his laughter quiet, and for the most part he succeeded, but the whole situation was too comical for him to control his mirth. Finally, wiping a tear from his cheek, Horial caught his breath. "You sold me," he said, still chuckling. "Where is darling Hetta?"

At that question, the Abreeant seemed to wilt slightly. He held out his hand, offering something to Horial. The sergeant caught a glint of red, and he reached out and clutched at a jeweled ring.

Well, you're a fine sight, Horial Rohden. Where is Vambran?

Horial nearly dropped the ring. *Grandmother Hetta?* he asked, unsure of where the voice was coming from. *Are you at House Matrell? Vambran said you were in trouble.*

Yes, trouble is the short way to sum it up, Hetta's voice replied. *And no, I'm not at the house. I'm in here. Now where's Vambran?*

Horial stared at the ring in the moonlight, aghast. *He is still in Reth, trying to save the rest of the men,* the sergeant answered. *He sent us back to help Emriana after she called to him.*

Well, good, Hetta said, and relief radiated from the disembodied voice. *Pilos and Quill need your help. There's too much to explain right now, but Emriana and Xaphira are in trouble. We all have to get out of the Generon, and quickly, before Junce and the palace guards catch us. Can you help them?*

Horial nodded, then thought, *That's why Vambran sent us back here, Grandmother Hetta. Just tell us what you need.*

Pilos will explain it all to you. For now, just pass me back to him. Oh, and Horial?

Yes?

Thank you for coming. You and Adyan are both good men, and Vambran is lucky to have you as friends.

Horial grinned as he handed the ring back to the young priest. "All right," he said, turning to look at everyone in turn. "Hetta says we've got to get out of here. Pilos?" he said, looking at the priest. When the Abreeant nodded, Horial said, "Tonight we're at your disposal." He made quick introductions and they set out, and he noted that the first pink light of morning was beginning to brighten the eastern sky. Their intentions were to proceed as before, strolling toward the front gates and out as though they didn't have a care in the world.

That plan lasted for perhaps ten paces before someone began to shout from a distance.

Horial spun around to see a contingent of Generon guards running toward them. When he turned back, a second collection of soldiers was assuming a formation to block the way out.

"I guess they know we're here," the sergeant said. They ran.

...

The sun was well above the horizon when Arbeenok woke Vambran. The lieutenant felt refreshed and immediately got to his feet, but Elenthia groaned and coughed. Arbeenok frowned and pulled the mercenary aside. "She is too weak to go with us," he said. "My magic is holding, but the disease has still taken most of her strength."

Vambran nodded. "Then we take her to her father before we depart," he said.

Arbeenok shook his head. "No. She is a carrier. She will infect those around her, even though she is not growing sicker. Do you see?"

Vambran rocked back on his heels, then, understanding at last. He looked over at Elenthia, who was staring at both of them as they whispered together, shifting her gaze back and forth, worried. She knew they were speaking of her. "We'll find you a safe place," the mercenary said.

Elenthia's eyes widened in fear. "You're not going to leave me here, are you?" she asked, a nervous edge to her voice. She didn't really want the answer to her question. "You can't leave me here!" The exertion brought on a coughing fit, and she doubled up in pain.

Vambran dropped down beside her and held her, then held a water skin to her mouth, waiting for her to drink when she was able. Finally, after she had caught her breath, he said, "You'll be all right. You're strong. If you don't let all the scheming society folk get the best of you, you won't let this beat you, either." He smiled at her kindly. Inside, he was in agony. *How can I do this to her? I left my men behind, too.*

Elenthia understood his little jest, though, and a faint smile played across her face. "You always know just the right thing to say to a girl," she said. Then her face turned a bit stony. "Even if you do cavort with druid women," she said, giving the lieutenant a ferocious glare.

Vambran started at her comment, then glanced up at Arbeenok, who was looking on as though he had no idea what the discussion was about. When Vambran looked back at Elenthia, he could see the faintest of smiles curling at the corners of her mouth. He rolled his eyes at her and gave her a reassuring pat, then looked at Arbeenok. "Is there anything else you need to do?" he asked, not wanting to delay the departure any more than necessary.

The druid seemed to consider, then nodded. "We should both have another dose of my powder," he said, producing two more earthen urns like the one he had administered to the lieutenant the previous evening. "We do not want to become sick before we find a cure," he added. After the druid had sprinkled the contents on both of them, they were ready.

"Then let's get moving," Vambran said, rising. "The sooner we get started, the sooner we'll be back." They left plenty of provisions with Elenthia—food and water they had procured from the pantry. She sat in a chair and watched them go, a brave smile on her face. At the door, Vambran turned to look back at her one last time, raising his hand in farewell. "Rest," he said, not knowing what else he could say.

"Come back," she said, her voice soft but earnest.

He only nodded then turned away.

Outside the room, beyond the woman's hearing, Vambran stopped and hung his head. "I can't believe I just left her there," he said, feeling the burden of failure wash over him. "Waukeen forgive me."

"It is the right choice," Arbeenok said, patting him on the shoulder. "It's her best chance of surviving."

Vambran sighed. "I feel like I'm leaving everyone to their deaths, lately." Then he squared his shoulders, took a deep breath, and said, "Let's do this thing." And he walked out of the house, through the garden, and out into the street.

Arbeenok was close behind.

The streets of Reth were littered with the dead. Many were the destroyed remains of those unfortunates who had died, animated, and died again, but a small few had simply perished by other means, somehow avoiding the terrible affliction that would have turned them to unlife.

For a long while, as the two of them walked, no signs of the living were to be found. The morning was filled with haze, smoke from fires that still smoldered. It blew across their path, acrid and hot. Whenever they got near a particularly thick cloud, Vambran grew cautious, unhappy at the thought of something lurking inside it.

After a while, Vambran began to hear something. A commotion, perhaps, but definitely the voices of many people mixed together. As the pair neared the docks, the lieutenant could make it out more plainly.

"Do you hear that?" Vambran asked. "Something's going on up ahead. Let's go see."

But Arbeenok hesitated. "I will not be welcome," he said. "I am too different."

Vambran stopped and looked back, surprised for a moment at his companion's words. He had stopped thinking of Arbeenok as a strange creature. The alaghi was just a trustworthy friend to him. "You have a point. Can you transform into a dog again?"

"I could," the druid replied, "and I will if that is the best course. But perhaps we should use my abilities more thoughtfully."

Vambran cocked his head to one side and looked at the druid quizzically. "What do you have in mind?"

"We only waste time dealing with the people of this city right now," Arbeenok explained. "They do not understand our purpose, and they might fear that we carry the plague."

"I think it's pretty clear we don't," Vambran replied, frowning.

"But why waste time in proving it?" Arbeenok
asked. "Our goal is to reach the water. Why do we
want to mingle with the people?"

"Well, unless you have a better idea," Vambran
said wryly, "walking to the docks is the only way I
know of to get to the Reach. And in order to walk to
the docks, we have to see what's happening."

Arbeenok smiled then. "I do, as you say, have a
better idea," he replied. And he drank deeply of the
morning air, sighed, and began to change.

The druid's arms snaked out, elongated and
lightened, sprouting feathers. His face shifted and
changed, rounding and enlarging, producing a beak
where his mouth and nose had been before. His feet
shortened and grew talons. His weight adjusted, re-
distributed, and his belongings vanished, melding
into himself, becoming rich brown feathers. When
the transformation was complete, Arbeenok regarded
Vambran with a critical and very piercing eye.

The mercenary gaped for a moment, shocked once
more by the feats Arbeenok was capable of. Then he
smiled and said, "You're one damned large hawk."

Arbeenok squawked once in reply and leaped
upward, beating his wings to gain speed and alti-
tude. Swooping forward, the druid reached down and
grasped Vambran by the shoulders, squeezing his
talons together just enough to take hold of the man's
armor without puncturing it and piercing his flesh.

Vambran gave a tiny yelp of surprise, but he
did not struggle as they soared together skyward,
Arbeenok beating his new wings furiously, hauling
the extra weight up beneath him. For a moment, Vambran was aghast, but once he convinced himself that
the druid would not drop him, he began to enjoy the
moment for what it was.

The feeling of flying was exhilarating, and he reveled in it. The morning air was crisp as it whistled past him, cooling after the heavy smoke. Still, it was a long way down, and Vambran swallowed hard a couple of times, especially when the druid shifted and turned. He did not like to imagine dying such a death. Arbeenok circled about a few times, allowing Vambran a chance to study the ground as they rose higher and higher.

"This is incredible!" the mercenary shouted from below the druid.

The buildings of the city dwindled below them, and quickly, the pair was high above, able to see most of the settlement spread out below. Even the highest structure, the great tower of the Palace of the Seven, shooting upward near the center of the city, shrank beneath them. Much of Reth had burned in the night, and many fires still smoked. Bodies were strewn everywhere.

"There," Vambran said, pointing to the docks, and Arbeenok had to arch his head downward to see where the man pointed. "All those people. What's going on down there?"

Arbeenok swooped in closer, and Vambran could make out lines of soldiers holding a position, weapons readied. Crowds of people were strung out facing the soldiers, with a sizeable space between them. As the lieutenant watched, someone tried to run toward the soldiers, dodging and weaving. The soldiers fired bows and crossbows, and Vambran even saw a flash of magic. The runner went down, lying still. As they circled, Vambran realized that the soldiers surrounded the city. And they were holding the people inside.

They are preventing the citizens from spreading

the plague, the mercenary thought. They won't let them leave the city. It made sense to him, though he was saddened by the soldiers' tactics. And when they swooped lower, the emblem on the soldiers' uniforms stirred anger in Vambran's heart.

They were men of the Silver Ravens.

The duo's shadow passed over a group of soldiers and the men on the ground looked up. Many began shouting and pointing. Though he knew that none of their weapons had the range necessary to be a true threat, Vambran feared a lucky shot. Nor, for that matter, did he wish to be a target for some wizard's clever magic. As if thinking the same thing, Arbeenok began pulling air beneath his wings with a few powerful strokes, and the pair quickly left the city behind, racing out over the open water of the Reach.

...

The arbor Patimi had spoken of was not far from Lobra's balcony, but in order to reach it, the two Matrell women and their prisoner had to descend a series of terraced flower beds that had been filled with numerous robust blooming plants, then cross an open lawn. Some of the flowers grew as tall as Emriana herself, and in addition, there were thick hedges, stands of swaying grass with razorlike leaves, and jumbles of thorny bushes. Beyond the flower beds, in the sliver of Selune that shone on it, the arbor loomed dark and forbidding, all overgrown and neglected.

At least we can hide in this mess, the girl thought as she shifted Lobra's weight and struggled down another level. No one would think to hunt for us in here.

On the other end of Lobra's limp form, Xaphira's labored breathing signaled to Emriana that her aunt was losing her energy quickly. That realization made her shudder, wondering what had happened to the older woman while she had been imprisoned in the dungeons of the Generon. After her own suffering at Lobra's hands and the bruises Xaphira sported, the girl's imagination lent itself to some pretty awful possibilities.

"You all right?" Emriana whispered as they shifted sideways to squeeze through a hedge. "You want to stop and rest?"

"No," Xaphira whispered back. "I'll be fine. Just winded."

"That's what I'm worried about," Emriana replied. "As much as I want to make Lobra pay for … this is a bit much. Maybe we ought to leave her here."

"No." Xaphira hissed, making it clear she wasn't going to change her mind. "She's the one advantage we have right now. I'll be all right. Keep moving."

Emriana started to argue, then snapped her mouth shut as she thought better of it. Xaphira could be as stubborn as Uncle Dregaul sometimes, and the girl sensed that it was one of those moments. *That and the fact that I just casually mentioned that her own mother had died,* Emriana thought, angry with herself. *She must have a thousand questions, and we can't even talk about it.*

Finally, the two of them reached the last terrace and stopped under the cover of a trellis heavy with some vine sprouting huge, sweet-smelling white blossoms. Emriana could feel Xaphira letting Lobra sag down to the damp, rich earth beneath them, so she did the same. They sat for a while, Emriana wondering what Xaphira was thinking. Finally, she leaned over and said, "I'm sorry."

Xaphira jerked her head around to peer at her
niece. "Sorry?" she asked very faintly. "For what?"

"For whatever happened to you. For springing the
news about Hetta on you the way I did. There's a lot
to be sorry about."

"It's all right," Xaphira replied, and she reached
out to find Emriana's hand with her own. Giving it
a comforting squeeze, she whispered, "Hush. They'll
hear us. Like you said, we'll talk later."

Emriana sighed but nodded, knowing her aunt was
right. I hope there is a later, she thought, eyeing the
open space between themselves and the trees.

After a moment longer, Xaphira got to her feet.
Lobra was beginning to stir. "We've got to hurry,
before she wakes up," the older Matrell woman whispered. "Come on."

Emriana joined her aunt and together, they
hoisted the woozy woman up from the damp ground.
Sticking her head out from the shelter of the shrubs,
Xaphira surveyed the grounds, then motioned to
Emriana that all was clear. They stepped out into
the open.

The first several steps seemed the longest. Emriana's heart was pounding from her fear of being
seen, but no one seemed to be about. When they were
halfway across, she started to think they would
make it.

Bells started ringing all around her.

The sound made her jump and yelp a tiny bit, and
she felt Xaphira react in a similar fashion. Both
women wasted no time trying to figure out the source
of the alarm bells. They broke into a lumbering run,
struggling to stay abreast of one another and not drop
their prisoner.

In the distance, dogs began to bark. Emriana thought she could hear the sounds of horses riding closer at a gallop. The guards were alerted. They were being hunted.

"Go on," Xaphira said, trying to take the full burden of Lobra on herself. "Run ahead, get over the wall before they catch us. I'll be right behind you."

"No," Emriana said. "I'm not leaving you again."

"Em, there's no time to argue. Go!"

"I'm not leaving you!" the girl almost screamed, fear making her voice rise in pitch. "I lost you once already. Forget it!"

Xaphira didn't reply. The two of them just kept moving, managing to get in among the trees just as lights appeared around the corner of the estate, moving rapidly toward them. The barking of the dogs grew more feverish, more insistent, and louder. Emriana wondered if their masters had released them from their leashes yet. She didn't dare turn around to see.

The arbor turned out to be harder to maneuver through than it might have seemed at first blush. The arching passage was filled with downed limbs, waist-high grass, and brambles. Emriana imagined that no one had tended to the place in at least a generation. More than once, she or Xaphira tripped over something hidden in the undergrowth, falling to one knee or sprawling against the trunk of a tree. Xaphira hit the ground particularly hard at one point and just lay there for a moment, groaning softly. Emriana had to help the woman to her feet.

To make matters worse, Lobra was becoming more awake by the moment, and she was beginning to thrash in her bonds, making it difficult to hold her. Finally, Emriana put her mouth to the woman's

ear and said, "If you want to live to see the light of
morning, I suggest you stop wiggling. I don't have any
compunction against slitting your throat and leaving
you here to bleed out, do you understand?"

After that, Lobra was much more compliant.

When they reached the wall, Emriana eyed the
barrier, which loomed a good ten feet high, uncertainly. "I've been climbing over too many of these
lately," she muttered.

"Get up there," Xaphira said. "I'll boost her up to
you once you're on top."

"No," Emriana said. "We go up together."

"Em, we can't! We can't both balance in the tree
and hold her. The dogs are coming! You don't have any
weapons to fight them! Get up there, now!"

Angry both at being scolded and knowing her
aunt was right, Emriana scrambled up the closest
tree and easily hopped to the wall. She turned and
lay across the top of it on her stomach, then reached
down. "Hand her up," she said. "Hurry!"

At the far end of the arbor, lights were bobbing
about and men were shouting. The dogs were howling
up a storm and charging through the underbrush
right toward them. Lobra began to squirm, resist-
ing Xaphira's efforts to heave her up to the younger
girl. Xaphira planted one fist into the prisoner's gut,
and Lobra crumpled. Xaphira slammed Lobra right
up against the wall, and the bound woman let out a
stifled grunt of pain. Then the mercenary got under-
neath her, gaining leverage, and shoved with her legs.
Even with her effort, though, Emriana couldn't quite
reach down far enough to grasp Lobra.

"It's no good," Emriana said. "We have to leave
her."

"No!" Xaphira yelled, and with a final heave, she

straightened her arms, pushing Lobra high enough.

Emriana grabbed hold of Lobra's shoulders, but she didn't have the strength to pull her to the top of the wall. "I can't lift her!" she cried. "I'm going to drop her!"

"Just hang on," Xaphira said, moving toward the tree. "I'll be there to help."

A dog lunged out of the grass, leaping right at Xaphira. The older Matrell woman spun and sidestepped the hound, which struck against the wall with a yelp and dropped to its feet. Spinning, it charged her again just as another dog appeared. Xaphira kicked out in front of her, catching the first dog on the nose, then she raked her heel back and out to the side, catching the second dog across its muzzle. Both hounds yipped in pain and scurried back, out of range.

Emriana watched all of it in dismay as she felt her grip on Lobra beginning to slip. "Xaphira!" she cried out. Lobra, she thought, don't you dare start squirming now. "Xaphira, hurry!"

With the two dogs cowed, Emriana's aunt spun and leaped to the lowest branch of the tree and began to clamber up. Below, another dog appeared, barking frantically as it danced around the base of the tree, as though it had trapped a raccoon. The lights were close, and Emriana could almost see the faces of the men carrying the lanterns.

Xaphira landed on top of the wall right beside Emriana just as one of the younger girl's hands finally slipped. Her aunt reached down and grabbed at Lobra's hair, pulling the woman up to the sound of a muffled shriek. Little by little, the two of them hauled their prisoner to the top of the wall while the dogs bayed below.

Just as the first of the Pharaboldi House watch arrived, Emriana and Xaphira managed to slip over the other side, their prisoner still in tow.

By the time more men from the estate worked their way around to the lane on the outside of the wall, the three women were gone, and the first pink rays of dawn were just beginning to spread across the sky.

CHAPTER 9

"This way!" Pilos gasped, turning and sprinting through a gap in a thick hedge. Behind him, Quill, the three mercenaries, and the druid Edilus scurried after him. Pilos's lungs burned and he thought he would collapse soon from exhaustion. The other five men didn't seem badly winded, though the dwarf Grolo was huffing pretty hard as he charged along on his stumpy shorter legs.

I'm soft, Pilos realized. Temple life is too cushy.

When he could run no further, the young priest dropped in a heap among some ferns and plantain trees that created a dense tangle, shielding the world from view. Beside him, the others gathered around, and Pilos was at least thankful to see the men breathing hard, hands on hips or knees. They stood without speaking. Aside from a few distant and muffled shouts, no one seemed to be getting closer to their hidden location.

"I think we lost them," Adyan drawled in a quiet voice, twisting his head to look back through the foliage the way they had come. "I don't hear anyone anymore."

"Good," Pilos muttered, flopping onto his back. "Because if they were still back there, I'd have to surrender."

Don't you dare, Hetta said, displeasure radiating from the ring. *Emriana needs you.*

I know, Pilos answered. *I wouldn't really. But I'm worn out.*

"City folk don't know how to run," Edilus said, his scorn obvious. Pilos looked over at the druid and noted with displeasure that the woodsman was breathing easily, looking at the rest of them as though impatient for them to get moving.

"You're right," Horial said, speaking between hard breaths. "We're more civilized, and we've figured out how to use things like wheels."

That elicited a soft chuckle from some of the others, which only made the druid scowl more. Since he had met the strange woodsman, Pilos had not seen him smile. He wondered if Edilus was capable of it.

"We can't stay here," Horial said, rising to his full height. "They will find us. We have to get over the wall and out into the city."

Pilos groaned and sat up. "I can barely lift my feet, much less climb a wall. It has to be twenty feet high!"

"Maybe you have some trick up your sleeve that

will get us over it," Horial suggested, looking askance at the young priest.

Pilos shrugged and shook his head. "I'm not a battle priest," he said, climbing slowly to his feet. "I served Mikolos personally before—" he stopped, feeling bitter. He took a deep breath. "The Grand Syndar rarely had a need to climb over palace walls," he finished, eliciting another chuckle from the mercenaries.

"There are trees," Quill said. "We might be able to climb one."

Grolo snorted. "Have you ever seen a dwarf climb a tree?" he asked gruffly, to which Quill shook his head. "There's a reason for that," the dwarf finished, giving the man a pointed stare.

Even Edilus cracked a hint of a smile. Then the druid said, "I have rope. If we can get to this wall and there are trees close by, I will get to the top and pull the rest of you over."

Pilos didn't feel it wise to point out that he hoped the guards would give them a sporting chance once they got to the wall. He figured they would work that part out once they got to it.

"Come on," Horial said, and Pilos climbed to his feet. "If they haven't figured out where we ducked out of sight yet, they will soon enough."

Together, the six men moved through the brush, trying to pass beneath the thick overgrowth that surrounded them without much noise. From time to time they heard a shout in the distance, guards who were coordinating with one another as they searched for the fugitives.

At one point, Horial and Adyan paused, giving each other a strange look. The six men had reached the bank of a small pond, the other side of which was open ground. In order to skirt the water, the group would have to move into the open, but that wasn't what concerned the two men. Pilos started to ask what was wrong, but they both shook it off and motioned for everyone to keep moving.

The six of them navigated the perimeter of the water and ducked back into the greenery, moving as quietly as they could. At one point, Edilus motioned for them all to freeze, then he slipped away, so silent as he disappeared that the young priest wasn't certain he was touching the ground at all.

They waited, no one moving, and heard a voice not far ahead of them. A second voice joined the first, and there was the sound of a conversation, though the discussion was muted enough that Pilos could not make it out. The longer they crouched in wait, the faster his heart beat.

Easy, Hetta said. *You'll send yourself to an early grave fretting like that.*

Pilos was too worried to answer the elderly woman.

Edilus returned, motioning for the rest of them to follow him. Pilos got to his feet and kept close behind the druid as he led them the rest of the way through the dense foliage. They reached the edge of the protective screen of greenery and saw that a peach orchard stood beyond, the ground open and more visible and the trees aligned in nice, even rows. No one seemed to be near, and the light of dawn was enough to reveal a wall on the far side.

"Sets of steps lead up to the top in various places along the wall," Edilus whispered to them, "and they are being watched by guards. But right there," he said, pointing toward the section that Pilos and the others could see, "the spot is vacant. No one watches.

If we can get there without being seen, I can get to the top and we will be out."

"And if we can't get there without being seen?" Horial asked, eying the druid. "What then?"

"Then we fight," the druid answered.

For a moment, no one said anything, then Horial shrugged. "Sounds like a plan to me."

Making sure that all six of them were ready, Edilus stepped out of the undergrowth and moved into the orchard. The druid crept from tree to tree, looking in every direction, watching for guards. The rest of the men trailed out behind him, using the trees for cover as he did. Dew coated the coarse grass growing in the orchard, glistening in the early morning light.

Pilos felt his hands shaking in apprehension, worrying that at any moment, someone would spot them. He kept waiting for a guard patrolling the area to come into view, to see him or the other men, and shout a warning to others.

When the young priest was halfway across the open space, as far from the protective canopy of the bushes as from the wall, Edilus signaled for everyone to halt and stay low. Pilos hit the ground, his heart thumping. He tried to look around to see what had startled the druid, but he didn't see anyone else in sight. Finally, Edilus rose up and continued, and the others rose with him.

Somehow, they all reached the wall without raising the alarm.

As they gathered together in a clump, Edilus produced a small charm, something woven of bones, feathers, and green vines, and he began to murmur as he moved it in intricate patterns. Behind him, Pilos heard the sound of ripping earth and snapping twigs, and he turned in time to see a rippling wall of plant growth rise up from the ground. The barricade of greenery twisted, wrapped, and thickened as it climbed, forming a nearly solid wall of protection against the rest of the orchard. It stopped growing when it was a good ten feet high, and it stretched between two of the closest peach trees, intertwining with their lowest branches. It formed an enclosure perhaps twenty feet long and about five feet wide with both ends open.

"That ought to keep us hidden for a few moments longer," Edilus said, examining the wall.

"Can you climb it?" Pilos asked. Until he had reached the wall, he was never certain that he might escape. Standing at the base of it, though, he began to feel some sense of hope.

"Yes," Edilus said, then he dropped to all fours and his physical shape began to alter. As Pilos watched, mesmerized, the druid elongated, his clothing and equipment absorbed into his form. His skin turned green and scaly. In the span of a breath, Edilus had become a lizard perhaps four feet long, not including his tail.

The lizard turned and scampered up the wall to the top. Once he was there, Edilus reverted to his human form and stood looking down at the men below him with a self-satisfied grin on his face.

That's twice now he's smiled, Pilos thought. Maybe he's human after all.

The druid yanked a coil of rope from his shoulder and tied one end of it around his waist. Then he motioned for Pilos to start up. "You first," he said, sitting down and bracing his feet as best as he could. "You're the lightest, and you can help hold it for the rest of them."

Pilos took hold of the rope and began to haul himself up, bracing his feet against the stone to help guide himself. It was not easy, for he was not adept at scaling walls, but he struggled to the top. Once he managed to swing his leg over and scramble to a sitting position, Edilus instructed him to sit behind him, grab hold of the druid's belt, and lean backward. Pilos hurried to comply, and once he was in position, the others began to clamber up the rope, too.

Once all six of them had attained the top of the wall, they prepared to lower themselves over the other side.

Horial, Adyan, and Grolo made it down easily, and Quill prepared to work his way down the wall next.

"Hurry," the druid hissed, looking back over his shoulder into the Generon. "Guards are coming. Go now, before we are spotted."

"I'm afraid it's too late for that," a familiar voice called from nearby.

Feeling his stomach turn somersaults, Pilos's gaze was pulled toward a movement to his side. Junce Roundface was on top of the wall, walking toward the three of them. He must have appeared there magically, for a moment before, they had been alone. Junce had a crossbow in his hands, and he was smiling, though the expression had a definite lack of joviality.

A scuffling of boots in the opposite direction caught the priest's attention next. Looking that way, the Abreeant saw Laithe strolling toward the three men. She held a wand in her hands.

The wizard saw Pilos looking at her and smiled at him. "Looks like the rat is not quite out of the trap, yet, eh?" she said. "I owe you one," she added, not smiling any longer. "For Lak and Borth."

As the two thugs closed the distance, narrowing
the gap, Pilos looked back and forth between the two
of them in dismay. Beside him, Quill got to his feet
and seemed prepared to pull his sword free, but Junce
steadied his crossbow and sighted down it.

"I wouldn't," the assassin warned. "You're not fast
enough."

The strum of a bow firing sounded from street
level and a crossbow bolt zipped upward at Junce.
The missile flew true and struck Junce in the ribs,
right under his arm, but it bounced away. Grolo, who
had fired the shot, swore.

Junce chuckled. "You didn't think I'd actually get
up here just so you could take target practice, did
you?" and quick as a cat, he turned and returned the
shot, sending the bolt right at Grolo's chest. The bolt
struck true and sank into the dwarf's flesh, causing
him to grunt.

As Pilos watched in horror, Grolo wavered on his
feet for a moment, staring at the fletching on the
end of the bolt, and his own crossbow slipped from
his fingers and he sat down hard.

"Waukeen," the dwarf muttered as he tipped over,
slumping to the ground.

Junce's shot had been quick, precise, but it had
taken his attention away from the three men in front
of him. That was all the opening anyone needed, and
all around Pilos, chaos ensued.

Edilus freed the rope from his waist and was on
his feet in an instant. Yanking his scimitar free, he
turned and advanced toward Junce, not giving the
assassin time to reload. The other man smiled again,
tossed his empty weapon aside, and drew his own
blade. At the same moment, Junce put something in
his mouth and produced a loud, shrill whistle.

A signal, Pilos realized in dismay. Summoning the guards.

"Go on!" Quill said to the priest, leaping to his feet. "Get down!" And the mercenary was turning away, drawing steel, facing off against Laithe.

Pilos glanced around, seeing everyone moving at once, and hesitated. Adyan and Horial were both shooting at the wizard, but like Junce, the missiles bounced off. She seemed more concerned by Quill's approach, however, and backed away as he tried to close the gap. Laithe brought up her wand and aimed it at the mercenary, and a blob of something sickly green streaked forth from it, fanning out until it was a spray. The droplets showered over Quill, who arched his back in pain and cried out, dropping to one knee.

Pilos winced, realizing the caustic substance must have been an acid, and wanted to go to the man, to soothe his pain with a healing touch. But Quill wasn't done yet. Staggering, he managed to rise, and Laithe leveled her wand to give him another dose.

She wasn't quite fast enough.

Quill threw himself at the woman, wrapping his arms around her just as her magical device burped forth another blob of acid. Quill smacked into the blob head-first, causing it to dribble on himself and spatter back onto Laithe. She screamed as she stumbled back, Quill still clinging to her.

In a dual cry of pain, the pair went over the side of the wall to the street below.

Horrified, Pilos could only watch the two combatants disappear. Then he realized that the two mercenaries were yelling at him.

"Come on!" Horial yelled. "Just drop!"

Pilos glanced over at where Edilus was still

fighting with Junce, and he saw a stricken look upon the assassin's face. The priest realized that Junce had seen Laithe go down, too. In his distress, he did not keep his guard up, and Edilus managed a lucky strike, cutting into the man's sword shoulder.

With a primal cry of pain and anger, Junce swung back at the druid, but his attack was awkward. Edilus bounced out of the way. With a curse, the assassin said something and vanished.

A crossbow bolt whizzed past Pilos's ear, and he saw then that guards had drawn near the base of the wall on the inside of the Generon grounds. He noticed more guards running down the street from both directions along the wall, closing in on the fugitives' position.

Jolted into action, Pilos tried to figure a way to lower himself down, but nothing prominent was available to anchor the rope. Just when he thought he might have to hang over the side and jump, Edilus was there. Thankfully, Pilos handed him the rope.

"No time," the druid said as another bolt flew past them. Reaching out, Edilus grabbed Pilos by the collar and shoved, and the two of them tumbled over the side of the wall together.

...

Vambran watched the waves crash against the rocks below him, squinting as the morning sun made the water glint. The smell of salt carried on the fresh breeze was strong, and the humidity was high, but the mercenary didn't mind. It felt clean to him.

Below him, among the rocks, Arbeenok prowled about, scooping up shellfish for a morning meal. The druid had a bundle of them already, and Vambran doubted the two of them could ever finish what was in that bulging satchel, but then his stomach rumbled and he grinned at the thought of such a feast. He had been eating nothing but dried meat and bread—when he wasn't being fed bugs by the druids, of course—and looked forward to a different sort of meal. The majestic scenery coupled with the warm morning was almost enough to let the mercenary forget all the difficulties of the last few days.

Almost.

The two of them had traveled west and south from Reth, speeding along the shoreline, until they reached a point of land that stuck way out from the coast into the Reach. They weren't far from where *Lady's Favor* had gone down, Vambran had realized, noting the miles and miles of beach below them as Arbeenok had swooped closer to land. The lieutenant wasn't sure what prompted his companion to alight on the outcropping of rock, but it seemed as good a place to start as any.

The next question, of course, was how to travel below the water effectively.

Vambran considered the possibilities, then settled down to pray to Waukeen while Arbeenok continued to gather food. The mercenary's thoughts were troubled, though, for he didn't merely want to ask for his goddess's blessings in the form of divine power. He needed more than just spells. He needed some sense of understanding, some feeling of peace, for all of the horrors he had endured in the last few days. A tiny part of him wanted some answers from Waukeen, to understand why she would allow those tragedies to pile up around him.

Rather than dive right in and begin asking for solace, Vambran started slowly, settling into a

meditative trance. For a long time, he felt nothing
but a growing sensation of tranquility, listening to
the waves crashing against the rocky beach and the
gulls screaming as they circled overhead. He imagined the sun bathing his face as his goddess's glorious
radiance showering down upon him, and he found a
center. He began to look inward, for he often found
that the best answers to his most spiritual questions
welled up from his heart, from his own sense of faith.
He hoped that would be the case that morning.

Why? was the question that had been plaguing
Vambran. Why me? Why has all of this been thrust
upon me? Did I in some way fail you? Did you want to
see my life take such a turn for some reason I cannot
fathom at the moment? Is this a punishment for some
transgression?

Once the question was clear in his mind, Vambran
began to mull it. Free of the guilt and the anger,
able to draw back and examine every aspect of the
circumstances with a calm eye, Vambran felt the
understanding flood into him at last.

Strength.

You're not punishing me, Vambran realized, accepting what he trusted his goddess was telling him.
You're asking me to take the burden because you
believe I can.

That realization, that true understanding at last
of what all of it had been about, flooded through
Vambran like a wave of pure joy. He felt the tears
flow then, not tears of sorrow for his losses, but tears
of unbridled love for Waukeen.

Thank you for your trust, he thought. I will do
my best.

Persevere.

I will try. Thank you.

For a long moment after his revelation, Vambran sat with his eyes closed, trying to absorb everything he had come to understand. Finally, with the burdens of his trials and tribulations lifted, he opened his eyes and took it all in—the sky, the ocean, the screaming gulls, the rocks. . . . Being in that place, in that time, was by deific design, certainly, but it was also a moment to be savored for its own sake, a celebration of service unto itself.

It's not a burden, he decided. It's a reward. Faith begets faith.

"It's beautiful, isn't it?" Arbeenok asked, standing beside the mercenary officer. "Savor it."

Vambran laughed. Really laughed. "I was just thinking the exact same thing, my friend," he said when he regained his composure. "We were brought to this place because we *can* savor it, and that is a gift not to be squandered."

Arbeenok smiled and sat down. "Then let us eat and savor a meal, too," he said.

The two of them ate in silence, appreciating the bountiful meal the sea had provided. When they were done, Vambran knew he was ready.

"We don't know what we will find beneath the waves today," he told the druid, "but I am willing to accept whatever is put in front of us. I have prepared for the journey with appropriate blessings. The only thing left to do is begin."

Arbeenok nodded. "Then let us trust our instincts and what nature shows us," he said.

They walked down to the beach together and looked for a passable route into the water, one that would not let the current dash them against the rocks. They found a small inlet, calm and still, and they began to wade out into the shallows. As they strode deeper into

the Reach, Vambran took his holy coin from inside his
shirt and prayed, thanking Waukeen for the abilities
he would be granted. Then, when the water covered
his shoulders, he ducked his head down.

The first breath was always the hardest. He had
to fight the urge to keep his mouth clamped shut, to
hold in the air already in his lungs. But he knew the
spell would work, and at last he relented and began
to breathe. The water gurgled and swirled into his
mouth, but only sweet air filled his lungs. Vambran
sighed in satisfaction and turned to Arbeenok.

The druid was still standing with his head above
water, but as Vambran watched, the alaghi began to
change, to transform. He became a manta ray, his
brown fur shrinking away and becoming firm, black
skin. He settled into the water and swam in a lazy
circle around Vambran, his winglike fins rippling
gently to propel him along.

Vambran watched the druid in fascination, and
when Arbeenok swam beside him, he shifted his flat
body sideways, running that sharklike skin along
Vambran's arm. The mercenary understood. He took
hold of the front of Arbeenok's extended frame and
began to glide through the water, letting the druid
propel them both. It was a magnificent beginning
to their journey.

The water was clear and blue, and the floor of the
Reach was shallow, luxuriously covered in smooth
sand. Coral groves formed arches and tunnels and
made homes for exotic fish. Vambran had often
watched such wondrous color pass beneath a ship
in calm, clear waters, but he had never imagined
the beauty of it from an undersea perspective. He
watched a school of bright orange fish scatter as he
and Arbeenok darted by.

Vambran found that he could indicate a direction to Arbeenok by gently pulling back with one hand or the other against the shoulders of the druid's wings. By giving such guidance, the mercenary was able to show Arbeenok that he wanted to move among some of the coral and see the abundance of sea life before going deeper into the water.

The remains of a ship came into view, and for a brief moment, Vambran wondered if it was *Lady's Favor*, but he dismissed the thought, for the wreck was older, smaller, and more intact. It had settled on its side upon a large expanse of red coral reef, and the abundant sea life had begun to cover its surfaces. Vambran wanted to sweep near the wreck for a closer look, but he sensed Arbeenok hesitate. When a large shark swam out of a hole in the side of the downed craft and began prowling close to them, Vambran was fully in favor of heading the other direction.

After getting over his initial sense of wonder, Vambran nudged Arbeenok further out from the shore, toward deeper waters. The floor of the Reach in that area remained shallow for several hundred paces, declining at a steady if gradual angle, but before long, the two searchers came to a notable boundary where the sea floor plunged rapidly downward to greater depths.

At first, Arbeenok chose to glide parallel to the edge of that steep slope rather than taking the plunge into its depths, for the light was dimmer there and large forests of long, twisted plants grew upward from the sandy floor, suitable hiding places for who-knew-what. Vambran was content to let the druid choose their route, for though he had taken great delight in drifting through the multicolored, brightly lit world of the shallows, he was more than a little apprehensive about descending into the gloom. The memory of the kraken was still too fresh in his mind.

Banishing their reluctance, the pair turned and began to drift downward, following the ocean floor as its rock-strewn incline dropped beneath them. Vambran was torn between having Arbeenok glide close to the top of the plant-forest so that they could dart in if a threat appeared, or nudging the druid to steer clear of the lush growth and evade whatever might be hiding inside. He chose to guide Arbeenok on a route near enough to make a sudden dive but not so near that they wouldn't have a chance to react to surprises rising from below.

Vambran considered again the notion that he had no idea what they were looking for—merely underwater ruins—and he wondered if any parts of ancient Jhaamdath still protruded above the sediment of so many centuries. The histories told him a great tidal wave had washed the Twelve Cities of Swords off the land and out into the sea, a magical scouring brought by the elves in retribution for unchecked logging of the Chondalwood. He couldn't imagine what might have survived such a catastrophe, for the wave was said to be a mile high.

Such force would surely have dragged hills and mountains down with it, he thought. Jhaamdath is probably buried down there, out of reach.

Just when the lieutenant was beginning to feel despair and wondering if they shouldn't return to shore to rethink their efforts, a figure darted toward him, whose movement he caught out of the corner of his eye. Suddenly, more figures were all around them, darting toward them as though to surround them, and he felt Arbeenok shudder with concern and begin banking to retreat. He crouched low against the druid's body, trying to reduce water resistance so they could swim faster.

But the creatures were too quick. Vambran fumbled for his sword, wondering how well he could swing it through water, when he realized he had seen the creatures' likes before. Blue-skinned and naked, the figures swimming toward him were remarkably similar to elves in appearance, though their hands and feet were webbed. As the sea elves swam around, large, friendly eyes regarded both Vambran and Arbeenok, smiling and reaching out gently to touch the two of them.

A female with short bluish hair, bedecked in shell bracelets and necklaces, swam right up to Vambran. Though he couldn't be certain, he thought it might have been the same member of the species he had encountered before, when *Lady's Favor* had sunk and he had nearly drowned while dueling the kraken. She smiled at him, those beautiful turquoise eyes with their gold flecks were unmistakable. She swam up next to the lieutenant and wrapped her arms about his head, embracing him and offering him a soft kiss. He didn't fight it. When she pulled away, he thought she might have giggled, though the sound was odd and distorted in the water.

The sea elf maiden rolled over once and regarded him as she paddled backward, and Vambran wondered if he was blushing at the sight of her unclothed, but then she motioned for them to follow her and spun around and darted away. Vambran shrugged and nudged Arbeenok to follow.

Around Vambran and Arbeenok, other sea elves swam in a sort of escort formation, maintaining a

distance on every side as well as above and below the
pair. As a group, they all followed the female downward, toward a jagged chasm that gashed the side of
the sloping ocean floor at an angle. When the sea elf
guide darted into the chasm and began descending
even faster, Vambran fought a brief sense of panic.
It was growing ever darker, and he was beginning
to feel the effects of the water pressure on his body.
But then the sea elf vanished from view, darting into
what must have been a cave. Arbeenok followed, not
needing Vambran's guidance to understand where
they were expected to go.

The mouth of the cave was large and dark, but
the mercenary noted a faint glow from its depths, as
the druid obviously did, for he rippled his wings and
followed the light source. Vambran hoped he was not
misplacing his trust in their guide, but something
told him their actions were right.

The cave continued for quite a distance. The light
turned out to be glowing coral positioned at intervals
on the walls of the tunnel. After several twists and
turns in the passage, the cave angled upward, and
Vambran could see brighter light ahead.

The water there had a surface, and the mercenary's
head broke through as Arbeenok glided up to it. They
were in a large chamber with a cavernous roof high
overhead. The whole of the place was lit with more
of the glowing coral, but brighter lights were also
placed along one side of the cavern. Vambran noticed
a sort of rocky beach, and the sea elf was sitting there,
out of the water, watching him with a bemused smile
on her face.

He and Arbeenok drifted toward her until the
water was too shallow for the druid to swim any closer.
Vambran climbed off his friend and stood up, letting

the water cascade off him. Beside Vambran, Arbeenok stood up, transformed back into his natural shape.

"Hello, land-walker," the sea elf said in a somewhat odd accent, but in a voice that was just as sweet as any land elf's. "We've been expecting you."

CHAPTER 10

As Pilos felt himself lose his balance and fall backward, he clutched at Edilus, whose sudden lunge had toppled the two of them together. But the druid's calm gaze did not waver, and as they began to plummet, Edilus shifted shape again, transforming into an eagle right before the priest's eyes. As the druid's hands became wings and his feet talons, he clutched at Pilos and began to beat his wings furiously. Their fall did not abate much at first, but Pilos could feel the power in Edilus's effort, and though the druid was not strong enough to hold his companion aloft, he managed to slow their fall enough so that the impact at the bottom would be less deadly. At the last moment, Edilus pulled up and released Pilos, letting him tumble to the cobblestones. Then he flew off, soaring over the landscape, leaving the priest and the other mercenaries behind.

Someone grabbed Pilos by the back of his tunic and helped him to his feet, guiding him along, running, stumbling, away from the wall. He looked back once and saw Generon guards, their uniforms stark white in the early morning glow of day, pursuing them. He also spotted the crumpled bodies of Quill and Laithe at the base of the wall, lying still. He wondered if either of them had survived, but there was no time to go back and check.

He realized that he did not see Grolo's form still lying in the street, and he looked up in time to see Adyan struggling to carry the dwarf into an alley. As soon as Pilos was able to sprint on his own, Horial released him and ran faster to catch up with his companion, sharing the burden of the wounded sergeant.

In the alley, Horial and Adyan led the young priest through several twisting turns between buildings, stopping at a court filled with crates, refuse, and rickety stairs leading to second-floor wooden landings.

"In here," Horial said over his shoulder, helping Adyan carry Grolo down into a cellar. Pilos followed the two men and turned to pull the door shut behind him. At the last moment, the eagle swooped in, and Pilos had to hold the portal open a moment longer. Once Edilus was inside, Pilos let the door swing shut, leaving him in near-darkness, and shifted a latch to lock it. Then he turned back to see where they had taken refuge.

Horial held a single lit candle and was looking over Adyan's shoulder. "Is he still alive?" the man asked as Adyan checked the dwarf's vital signs. After a moment, the mercenary nodded, but his face was grim. "Not for long, though, if we don't get him some help. Do you have any healing draughts left?" he asked.

Horial shook his head. "No, I used the last of mine back in the woods when we ran into those snakes. Edilus patched me up before, after the fight at the portal. How about it, druid, do you still have some healing magic?"

The man in eagle form cocked his head to one side and stared at the mercenary, then shook it in a clear indication of a negative answer.

Pilos moved over to the wounded and dying dwarf. "I can still conjure a minor spell or two," he said, "but it probably won't be effective enough to rouse him. Just enough to keep him from dying."

"Do it," Horial said, moving over to give the Abree-ant space.

Pilos didn't waste any time. Placing his hands around the bolt shaft, he felt the wound pulsing weakly. Closing his eyes, he pleaded with Waukeen to grant the dwarf who had aided them a little more time, and when he yanked the bolt free, he let healing magic flow forth into the gaping hole left behind.

Grolo twitched but did not move otherwise.

Pilos drew a deep breath and performed the magic one more time. It was his last spell, a minor orison that would do little more than stop the bleeding and help Grolo rest. When he was finished, he could hear that the dwarf was breathing a little better, a little stronger.

"That's it," he said, wiping his bloody hands on the dwarf's tunic. "That's all I have left. I hope it's enough."

Place me on his hand, Hetta said, startling the priest.

The Abreeant took the ring from his pocket and slipped it onto Grolo's smallest finger. It barely fit over the end, but Pilos could wiggle it into place. A little more color returned to the dwarf's face and his breathing sounded calmer, more restful.

"What was that for?" Horial asked, eyeing the ring as Pilos put it into his pocket.

"She seems to be able to pass some of her energy to others when they need it," he answered, not sure he understood it himself. "I just did what she told me."

Horial nodded, a satisfied look on his face. "Well, that will keep him alive for the time being. But now we've got to figure out how to get out of here without drawing attention to ourselves. The Generon guards are probably swarming the streets already, looking for us."

"They're looking for me and Quill," Pilos said. "But the two of you and Edilus might be able to get out without being noticed. I could stay here with Grolo while you go for help."

Horial shook his head. "No, I appreciate your offer, lad, but I'll bet those guards got a good description from Junce. They know we're with you, and besides, I don't want to leave you here alone. We'll figure out something else."

Pilos turned to Edilus, who hadn't transformed back into his human shape yet. "Are you waiting to change back because you have something in mind?" he asked the druid.

The eagle's head bobbed up and down.

"Are we supposed to guess what it is?" Horial asked somewhat wryly.

Again the nod.

"All right," Pilos said, finding the little game challenging. "If he's in bird form, what's the benefit?"

"Well, no one has to smell him," Adyan said, smirking.

That elicited a sharp squawk from Edilus.

Pilos shook his head, impatient. "Seriously, what do we gain? The ability to fly? Only for him—he can't carry one of us with him, we know that. But he could slip through the lines of soldiers searching for us, make his way to bring back help."

"Except that he has no idea where he's going, or whom to trust," Horial said. "But what if he scouted ahead for us? Checked to find the best way to travel to avoid notice, and when to duck out of sight when trouble was coming? Is that what you're thinking, druid?"

Edilus bobbed his head up and down rapidly.

Horial stroked his chin, considering. "It's worth a try," he said.

"It's either that or we sit here and wait," Adyan said, "and I don't like the odds of that working out."

"Me, neither," Horial replied. "All right, let's try it. We'll give a peek outside, and if there's no one about, you can fly out of here, do a quick reconnoiter, and come back to let us know. Since you can't communicate, we'll have to use some signals so we understand."

After a few moments spent perfecting a series of beak jabs and directional flying, the group was ready. Pilos pulled back the latch and peeked into the alley. No one was in sight. He opened the door enough to let Edilus hop out and lift off, then watched the transformed druid glide toward the exit of the dead end where they had chosen to hide. He pulled the door to the cellar nearly shut again and watched for Edilus's return.

While they waited, they debated which direction they should travel to seek help. Adyan and Horial wanted to get to their barracks at the temple, for they felt they would find shelter and acceptance there, but the temple lay a long way across Arrabar from the Generon, especially for a group on foot with an unconscious companion. Pilos suggested his own house, but the mercenaries thought that seemed a risky neighborhood for a group carrying a body.

Finally, they settled on a market nearby where they could beg, borrow, or steal a cart in which to hide Grolo while they transported him. They left the debate of who would be the driver for later. They did agree that they would be better off not wearing their uniforms, so they all stripped off their tell-tale clothing and dumped it in a corner. Pilos was saddened to leave behind his gold circlet of office, which symbolized his position as Abreeant, but he understood the sacrifice.

Edilus returned and signaled to the men that the way was clear. They gathered up Grolo and trundled into the alley, cautious but confident as they moved toward the egress. At the first corner, they waited until the druid signaled, then darted across the road to the other side, into another alley. They made their way easily at first then nearly ran into trouble, for the far end of the next alley had become a station for Generon guardsmen to congregate and share news of their manhunt. The mercenaries had to retreat and hide behind crates while figuring out what to do next. Eventually, the guards seemed to lose interest in the spot and moved on.

At last, after considerable sneaking and watch-ing, the group made its way into the marketplace. While Adyan hid with Grolo in a rundown lean-to

near the edge of the market, the other two found a
wagon owned by a man selling clay urns, and after
some haggling, they managed to purchase the entire
affair—wagon, donkey, urns, and all. Pilos doled out
a number of gold coins, sparing a scathing look to
Horial as he did so. When the man had been paid,
they took the wagon back to Adyan's hiding place,
unloaded enough urns to make space for Grolo, then
covered him with blankets they purchased from
another nearby vendor.

At last, they began moving out of the market,
trying to look like common laborers with a cart of
goods to be sold. Edilus remained an eagle, scouting
ahead, though as more and more people rose for the
day, the looping and circling eagle began drawing unwanted attention. Finally, Horial convinced the druid
to find a secluded spot and remain inconspicuous, but
keep the guise of an eagle.

The men walked together, talking casually, watching all around for any sign that they had been
recognized and were being pursued. The farther they
got from the Generon, the more Pilos began to relax.
He had convinced the others to return with him to
House Darowdryn, because he knew for certain they
would be received without question there. He also
wanted to let his family know that he was alive and
well, but that Emriana had been caught and was
missing. He finally sold Horial on the plan by telling
the man that Lavant might have turned the entire
temple against anyone known to have consorted with
House Matrell.

"All right," the mercenary said at last, "you win.
I just hope they'll let riffraff like us traverse the
streets of your neighborhood."

The group of fugitives worked its way into the

upscale neighborhood of the merchant villas, and
Pilos knew that just a few more streets over, they
would arrive in the wealthy section of town. He
was beginning to feel good about the situation, and
even considered what he should do next, when a
strange noise caught his attention from the side of
the street.

The young priest turned his head to peer in the
direction of the sound and spied a face peeking out
from behind a canopied store window.

"Emriana?" he asked, not believing his eyes.

...

"We have been watching the coastlines of your
land ever since we received the portent that we would
be needed," Serille the sea elf maiden said, leading
Vambran and Arbeenok up the rocky slope of the
cave floor to a brightly lit area. "Deep Sashelas spoke
to us and said that a human known to us by family
and marked thrice would appear in the sea during a
great battle, and that this human would seek powerful history."

As Vambran listened to the girl's explanation,
he admired the beauty of the cave. The entire far
end had been carved to mimic the shape of a nauti-
lus shell, and in the center rested a rounded stone
that reminded Vambran of a clam shell. The entire
cave was draped with the green plants he and the
druid had swum past. In addition, the cavern was
illuminated with magical glowing orbs, resembling
common pierced lanterns favored by Chondathans
on the surface.

"This shrine to the Dolphin Prince is normally
submerged," Serille said as she guided the two surface

dwellers toward the stone shell, "but we made some alterations in preparation for your arrival. We thought it would allow you to be more ... comfortable ... this way."

Vambran nodded as he walked around the large stone, which he took for an altar. Arbeenok chose to examine a strange script carved along the smooth walls of the place. As Serille followed the lieutenant about the shrine, other sea elves clambered out of the water. Many carried tridents or nets, and most adorned their bodies with necklaces of shells and coral, and wore belts of shark and eel skin. Some had odd satchels draped across a shoulder or hanging from a belt. Clothing was not worn by any, as Vambran was beginning to understand, feeling weighted down by his own soaking wet shirt, trousers, and boots.

"This is normally filled with water?" Vambran asked the girl as she came up beside him. He was admiring a particularly beautiful carving of a dolphin in the wall.

"Yes," she said. "We have little need for these bubbles, though we can tolerate being out of the water for brief periods of time."

Something the girl had said nagged at Vambran's mind. Then it hit him. He turned to look at her. "You said that you would know me by my family. What, exactly, does that mean?"

Serille smiled. "You are Matrell, correct?"

Vambran could only nod, feeling a bit overwhelmed.

"You have your aunt's eyes," the girl said, and she laughed at Vambran's reaction.

He finally snapped his mouth shut, then asked, "My aunt? You know Xaphira?"

"Yes, I do. She is a kind woman. Did you not know that your family and my people engage in trade? It has been quite beneficial to both sides," she added.

Vambran shook his head. "I had no idea. That must have been what Xaphira was doing all those years she was missing."

"I knew you were the one the moment you drove away the kraken," Serille said, coming close and looking at Vambran intensely. "As I said, your face was familiar to me, but it was these," and she reached up and touched the three dots, one by one, on his forehead, "that confirmed it." Then her bright smile clouded into a frown. "But you were unwilling to come with me then, and I thought perhaps I had made a mistake." She turned and looked at the altar. "I spent a number of tides praying, hoping the Lord of the Sea would help me to understand what I had done wrong."

Vambran chuckled. "I'm sorry," he said. "At the time, I had no idea I was destined for this, so the thought of sinking to the bottom of the ocean, even with someone as fetching as you, was quite intimidating. I was drowning, if you recall."

The smile returned to Serille's face. "Yes," she said. "I was happy to assist you, whether you were the one spoken of in our portents or not."

Vambran saw that Serille's gaze was just a little more provocative, a tad more suggestive, than it had been before, and suddenly, he was conscious again of her bare body. Turning away, he said, "I guess I should thank you for that, then," and walked back to Arbeenok to put a little space between himself and the girl. "But now that we're here," he said, changing the subject, "I have no idea what we need from you."

Arbeenok walked over to a small shelf of rock and sat down. "We are seeking great magic," he said in his rich, deep voice. The alaghi's words echoed through the cavern, making the elves turn and look at him in wonder. "A healing magic, to cure a terrible plague. And we believe what we need can only be found in the submerged ruins of a human city. One known as the Twelve Cities of Swords."

Serille's smile faded once more. "You seek great history," she said, repeating her words from before. "Deep Sashelas told of this, but I did not know what it would mean." She sat for a moment, as if trying to accept what the druid had revealed. Finally she stood again and said, "I don't know what magic you have come for, either, but I can tell you that what you wish to do is very dangerous. The ruins of your ancient kingdom lie buried under the ocean floor, with only a few places accessible from the water. There are tribes of creatures living near those entrances, bitter enemies to us. And other things lurk deeper in the ruins, slumbering beasts that we would do well not to awaken. But if this is what you wish, we will try to help you."

Vambran smiled. "The world above will thank you for it, if we manage to find what we're looking for."

Serille looked at the lieutenant. "And what about you, Matrell? Will you thank me, too?"

Vambran nodded, feeling a little unnerved. "Yes," he said. "I will be very grateful. People I care about very deeply up there are in trouble, and I want to help them."

Serille considered his comments, then nodded, too. "Then we must not waste time. First, we must consult with the elders of my tribe, to see what they might know of this magic you seek. If we cannot learn enough that way, then we will ask the Dolphin Lord to guide us."

Quickly, the elves were in motion, speaking among themselves in a language that seemed to Vambran to be a cross between elvish and the chittering of dolphins. However the conversation was resolved, shortly afterward, several of the sea elves dived into the water and disappeared, while others began to move about the chamber, searching the lines of script carved on the walls.

"I have sent my fastest swimmers to seek information from my home city," Serille said. "It should not take more than a quarter tide to learn what we need to know." Then she pointed to the other members of her group and said, "My companions are searching among our holy lore, trying to learn what might be revealed by our written histories."

Vambran nodded. "So, what can we do to help?" he asked.

"Rest," Serille said. "When we learn something, the journey to your goal will be long and arduous." She went behind the altar and brought out a platter. Vambran saw that it held small mounds of a green substance that reminded him of algae from the ponds back home, as well as clams and even some fish, freshly filleted. The girl brought the platter to him and said, "We have prepared food for you. It is not much by your standards, we realize, but we tried to guess what you would like."

Arbeenok moved over beside Vambran, dipped his finger in one of the piles of green goop, and licked it. His eyes widened in surprise, and he scooped up a handful and popped it into his mouth. He made a satisfied sound as he chewed the strange food and motioned for Vambran to try it.

Vambran gingerly took a sample and tasted it, not sure what to expect, Arbeenok's reaction notwithstanding. But the flavor was delicious. It reminded the lieutenant of a blend of a hot buttered bun and a lemon, and he eagerly took another bite. Serille smiled and set the platter down between the two of them, then went off to help her kin search among the ancient writings carved into the walls of the shrine. Vambran and Arbeenok continued to consume the tasty meal. The fish was even better than the green concoction, and before long, the platter was empty and the two companions sat back, full.

"I feel as though I am on the verge of a vision," Arbeenok said, standing. "I will pray and see if I can learn something useful for us." He went off to find a quiet spot, out of the way, leaving Vambran to sit and wait.

For a long time, Vambran simply contemplated the events that had unfolded in the previous few hours. It was hard to imagine that only one day before, he had been the unwilling guest of the Emerald Enclave, housed in a cave on a rock outcropping. So much had happened in that span. He considered the people he had met, from Shinthala the druid who had taken a liking to him, to Edilus, who had not. He thought about the loss of his troops, and Uncle Kovrim, and he spent a private moment grieving again, though his sorrow was not mixed with guilt any longer. After his prayers earlier that morning, Vambran understood again the vagaries of life and his role in the lives of other people. Instead of being angry with himself for not having done more to save the Crescents, he accepted that events had been beyond his control and that those who were responsible deserved his wrath.

Vambran was startled out of his thoughts by Serille's appearance again. "Would you like to take a little journey with me?" she asked somewhat shyly. "To a secret spot I like?" she added, gesturing toward the water. She was holding a necklace of brightly colored coral and shells, all reds and purples and blues.

"Sure," the lieutenant said, certain that he still had several hours to use his water-breathing magic. "I can travel with you for a little while," he said. Then he frowned. "Though I can't swim nearly as well as you, and without Arbeenok to carry me, I may just sink."

"This will help," Serille said, holding up the necklace. "It has some powerful magic that's perfect for you." She handed the jewelry to Vambran and said, "You won't need those," brushing her hand against his still-wet clothes. "In fact, the magic of the necklace is much better if you take them off."

Vambran looked at the sea elf askance, trying to determine her motives, but the look she gave him was so innocent that he couldn't be sure what he thought. Shrugging, he sat down and slipped his waterlogged boots off, then quickly got out of his breastplate and the rest of his wet clothes. He laid them on a rock shelf to dry, though he wondered why he bothered. Then, when he was as naked as Serille, he looked at her expectantly.

She came to him and motioned for him to bow his head, and she slipped the jewelry around his neck. Immediately, Vambran could feel a change come over him. He gasped as he felt his hands and feet alter, elongating and growing webbing between fingers and toes. He suddenly had an urge to dive into the water and swim, knowing that it would feel like the most natural thing in the world. He reached up to feel the necklace and his hand brushed against gills along his neck and breastbone.

In a sudden panic, Vambran wondered if the transformation was permanent, and he yanked the necklace off again. At once, his body returned to its human anatomy, and he breathed a sharp sigh of relief. He slowly slipped the necklace back into place and felt the aquatic adaptation happen again.

"We have one for your companion, too," Serille said, "but we can give it to him later. He looks content."

Vambran looked over at Arbeenok, who had chosen to meditate, and saw the alaghi sitting very still with his eyes closed. He had to agree with the girl's assessment.

"Come on," Serille said, trotting toward the water. She looked back at Vambran.

The mercenary hesitated, turning back and reaching for his sword. "I don't feel right without this," he said, but he had no idea how to swim with it in his hand, since he no longer wore its scabbard.

"Leave it," Serille instructed. Instead, she took up a trident, one that had been borne into the cavern by another sea elf. She handed the new weapon to Vambran and said, "Can you use this?"

The lieutenant considered the aquatic weapon for a moment and gave it an experimental thrust, then nodded.

"Then let's go," the girl said, and laughing, she turned and splashed into the water.

Vambran followed her into the ocean, wondering what it would feel like, swimming with webbed hands and feet. It took him a moment to acclimate to his natural buoyancy and to learn to thrust properly, but soon enough, the mercenary was scooting through the water, able to keep up with Serille most of the time. Occasionally, she would swim circles around him, tickling him, and he would find it difficult to keep her at bay. Then, once she swam away, leaving him behind, he would stroke hard to catch up. When he realized that he had lost her, he began to worry, wondering if he could find his way back to the cave, but at the next moment, she popped up from behind a rock, laughing at him.

The most wondrous thing about the necklace, Vambran soon learned, was that he could speak with the girl and hear her speak.

"This way," she said at last and swam toward a large forest of the green plants growing from the ocean floor. It was a fairly flat place, and the plants grew thick and tall.

"What is this?" Vambran asked as they drifted among the treelike growths.

"It's called kelp," Serille answered. "Isn't it beautiful?" And she darted away, vanishing, beginning a game of hide and seek.

Vambran tried to keep up with the girl, but he kept getting his trident tangled in the kelp, and finally he called out, "I give up! You're too good!" Serille poked him from behind with her toe. When he spun to look at her, she swam to him, wrapping him in a most suggestive embrace, and kissed him.

CHAPTER 11

"Getting to House Darowdryn should be quite an adventure," Pilos said. The Abreeant, Edilus, and the mercenaries had pulled the wagon into an alley near the store where Emriana and, to their extreme surprise, Xaphira were hiding. They were all circled around the trussed up form of Lobra Pharaboldi, who was scowling at them, her mouth stuffed with cloth. "I can't believe you're here," he said, beaming at Emriana.

The girl returned his smile, but there was a sadness in it he had never seen before. "Tymora smiled on us a few times last night," she said.

"What happened? How did you get free?" he asked, eager to hear of the girl's exploits.

Emriana shook her head. "Not now, not

here," she said, still in that soft, sad voice. "We have to get her off the street before someone sees her."

Pilos nodded, though he did not understand and wanted to. Later, he decided. She's obviously been through a lot.

Horial was doing some quick rearranging in the cart. "All right, lift her up here," he said after making room next to Grolo.

Lobra thrashed and kicked but Emriana gave her one hard smack across the cheek and the woman stopped struggling. Adyan and Edilus hoisted the bound prisoner up off the cobblestones while Pilos kept a nervous watch over their surroundings. The last thing they needed was a city watchman strolling by at just the wrong time.

In the end, the two Matrell women had to ride on the cart, sitting on Lobra, who was pinned under a blanket beside the still-unconscious Grolo. Along with Edilus, they looked like some sort of traveling carnival, and a dirty one at that.

As they set off, Pilos suddenly remembered. "Em," he said, pulling a satchel out from under the seat of the cart. "I think these are yours."

Emriana eyed the bag in puzzlement for a heart-beat, then her expression brightened immeasurably and she grabbed at it. "Hetta!" she cried, digging into the satchel. Finding the ring, she slipped it onto her finger and turned all her attention to something unseen. Pilos smiled, happy to have cheered the girl. After a moment, she removed the ring and held it out to Xaphira, who stared at it with wariness. "Go on, take it," Emriana said. "She wants to speak with you."

Gingerly, Xaphira took the ring from her niece's hand and slipped it on. Her eyes glazed over and she stared at nothing, and Pilos knew she was in silent conversation.

Emriana leaned forward and gave the young priest a tight hug. "Thank you," she said. "Thank you for bringing her back to me."

Pilos smiled. "It was more like her bringing me back, but you're welcome."

The girl dug around in the satchel some more, then gasped in delight as she pulled out her opal pendant. "I can contact Vambran!" she exclaimed, slipping it over her head.

Emriana took hold of it to make use of its magic, but Xaphira reached out and stopped her. "Wait," she said. "Wait until after everyone has heard each other's stories. He'll want to know as much as we can tell him."

Emriana frowned for a moment, then nodded. "All right," she said, tucking the pendant away.

They rode on in silence for a time, partially because it seemed to Pilos that Emriana did not want to talk, but also because he was concerned that palace guards or the city watch might still be looking for them. At one point, Xaphira turned to Emriana and said, "Quill is dead." Pilos watched as her niece reached out and took Xaphira's hand, squeezing it in a comforting manner, but Pilos wasn't sure from the older woman's expression whether she was grieving or gratified. She remained silent for the rest of the ride.

The united group succeeded in reaching the Darowdryn estate without further trouble. As they rolled through the gates of the estate and word was sent ahead that they had arrived, Pilos felt himself finally relax. He could sense the others reacting the same way. At the front steps of the house, Ariskrit immediately took control of the situation, sending servants scattering in every direction and ordering every one of the new arrivals into baths and clean clothes. There were no complaints.

After everyone refreshed themselves, the entire group convened to discuss events. Pilos stifled a big yawn as he waited for everyone to gather in his family's sitting room. He had been one of the first to arrive.

Long night, he realized. *When was the last time I slept?* He realized it had been the night before the last, and fitfully at that. *When Mikolos died*, Pilos remembered, feeling his throat constricting in sorrow. *Has it only been one day?*

The Abreeant felt much better, though, even if he was tired. A hot bath and clean clothes could do wonders for a person who had been nearly stabbed, drowned, and shot at numerous times throughout the day and night. Everyone else who drifted into the room looked better, too, though Emriana still had that strange, haunted look on her face. It troubled Pilos, but he resolved to give her whatever time she needed and not press her about it. *She'll tell me when she's ready*, he told himself.

The sitting room quickly became crowded as everyone packed in. In addition to himself, Uncle Tharlgarl, and Ariskrit, Pilos counted Emriana and Xaphira, Horial, Adyan, Grolo—looking much better after substantial healing—and Edilus, and a pair of House guards sitting on either side of a still-confined Lobra.

Ariskrit cleared her throat and everyone grew silent. "Well, now," she said in a bemused tone. "It seems that a few of us have had a rather interesting evening. Lots of news to share and plans to be made.

But before we begin, let me just say that House Darowdryn has always been and will continue to be
staunch allies of the Matrells and their associates.
Let that never be in doubt." She looked pointedly
at Emriana and Xaphira, and the grand dame sent
an icy stare toward Lobra, who sniffed. Pilos wasn't
buying into the woman's airs, though. She looked
beside herself with apprehension.

She knows she's in a pickle, the young priest
thought.

In turn, everyone told their stories. Along the way,
there were more than a few gasps and murmurs, and
when Emriana described how she had come to be free
of the mirror, she seemed to leave a large gap in the
tale. At one point, she had to stop and clutch at her
aunt's hand, but she got through her part of things
without ever revealing what Pilos was beginning to
suspect was the reason for her demeanor.

When everyone had explained their adventures,
and after considerable back-and-forth questioning,
the room fell silent.

"All right," Ariskrit said, turning to look at
Lobra. "Let's see what you have to say." She gestured for the two guards to remove the woman's
gag. Once she was free to speak, she looked around
the room, her expression sullen. "You might as well
go ahead," Ariskrit said. "We'll beat the truth out
of you eventually, but you can spare yourself quite
a bit of misery by just spilling it now. And don't
think we won't know if you lie. We've got plenty
of enchantments to reveal falsehoods. Well?" she
demanded and tapped her toe.

Lobra, still looking sullen, finally began to speak.
"My husband did most of it," she said. "I was too distraught with family deaths to participate much."

"And is it true that your husband has been conspiring with House Talricci and the newly appointed Grand Syndar to bring about all this chaos?"

"I suppose so," Lobra muttered.

"Speak up, girl," Ariskrit demanded, crossing over to where Lobra was restrained. "Your mother isn't here to see this, rest her soul, but if she were, I'm sure Anista Pharaboldi would be more than a little upset with your antics of late. Now then, did your husband conspire with Grand Syndar Lavant and Grozier Talricci to start a war?"

Lobra began sniffling then, all of her stoicism lost. "Yes!" she blurted. "Yes! They wanted to corner the lumber market! And they wanted House Matrell out of the way while they did it! I went along with it because I was so angry with the Matrells for what happened to my brother and mother! Falagh hates you all so much, and I just learned to hate you, too." At that point, she broke off speaking and sat there, looking miserable.

For a moment, Pilos started to feel sorry for the woman, for it seemed to him that she had been manipulated by others into her participation. Emriana stood up, walked over to Lobra, and glared at her. Then, out of nowhere, she smacked the sniveling woman. And it was no slap, but a full-on, hand-balled-into-fist punch in the mouth. The blow knocked Lobra backward with a grunt.

Everyone in the room gasped in surprise and began to talk at once. Xaphira jumped up and grabbed Emriana, pulling her back, while Lobra, chastened, stared at the floor, a trickle of blood running from the corner of her mouth. Whatever sympathy Pilos had felt for the woman before, it was gone with that outburst. Emriana didn't say anything as she was led back to her seat, but she continued to glare at Lobra for a long time.

Once calm had been restored, Ariskrit turned to Pilos. "Do you think the other priests of the temple would be interested in hearing what our dear Lobra has to say?" she asked.

The Abreeant nodded. "I don't think they'll be too happy with their new Grand Syndar," he said. "The Waukeenar are not in the business of starting wars for profit," he said firmly.

"Then I think it's time you went to them and told them what evidence we have," Ariskrit said. "But you can't go alone. You need some other folk who can help you convince them to listen."

"Horial, Adyan, and Grolo should go, too," Xaphira said. "I can't imagine the clergy will be happy to hear that Lavant and Falagh tried to exterminate an entire company of their finest troops."

Horial began shaking his head. "We promised Vambran we would look after you and Em," he said. "We gave our word."

Xaphira gave the mercenary a cold stare. "I was fighting in skirmishes before the two of you and Vambran were old enough to kiss the girls," she said. "Vambran means well, but Emriana and I can take care of ourselves. Now that we know exactly how widespread this whole horrible scheme is, House Matrell is not the only entity in danger. We need to make certain everyone in the city is aware of it. Lavant cannot be allowed to continue to rule the temple. You three are going with Pilos."

Horial shrugged and said, "Yes, ma'am." He cast a quick glance at Adyan, but the other sergeant was just grinning and shrugged back.

"I would go with them, too," Edilus said, bringing

the room to absolute silence as everyone turned to look at the druid. "Though I did not intend to come here with the soldiers, I see that they have been honorable in their words to me, and I want to aid them." He turned and looked directly at Horial. "And my debt to you for saving my life is over!" he grumbled, folding his arms across his chest.

"Suits me just fine," Horial said. "I think maybe it's time for the temple to meet one of you druids, anyway. Might get a better idea of what you stand for, which to my way of thinking would be a good first step toward repairing relations with the Enclave."

Edilus seemed surprised at the sergeant's words, and he inclined his head in acknowledgement.

"Then it's settled," Ariskrit said. "Pilos and the boys will go to the temple to expose Lavant for the liar that he is. And you," she said, looking at Lobra again, "will remain our guest until the priests are ready to talk to you themselves."

"Emriana and I are going back to our house," Xaphira announced. "We have some unfinished business there."

Ariskrit looked worried for a moment, but when she saw the determined look in both women's eyes, she nodded. "I see by your expressions that you're every bit as determined as Hetta always was, so I don't think I could talk you out of it if I tried. Very well, then, I'll just wish you good luck and offer you whatever I can from our House to aid you."

Xaphira smiled and nodded her thanks.

The mercenaries wasted no time setting out with Pilos. At first, they considered taking a contingent of Darowdryn guards with them for additional force, but they decided it would draw the wrong kind of attention, suggesting that they intended to

be confrontational. Instead, they took advantage
of Darowdryn coaches and rode through the city
streets in relative obscurity. From time to time they
spotted Generon guards about, but it didn't look as
if a concerted effort to track them down continued.
After they rolled past the third such group without
incident, Pilos began to relax.

The coaches made their way through the crowded
streets and reached the temple complex by early
afternoon. They rode right up to the front entrance,
and Pilos and the others climbed down, ready to
stride right into the middle of the council chambers
and declare Lavant a traitor to the Waukeenar. The
temple was bustling with activity as they entered, but
more than a few clerics stopped dead in their tracks
as Pilos and the others passed.

At first, the Abreeant thought it was simply because Edilus was with them, but as they approached
the council chambers, he began to realize that
temple guards were everywhere, watching them.
They reached the door and prepared to go inside,
but one of the guards stepped in their path, barring
them entry.

"By order of the Grand Syndar and the entire high
council," the guard said, "you are all under arrest for
crimes against the temple and the city."

...

Arbeenok was waiting, about as agitated and
impatient as Vambran ever remembered seeing the
alaghi, by the time he and Serille returned from their
swim. As the mercenary climbed out of the water, the
druid paced back and forth.

"I had a new vision," Arbeenok said, cocking his

head to one side and looking at Vambran quizzically once he realized that the lieutenant sported aquatic features.

Vambran held up the necklace as he shook the water from his body. "They have one for you, too," he said, gesturing back at Serille, who had emerged with him from the water and was moving to speak with other sea elves. "So what did your vision reveal?" he asked. It seemed to Vambran that some of Serille's companions who had been sent to consult with the elders had returned. He wasn't sure by faces, but there seemed to be more figures in the room than before.

"There is a great chamber, a hall of some sort," Arbeenok said, "and many people are in the chamber, a gathering, an official ceremony. And everything has a green tinge to it."

"Green? Is it a trick of the light? Is this place underwater?" Vambran asked. He considered putting his clothes back on, but didn't really see the point. *If we're going swimming again once we know something,* he told himself, *why bother?*

"No," Arbeenok said in answer. "I think this must have happened a long time ago, before the city was washed away by the tidal wave."

"But green is significant," Vambran said. "Maybe we're looking for something green."

"That is quite likely," Serille said, returning to the pair after an extended conversation with her kin. "We believe we may have uncovered information about this magic you seek." She entwined her hand into Vambran's as she explained. "Many hundreds of years ago, in the Year of the Stricken, right before the cataclysm that destroyed the human kingdom on the surface, our landed brethren of the forests came to visit the leader of your people, in a city known as Naarkolyth."

Vambran started to explain to Serille that they were not his people. Though he had little knowledge of the history of Jhaamdath, what bits he did know suggested that they had been introverted and decadent, suspicious of all outsiders. He held his tongue, though, figuring it wasn't germane to the story.

"One of the things they brought with them was an item of powerful healing. We believe this is what you seek."

"I don't suppose you know where the remains of this Naarkolyth are, do you?" he asked.

Serille adopted a serious mien. "As a matter of fact, I do," she said. "But it is well hidden, hard to reach, and in dangerous waters."

"Perfect," Vambran said. "Just what I wanted to hear. What do we need to do now?"

"We are prepared to guide you to the remains of the city," the sea elf answered. "And a few among us are willing to accompany you into its depths. We have gathered provisions for this trip, and by Deep Sashelas's will, we will find your magic and help you save your people."

Vambran nodded his head. "Then let's get going," he said, "the plague is undoubtedly spreading above. And you can tell me more of this history along the way."

Serille smiled and nodded.

Along with Arbeenok, Vambran, and Serille, ten more sea elves began the journey to Naarkolyth. Serille led them out of the cave and into the depths of the Reach. They traveled along the slope of the continental shelf, rather than descending deeper into the water, for the elves had explained that they would encounter fewer enemies at a shallower depth, and they would wait until the last possible moment before turning and dropping into the murk.

As before, Vambran found the travel exhilarating, because he had the freedom to swim himself rather than relying on Arbeenok to tow him. He worried that he would miss his armor, but since none of the elves in the group wore any, he decided to trust his instincts and learn their ways and culture as best as he could.

Arbeenok did not seem quite as exuberant about swimming as the lieutenant did, and Vambran imagined that being able to transform into a multitude of animals would make the druid less amazed by such new experiences. Still, the alaghi took the opportunity to observe the many wonders of the sea, pointing out flashing schools of fish darting back and forth, great spreads of coral covering the sea floor, and an amazing variety of kelp and other aquatic plants, all of which provided the swimmers with a spectacular vista. They passed the occasional shipwreck, too, in various stages of decay. Vambran pondered the fates of the sailors who had been on board those vessels, wondering how *Lady's Favor* might look at the moment, sitting in the sandy bottoms where she went down.

His thoughts were interrupted as Serille began to relate some of the history of Naarkolyth. "The elves of the forests and the people of the coastal lands did not agree on a great many things, but in the Year of the Stricken, as I mentioned, they made a last effort at peace. The elves brought with them many gifts, tributes that they hoped would create a bond, a friendship between themselves and the humans of the Cities of the Twelve Swords. Among those gifts, apparently, was a scepter. Though the portions of our histories that describe this scepter in greater detail are lost, what does remain tells of a beautiful natural object, woven of plants and other items of the land. The histories claim that this scepter was powerfully enchanted to bring health to the citizens of the cities."

"And this is the object we seek?" Vambran asked. He felt skeptical. Who's to say this is the right item and not something else, something lost even to the annals of history? he wondered.

Serille shrugged. "It is the only reference to anything with the power to heal that we know of," she said. "If that is not the magic you seek, then why would the Dolphin Lord bring us together?"

Why, indeed, Vambran thought, remembering his swim with the girl earlier.

"I believe the item she describes is the one we are looking for," Arbeenok said, swimming beside the two of them. "I cannot explain it with clarity, but everything she described feels right with my own intuitions."

"Well, even if it is the right one," Vambran said, feeling a sense of gloom wash over him, "we don't have any idea where it is now. A leader of the city could have taken it home with him, could have placed it in some vault somewhere, or it could have shattered during use," he continued. "Jhaamdath stretched all along the coast, just as Chondath does now. Without some sense of reference, that fable doesn't give us much."

"Oh, the histories tell more," Serille said, her smile bright. "The elves chronicled their visit in detail, for they wanted history to understand why the cataclysm came to be. The elves gathered in the midst of Naarkolyth, the largest of the twelve cities, in a great palace, and met with the king. He accepted the gifts the elves had brought and sent them away, promising better relations, but they were empty words, as we now know. The elves believed that the king, fearing a trick, had the gifts sealed away in a vault beneath the same audience chamber where they had been bestowed. He never once took them out and put them to use. Two years later, after more bickering and slaughter, Jhaamdath was wiped from the face of Toril."

"So we know it's in the center of the city of Naar-kolyth," Vambran said, imagining what it must have been like in those final hours, as an immense tidal wave scoured the coastline clean. Turning to Arbeenok, the lieutenant asked, "Do you suppose this great palace chamber is the same as in your vision?"

The druid nodded. "I believe so."

"Then you'll know we're there when we actually get there," the mercenary quipped.

After her tale-spinning, Serille took the opportunity to play, cavorting around Vambran, sneaking up beneath or behind him and tickling him when he wasn't expecting it. The lieutenant took some delight in her affections and tried to chase her down once or twice, but she was a far better swimmer than he and easily evaded his lunges. At one point, after she had come at the mercenary officer from above and wrapped her hands across his eyes as if to play guess-who, Vambran noticed one of the male elves scowling at him. As soon as Vambran returned the look, though, the sea elf turned away and swam out a little distance, as though watching for trouble.

I've seen that kind of scowl before, the lieutenant

thought, rolling his eyes. He swam over to Serille and said pointedly, "A couple of your companions are acting a little possessive of you, and don't seem to like our carrying on. Is there something I should know?"

Serille's eyes narrowed the slightest bit, but Vambran wasn't certain whether her irritation was directed at him and his blunt question or at the other sea elf's resentment. She asked, "Which one?" in a very serious and somewhat icy tone. When Vambran pointed out the fellow, the girl swam directly over to him and began a rather one-sided conversation, with quite a bit of gesticulating to accompany it. On more than one occasion, the male turned to look at Vambran, but Serille quickly dragged his attention back to her. When the discussion was finished, she swam back to the lieutenant and said, "That's Ishuliga. He doesn't think I should be consorting with surface dwellers. I changed his mind, and he shouldn't be a problem any more." Then she swam away, toward the front of the procession, apparently no longer in a playful mood.

Vambran considered swimming over to Ishuliga himself, to try to settle things in a more comfortable manner, but he decided against it, at least for the time being. *If a better opportunity arises, then I might,* he decided. With that decision, the mercenary forgot about the matter and returned his attention to the journey at hand.

The sea elves and their visitors traveled for several hours before they arrived at a spot overlooking a region of rough and rocky terrain. Vambran studied it and noted that the contrast between that area and the rest of the seabed seemed remarkable. The idea occurred to him that perhaps it was debris from the great tidal wave. He wondered if certain parts of the coast of Jhaamdath had been harder hit or were more susceptible to destruction than others. It made sense to him that regions along the coast that were formed of loose soil would settle more evenly once dragged into the water, while rocky terrain would form a more uneven landscape—or rather seascape—such as the scene they faced at the moment.

"This is where Naarkolyth is buried," Serille said, swimming closer to Vambran and Arbeenok. "A couple of locations can be found where fissures open into the depths of the ruins, but most of the build-ings were crushed beneath all of the earth that was dragged off the land with it."

"I wish we had some sort of map of the city," Vam-bran lamented. "It might help us determine the layout once we get down there."

Serille chuckled. "No map from the surface would aid you now," she said. "The city was literally tumbled down upon itself. What little survived was most often turned upside down or sideways. Whole sections of the city were rearranged as the waves dragged it out to sea. It is simply a different place."

"What should we expect in the way of trouble?" Vambran asked. "You said these were dangerous waters."

"They are. Koalinth live in the cracks and crevices of this part of the Selmal Basin, brutes who wage war upon one another almost as often as they attack my own people. They are not overly bright, but they prefer overwhelming numbers. We would do better not to have to face them at all, but if we cannot avoid a skirmish with them, do not show them any hesita-tion, any fear. That's what inspires them to continue to fight."

Vambran glanced over at Arbeenok, who was

nodding. "They are distant cousins to hobgoblins in the hills above," the druid said. "They fight with similar tactics."

Vambran found himself wishing he had his sword. He looked at the trident in his hands. I'll make do, he decided. "All right," he said at last, "Lead on."

"We cannot risk light here," Serille said, turning to begin the descent. "Not until we reach the mouth of the fissures. We will attract too much attention to ourselves. So until then, stay close so you don't get lost."

The procession of sea elves and surface visitors began to swim out over the edge of the continental shelf, following the steeper slope as it angled down, deeper into the gloom below and away from the sunlight. The rough and tumble appearance of the sea floor put Vambran on edge, for he imagined a horde of swimming, swarming hobgoblins springing out of every gorge, charging from around every craggy outcropping. Hiding places were plentiful, and because the sea elves had explained that they should stay close to the sea floor rather than risking visibility by swimming high, it felt as if they were ripe for an ambush.

Yet nothing attacked the group and they continued on, swimming downward, deeper than Vambran could have managed on his magic alone. The pressure would have taken its toll on his body long before, without the aid of the necklace Serille had given him. Even so, he was beginning to feel the effects of the gloom, for the water was growing colder, cut off as it was from the warmth of the sun shining on the surface.

This is the sea nightmares are made of, the mercenary realized. This is what the sailors imagine when their ships are slowly receding beneath the storm-tossed waves. They both love and fear it, and this is why.

As Vambran paddled along, keeping an eye on the rocks below him, he passed a particularly unusual outcropping. It was covered in brown coral, not nearly as colorful as the species that grew in shallow water. The coral was interspersed with unusual anemones and strange, frondlike things. But what really caught the lieutenant's attention was the shape of the undersea promontory. It had the distinct likeness of a broad, round dome, and though the growth of the sea hid it well, he thought he could see columns, evenly spaced and perfectly parallel, running from one side of the dome. Its orientation suggested that it was lying on its side, but Vambran could easily imagine it as a central structure in a broad plaza somewhere on the surface. A temple, perhaps, or a civic building with steps surrounding it.

The mercenary stopped, peering, for he was suddenly certain that he had spotted an opening, a tiny crevasse, where a wide doorway might once have been. He rubbed his eyes and swam closer, fighting the gloom. Yes, it was definitely symmetrical, and centered.

A way in!

Vambran popped his head up to call to the rest of the group, to tell them of his find, and discovered to his great dismay that he was alone. Serille, Arbeenok, and the other sea elves had vanished. Frantically, Vambran began swimming forward again, looking for his companions. He did not want to lose track of the discovery he had made, but the thought of being left alone in such a dismal, murky location made his heart race with fear.

Fool! Vambran berated himself. *What did she tell you about getting lost?*

The mercenary glanced back once to see if he could still make out the building behind him, and he froze in the water. A huge dark shadow was approaching, slightly above him, blotting out all the light. It seemed to swim lazily back and forth, but as it got closer, its shape became clear.

It was a shark, and the biggest Vambran could ever have imagined, easily the size of a small ship. Vambran was awestruck even as his heart pounded in his chest.

The shark suddenly accelerated and came straight for him.

Vambran nearly dropped his trident as he turned and dived as quickly as he could downward, toward the uneven formations of rock below. The shark, a gargantuan thing that seemed to go on forever, altered its course slightly, still bearing down on him. Pulling through the water with all his might, Vambran was still not fast enough to evade the thing.

Opening its jaws wide, the enormous shark engulfed him.

CHAPTER 12

I n the end, Xaphira acquiesced, agreeing
that being accompanied by an armed
force was more practical than the two
women going alone—even if she did insist
she was ready to knock the very walls down
to reclaim what was hers. Emriana had not
blamed her for wanting to stalk right up to
the gates of House Matrell, just the two of
them, and demand to be let in, but she knew
better than to trust that the guards would
make way for them to enter the dwelling.
Grozier and Marga had turned them out, and
it had seemed to be all on the level.

So Tharlgarl Darowdryn and twenty of
his best House guards approached the front
gates of the Matrell estate with Xaphira and
Emriana, and though she was ready to mete

out some serious revenge all on her own, Emriana realized she was thankful for the support.

Xaphira wore her red mercenary outfit, while Emriana had donned her more comfortable and practical black shirt and trousers. "The better for skulking," she had said. She had told Xaphira to keep Hetta's ring, for though she immensely loved her grandmother's presence inside her head, she thought it only fair that Xaphira have an opportunity to share time, too.

They arrived on horseback, for Steelfists had insisted on wearing his elaborate armor to the fray, and there was no way in the Nine Hells, he had said, that he could walk to the end of his property in it without passing out from exhaustion. Emriana doubted the veracity of that statement, for the man's arms were as thick as small trees, and she could sense the strength radiating from him. Nonetheless, she was also thankful for a mount, for it made her feel more in charge and less ... pleading. Yes, on horseback, it felt less like they were asking to be allowed to reenter their home.

As they trotted up to the gates, Xaphira was the first to speak. "Get the damned gates open right now before we ride them down," she said simply.

Emriana nearly laughed out loud at the wide-eyed expression of the four guards there, at least two of which she knew. Despite whatever Grozier and Marga might have told them, the House guards did not seem the least bit interested in denying the woman who was ostensibly their lady and mistress. They nearly stumbled over themselves in an effort to get the portal open before Xaphira actually had to rein in.

Emriana wondered whether her aunt would have

slowed down to wait or if she would have plowed right through the gates. She was thankful they hadn't had to find out.

"As of right now," Xaphira said, not deigning to look at any of the four guards as she rode through, straight and proud, "you are either still employed by me, in which case you had damn well better consider Grozier Talricci a threat to this family, one to be apprehended at once, or else you still operate under the illusion that he is in control of this House, in which case I'd better not see your faces again. Because by the time I come back this way, he will either be dead or in a pillory."

Emriana stole a glance to one side and saw the two guards looking at one another in amazement. The first bowed deeply and said, "We are at your service, m'lady," and quickly, the other three piped up with similar oaths of loyalty.

"Good," Xaphira said, still not turning to meet them eye to eye. "Then start earning your coin."

It's good to be home, Emriana thought, almost giggling.

The procession rode up to the front steps of the house, where servants began pouring out the front doors, many of them exclaiming how stunned and delighted they were that the two Matrell women were both alive and well. A few offered hugs, which Xaphira accepted graciously, but it was clear that she was in no mood for reunions, and neither was Emriana. She dismounted beside her aunt and together, they stepped into the front hall of the estate. Steelfists ordered his men to dismount and be at the ready.

"Talricci!" Xaphira called out, already taking hold of her holy coin and muttering a prayer. "We have unfinished business, *now!*" She strode from the front hall into the main sitting room, and into the dining room, looking for her quarry. All around her, servants fell over themselves either welcoming her back or trying to tell her that Grozier and Bartimus were no longer there.

It took a few moments of chaos before Xaphira and Emriana finally got a straight story. It seemed that the moment word had reached the house that the two Matrell women had returned and were riding at the front of an armed escort, Grozier and his wizard had bolted.

Liezl, the serving girl who had told Emriana of Hetta's death, saw the man depart and was happy to share the experience. "He heard the commotion and stood up from that very chair to look out the windows there. When he turned back around, he was pale as a ghost, and he said, 'Bartimus, get us home, now!' Just like that."

Emriana was almost sorry they hadn't caught him in the middle of their house. She really did want to thump him. "That still leaves Marga," she told her aunt.

"Right," Xaphira said, turning about. "Where is she?" the woman asked of anyone willing to answer.

"Why, Marga hasn't come out of her rooms in the last couple of days," Mirolyn said, standing at the doorway. "She doesn't seem sick, but she doesn't want any visitors."

"We'll see about that," Xaphira said. "Tharlgarl, will you and your men kindly begin rounding up the rest of our House guards and explain to them exactly what is expected of them?"

"It would be my pleasure, Lady Xaphira," Steelfists

boomed. He turned and barked orders to his men.

With that, Xaphira turned and stalked down the hall toward Marga's chambers. Emriana was right on her heels.

Xaphira made the door slam open as she entered Marga's rooms. There had been no knock, Emriana observed in delight. "Either you have a very good explanation for why you let your brother take over this House, or you're out on the street by nightfall," Xaphira said, staring at the woman seated in a chair on the far side of the room.

Marga only looked up calmly and said, "I don't wish to be disturbed at the moment. Perhaps you could come back later?"

Xaphira's shoulders hunched in rage, but Emriana thought that Marga's expression was odd. Sort of pained, the girl thought, like she's struggling with something. That was when she noticed Marga's hands twitching, and Emriana saw that she was clasping something in them.

Xaphira began to stride across the room. "Why you thankless little wench," she said, reaching out, intending to grab Marga by the shoulders. "I ought to—"

"Xaphira, wait," Emriana said, pointing at the item, which seemed to be a letter. "What is she holding?"

Marga only smiled and said, "I really don't want to be disturbed. Can't this wait?"

"Probably the deed to the property," Xaphira snapped, yanking the paper from the woman's grasp. She glanced at it as if ready to discard it, but then the woman did a doubletake and began to read in earnest.

Emriana noticed a single tear form in the corner of Marga's eye, and as Xaphira finished reading the letter, that tear began to make its way down the woman's cheek.

"Oh, by the gods, I'm so sorry," Xaphira said, dropping the letter and grabbing at Marga to hug her tightly. Though Marga wrapped her arms around Xaphira in return, Emriana heard her say, "This really isn't necessary. I would like to be alone right now."

The girl snatched up the fallen missive and read it.

> *Please help me! I am being magically compelled to say these things, but in truth I want very much to come out of my rooms. Grozier has kidnapped Quindy and Obiron and is holding them at the Talricci estate. Bartimus made sure I couldn't say anything to anyone, but he slipped up because I can write the truth. Please help me and my babies!*
>
> *Marga*

Emriana was beside her aunt, hugging Marga just as hard, even before the paper hit the floor. Marga still seemed unwilling to admit what was going on, and Emriana shuddered to think of how hard it must be, wanting to say something and not being able to make the words come out.

"Can you remove this foul magic?" Emriana asked at last, pulling back and studying Marga's smooth, emotionless face.

"Oh, yes," Xaphira said. "I've got just the thing to deal with this. And when I get my hands on that damnable wizard, he's going to wish he had never set foot in this house," she muttered, fumbling for something in one of her satchels.

"Not if I get to him first," Emriana said, imagining planting a well-placed kick right into the paunchy wizard's nose. "Hurry, Aunt Xaphira. We need to get to the Talricci estate before he does—" Emriana cut herself off then, not wanting to suggest injury to the twins in front of Marga. It must be hard enough to be thinking about them and unable to plead for help, she thought. But hearing someone else talk about them in that way . . .

Xaphira produced a small scroll tube from her satchel and withdrew a curled sheaf of parchments. She thumbed through them, finding the one she wanted, and replaced the rest in the tube before tucking it back in the satchel.

Emriana watched her aunt scan the page for a moment. "Will that do it?" she asked, not wanting to interrupt but unbearably curious. She had never seen her aunt draw magic from a scroll before and she wanted to understand how it was done.

"I never had much need to obliterate a curse on the battlefield," Xaphira said at last, "but I always thought this would be handy to have around. All right, here we go." And she began to chant, her eyes scanning the page. Emriana heard the woman singing the words, but she couldn't understand any of it. Xaphira's song reached a quick crescendo and she stopped.

Marga burst into tears. "Oh, by the gods," she sobbed, jumping up and running out into the hall. "Please go get them," she begged, turning around to face Xaphira and Emriana. "Don't let him hurt them," she said in a near-whisper.

Both women ran to Marga and took her in their arms again. "It's all right," Xaphira said, shushing her and stroking her hair. "We'll get them back for you."

Emriana just wrapped her arms around the woman's waist and clung to her. I know how you feel, she thought. I was helpless for a while, too.

By the time they had gotten Marga comfortable and had heard her entire story, Emriana was seething mad. Shapeshifters! That day by the pond, she thought, understanding the twins' odd behavior at last.

Denrick.

Somehow, realizing the truth of the previous night made her feel worse. She shuddered, trying not to relive the ordeal again. She knew that Lobra had preyed upon her worst fears, and in a way, she was angry with herself for letting it be such an effective fear.

No! She thought, shouting at herself. Don't you accept any blame for that. *They* did it to *you!*

It was time to put a stop to it, Emriana decided. Right now. "Xaphira," she said, and something in the tone of her voice must have made her aunt realize the gravity of what she was about to say, for the woman looked at her intently. "We still have unfinished business to deal with." When Xaphira didn't say anything, Emriana continued. "It's time to pay Grozier Talricci a visit."

. . .

Several rows of teeth the size of Vambran's torso flashed toward the mercenary, white blades designed to shred him into bloody pulp. But when they snapped together, the yawning blackness of the shark wholly enveloped him, and those great daggers missed his flesh. He was swept into the blackness, fighting the churning water, thrashing against the current, but it was futile. The undersea world, the light, receded.

Trapped inside the shark's mouth, the current still propelled Vambran, and he found himself sliding deeper into its cavernous insides. Fighting the terror of what had befallen him, the lieutenant tried to reason. He still had the trident Serille had given him, though he doubted it would do much against such a massive creature. Still, he might be able to use it to slow his descent into the thing's belly. He rammed the weapon down hard, feeling it sink into the flesh. He clung to the haft, fighting the flow of water, and peered around.

Ahead, he could see the light beyond the enormous mouth as the shark swam about, allowing water to flow in. Indeed, the current that was trying to sweep him along reminded him of something. Turning to stare in the other direction, deeper into the beast's gullet, he spied the twin glimmers of light he was hoping for.

The gills.

Uprooting the trident and paddling furiously, Vambran swam toward one side of the shark, aiming at those slits, letting the flow of the water carry him. As he neared the first of the gaps in the shark's body, he jabbed the trident into it, using the weapon as a handle. The force of the water was strong, but Vambran wasn't sure he could slip out through the gill. He pushed on the flap experimentally to see how flexible it was. It did not give much, but it was the only means of escape that he could see. Bolstering his courage, the mercenary began to climb through the gill. He led with the trident and his arms. Once he got his head wedged into the gap, he began shoving himself through, using the trident like a pry bar.

The shark, perhaps sensing the man's assault

on a sensitive body part, thrashed about, buffeting
Vambran. He nearly lost his grip on his weapon and
he was slammed about painfully, all the while still
desperate to free himself. When, the shark jerked
just right, the gill slit opened enough that Vambran's
body slipped through. He went tumbling along the
shark's flank, buffeted by its motion and scraping
painfully against its rough skin.

But he was free.

And bleeding.

It was no more than a scrape, trickling only a little
blood, but the great brute was making a wide turn,
and Vambran feared that it could smell his wound in
the water already. Terrified of another attack, of not
being so lucky as to evade the teeth again, he dived
downward to the sea floor and discovered a small
fold in the coral and the anemones where he could
wedge himself in. He plunged into the crack and fell
still just as the shark glided past again, snapping
its jaws where he had been only a heartbeat before.
The ferocity of the bites churned the water, swirling
it and buffeting Vambran severely. He cradled his
head in his arms as he bounced against the rock,
and when the water grew calm, he glanced up to see
the skin of the beast moving past him at less than
an arm length away.

Even after the creature had moved past, Vambran
remained still for several long moments more, unwilling even to turn his head to see where it had gone.

Finally, when his heartbeat had slowed to an even
rate, the lieutenant did rise, barely enough to peer
around. He saw no sign of the immense shark.

Thank Tymora, he thought, sagging down again.

After gathering his strength, Vambran rose up
from his protected hiding place. He saw no evidence

of the rest of his companions. Dismayed, he considered the best course of action.

On land, he thought, if a soldier gets lost in the woods, he's instructed to stay put and let others find him. Maybe that works in the water, too. But how long do I wait for them to come back? he wondered. It's bound to get even darker down here. I can make a light, but Serille said that was a bad idea.

After weighing his options, the lieutenant decided to follow his instincts, which told him to return to the domed building he had discovered before the arrival of the shark. He rationalized that it was the place where he had first lost his companions and thus, if they followed the same methods as on the surface, they would backtrack to that spot and find him. But the truth was, he felt drawn to the location. Curiosity was driving him to find out what was inside, through that narrow space that he had imagined being a doorway.

The only problem was, how could he leave a clue for the others that he was there? Vambran needed some way to mark the spot, leave some sign behind—subtle enough not to attract the attention of unwanted species, but obvious enough to those who knew what to look for.

Vambran had no idea how long it took him to find the unusual formation again, but eventually he spotted the strange dome. With a sigh of relief, he settled down near the rocky crevice that he thought might allow ingress. The fissure was pitch black within and Vambran was reluctant to use his magic to generate light, but he would never work up the courage to descend without being able to see. He also knew that blindly entering the unknown space might bring him face-to-face with Waukeen in no time.

Vambran considered how best to mark his passage. Using the trident, he chipped off some of the coral along a flat area that was more or less vertical. The growth broke off in large chunks, exposing a lighter color beneath. The revealed surface didn't appear to be natural rock, but what Vambran believed to be worked stone. Elated, he quickly chiseled away two more identical spots. He carefully rounded all three of them, making sure that they were sizeable enough to be seen from a considerable distance. Then he retreated from his work and looked down on it. From several vantage points, three dots were clearly visible, identical in formation to the three dots he bore on his brow.

Perfect, the lieutenant thought. They'll figure that out.

Satisfied that he had left a reasonable trail, Vambran moved down toward the gap in the rock. He sat for a time, trying to build up his courage. He didn't know if his hesitation was a fear of being sucked into a great blackness for a second time that day, or if he felt some sense of trespassing on a scene of ancient death. If the place was truly a portal into the forgotten ruins of Naarkolyth, he might very well be the first human to pass through its halls in over a millennium. The thought was both sobering and exhilarating.

Sitting on a rock under the ocean wasn't helping anyone on the surface, Vambran convinced himself, and finally, he took hold of his holy coin and muttered a prayer. He worried briefly that the changes in his voice due to his gills might cause the magic to fail. With the final word of the spell, though, his coin glowed with a soft light.

Before the illumination could attract the attention

of predators or enemies nearby, Vambran ducked down and sized up the gap. The passage was wider and the way was easier than he had imagined. He slipped through the opening and found himself in a narrow gash in the rock. He disturbed a few fish and some crabs, which scuttled away at his approach.

The slit opened downward to the edge of his light and beyond and was so narrow that Vambran would not be able to maneuver much as he descended. He considered giving up and returning to the surface to wait for Serille and Arbeenok to find him, but his curiosity won out. The mercenary allowed himself to drift down through the crevice.

The rock became smoother as Vambran swam farther down, for no plant or coral could grow upon it without at least feeble light to feed on. The passage he was traversing eventually widened enough to become recognizable as a hallway or tunnel, and the thought sent chills down his spine. He was moving through a corridor that humans had walked hundreds of years earlier.

After descending into the unadorned passage for a few more moments, Vambran's light suddenly illuminated a dead end. Silt and mud filled the bottom of the shaft and no other passage was visible. Disappointed, Vambran probed the silt with the butt end of the trident, hoping to find an opening, or some clue or secret, that would let him explore farther.

The lieutenant was on the verge of turning back when something caught his eye. A tiny plume of bubbles streamed forth from the stone wall of the shaft. Vambran got close to the trail of bubbles and peered at the stonework. He wasn't certain, but a very small, very straight crack seemed to run the length of the rock.

A hidden passage? he wondered.

Vambran spent several minutes searching and discovered a barely discernable seam that looked like the outline of a hidden door. He tried pushing on the stone in various locations and examined other sections of the wall to locate a lever, stud, or other release mechanism, but his search was in vain.

Only mildly discouraged, the mercenary again considered returning to the open water to wait for his companions, but then he felt the familiar tingle of magic. Inspiration flowed through him and an understanding he couldn't explain washed through his mind. The lieutenant believed he had the workings of a new arcane power at his fingertips. He simply knew, and though the feeling was startling, it wasn't as unnerving as it had been the first time he had discovered the innate ability.

Thanking Waukeen for whatever role she had played in the manifestation of his power, Vambran placed his hands on the concealed portal once more and spoke a phrase that simply came to his mind. A low, deep click sounded and the stone shifted beneath his touch, settling slightly. Elated, Vambran started to push against the door to see if it would open, but before he could react, a second click became audible and the door sank away, releasing a great burst of air that buffeted the mercenary.

At the same moment, a sudden suction took hold of the man, drawing him inextricably downward, into the hole he had created. As his body slid through the ever-widening gap in the stone, his trident wedged across the opening. He dangled for a moment, his iron-tight grip on the haft of the weapon keeping him from being sucked away by the force of the water. Huge bubbles surged upward out of the void beyond the doorway, slamming into Vambran and tossing him about.

The lieutenant tried to pull himself out, tried to remember a spell that might rescue him, but the pain in his arm and shoulder became too great. With a frantic cry of fear, Vambran lost his grip on his weapon and shot downward into the darkness below.

...

For several long moments, no one moved.

Pilos had trouble believing what he had heard. Arrested?

Then chaos erupted in the halls of the temple of Waukeen as everyone began talking at once. The Abreeant heard someone shouting behind him, but all he could focus on were the doors to the council chamber, only steps away.

Arrested?

"Edilus, no!" Horial shouted, and Pilos whirled around to witness the growing commotion.

The druid had jerked his scimitar free and was menacing a tightening circle of temple guards, all of whom had a distinct advantage with the longer reach of their half-spears. Horial was trying to push past one of the guards, to stop Edilus before he drew blood. Somehow, he managed to convince the druid to lower his weapon. Adyan stood with his hands up, unthreatening, but Pilos could see that the sergeant's jaw was clenched, for the scar along his chin was flexing. Grolo stood beside Adyan, jabbing his stubby finger into the chest of another guard, who was arguing right back.

Pilos had never seen so much uproar within the

confines of the temple, then he realized that it had
begun prior to their arrival.

A guard attempted to take hold of the young
priest by both arms and Pilos spun around, jerking
his hands free. "No!" he said, shouting to be heard. "I
must see the high priests, immediately!"

The guard was shaking his head and held one
hand on his weapon as he advanced toward Pilos
again. "They are in emergency session and are not
to be disturbed," the soldier said. "Now don't make
this harder than it already is."

Emergency session? Pilos wondered, his mind
awhirl with confusion and fear. "Why?" he asked the
man, even as he relented and allowed the guard to
begin locking manacles onto his wrists.

"Trying to decide what to do about the plague,
of course," the guard answered, sounding surprised.

Pilos's mind reeled. "Plague?" he blurted out.
"When? Where?"

The guard spun the priest around and stared at
him. "You haven't heard? There's a plague in Reth.
Zombies are walking the streets. The Generon is
calling for immediate troop relocations. The temple's
sending every last able-bodied mercenary and priest
it can spare."

"No," Pilos said, piecing it together. Lavant is
behind this. He can't truly mean to . . . "No!" he
shouted. "I demand the right of immediate sentencing!" The din was too loud, though. The hall
was packed with priests and soldiers and each one
was shouting, arguing. No one could hear him. He
screamed at the top of his lungs. "I demand right of
immediate sentencing! I want to be heard in a Truth
Inquiry!"

The guard facing the Abreeant stared, awestruck.

The sounds of arguing faded, replaced by urgent shushing noises and whispered explanations, until everyone had gone so still that Pilos imagined he might have been able to hear a mouse squeak. Everyone looked at him.

"I demand right of immediate sentencing," the Abreeant repeated, "to be heard in a Truth Inquiry!"

"Pilos," Horial said behind him. "Are you sure?"

Pilos nodded. "The truth will come out," he said. "I have faith in the will of Waukeen."

Several people began to talk again, but in muted voices. What the young priest had demanded had not been requested in many years. For Pilos, should the Inquiry find him guilty, the sentence would be immediate death.

Shrugging as if absolving himself of the foolishness of his prisoner, the guard who had restrained Pilos turned and opened the twin doors into the council chamber. He strode forward and Pilos followed. The high priests nearest the door turned and looked, many of them visibly annoyed.

"We gave strict instructions not to be disturbed," one of them said. "What is the meaning of this intrusion?"

The guard bowed. "My apologies, Grand Trabbar Perolin, but this priest has demanded right of immediate sentencing in accordance with a Truth Inquiry."

There were numerous gasps throughout the chamber. Pilos looked straight ahead, ignoring them all. All, except for Grand Syndar Lavant, who sat regally upon a central chair, leading the discussion. When the fat priest spotted the Abreeant watching him, a strange, cold look came over his face.

"There must be some mistake," Grand Trabbar

Perolin said, sounding doubtful. "Young Pilos, are you certain this is what you want? You understand what you're asking for, correct?"

Pilos merely nodded, never taking his eyes from Lavant. He began to quote. "Upon hearing of a demand for immediate sentencing, the high priests of Waukeen have before them two paths. They may either dispense justice for the perceived crime without an investigation, or they may suggest a Truth Inquiry be held on the spot. If one submits to such an inquiry and is found to be guilty—or worse yet, lying—the sentence is death," he said, reciting the dictums of the temple from his youngest days of lessons within its confines. "I want to be heard in Truth Inquiry," he repeated. "I have faith in the will of Waukeen to clear my name, and those of my fellow prisoners."

Lavant stood up. "This is the young priest who has been charged with treasonous crimes against the entire temple," he said, his tone deprecating. "And this is nothing more than a ploy to stall the inevitable. It is fortunate he turned himself in. But I see no reason to waste the council's time in deliberations. We know what he has been involved in, and we have more pressing matters to attend to."

As outside, the murmurs of many voices began to fill the chamber. Pilos could hear some of the high priests arguing in favor of Lavant's suggestion, while others railed against the notion of denying a Truth Inquiry when one had been demanded. By right, Pilos deserved to be heard.

"I have evidence that reveals corruption in the temple," Pilos said, loudly enough that the Grand Trabbar Perolin caught his words.

Suddenly, a ripple of "Shhh!" and "Be silent! Let

him speak!" spread through the chamber. When the room had quieted, the Grand Trabbar asked in a hesitant tone, "What did you say?"

"I have evidence of corruption within this very chamber," Pilos answered. "Testimony from myself, as well as several others, that all of you will very much wish to hear."

"Are we to let this whelp of an Abreeant come in here and spread his lies? He has already demonstrated that he is capable of grand subterfuge, sneaking into the Shining Lord's palace uninvited, associating with known criminals, and attempting to escape custody in the company of outlaws to all of Arrabar. What value is there in letting him further deceive us?"

"You know the laws, Lavant," Perolin said. "It's his right to call for it."

Again a murmuring arose, but Pilos shouted before it could grow too loud, "And you're the center of the rot in this temple!"

A heartbeat of muffled words followed, then utter silence. In the next instant the chamber exploded in voices, all of them clamoring for a hundred different things. Through the cacophony of shouting, Lavant stared daggers at Pilos.

CHAPTER 13

Vambran clunked against the sides of another narrow passageway as water washed him down into the depths of the world. He tumbled and bounced and was forced to tuck his head between his arms to avoid being knocked unconscious. When he finally slowed, drifting in an open space with water still churning and tossing about, he uncoiled himself and risked a glance.

The lieutenant appeared to be in a void, his glowing coin the only light. The illumination formed a bright bubble around him, allowing him to see the disturbed sediment in the water, but nothing visible lay beyond the range of the light. Vambran had no idea what place he was in. He felt exposed to unseen enemies by his glowing light. He wondered if things swam beneath him, detecting the light and rushing forward to attack him.

Vambran had to fight a panicked urge to douse his light, to cancel the magic so he wouldn't feel so much like a target. But he didn't want to be in utter darkness, with no idea where he was and no idea how to get out. He calmed his fears, used his soldier's training to force himself to focus on the elements he could control.

If it's so dark, I must be inside something, he mused. There must be walls. A roof, at least.

The mercenary oriented himself and determined which way was up, then began to swim in that direction, slowly. He had no wish to strike against rock without warning. As he swam, he tried to control his terror.

If I sank down here, I can swim back out, he reasoned.

If you can find your way out, a little voice told him.

I will.

Suddenly, Vambran's head broke through the surface. He coughed for a moment as his body tried to adjust to air after so long underwater. Water flowed from his lungs, spilling out of the gills the necklace had magically produced, and at last, he could draw in a solid breath.

The air was terribly cold, so cold in fact that Vambran could see his breath in the dim light of his coin. It smelled stale, musty. Old.

Knowing that he must be inside a sealed area for air to still be present, Vambran held his light up, as high as he could reach, hoping to catch a glimpse of a ceiling overhead. He could not.

Well, then, I guess I'd better start swimming, the

lieutenant decided. Somewhere around here there must be walls, something that's keeping the air trapped inside.

Vambran tried to select the direction that would lead him toward the opening he had tumbled in through, but he had become so disoriented that he had no clue. He paddled along slowly, again not wishing for his face to meet stone. Even so, he was startled when something solid appeared in his view.

It was a wall, not just of rock, but of worked stone blocks. The seams of the blocks were slanted, angling sharply, giving him the impression that the wall was tilted, cocked to one side. He began to follow the wall, swimming in the direction that the seams angled upward, hoping that he might find the bottom of something and perhaps dry land beyond.

When his feet brushed against something, Vambran yelped and flailed, certain that some creature had nudged past him, menacing his toes. But then his foot struck again and he realized it was a surface, a smooth stone surface, and a moment later, he was ascending a steep, paved slope. Wet and naked, he was keenly aware of the cold air.

The incline was sharp enough that Vambran had difficulty walking up. More than once he nearly lost his balance, but he hunched forward and picked his way with care, following the wall, which seemed to have a gentle curve to it.

All at once, Vambran found himself at the edge of the slope, reaching up and grasping for a handhold to pull himself the last few feet. Beyond was more blackness.

He shivered in the cold, wondering what was beyond his puny little light.

I need more illumination, Vambran thought. To

the Hells with it, he decided.

The mercenary spoke the familiar magical phrase aloud and pointed his finger upward and ahead. A searing, bright flash of light shot forth from his fingertip and raced ahead. For the first few seconds, Vambran simply could not see, for the brightness of the flare hurt his eyes. But as his eyes adjusted, he began looking around, and what he saw amazed him.

The remains of a city block spread out before him, as if at the bottom of a steep hill, tilted at an awkward angle. The place where he stood had cracked and folded somehow, so that he was at the crest of a ridge between two downward slopes. Behind him, sliding back into the water, was the paved slope he had ascended, with portions of ancient walls enclosing it on either side. Only parts of those walls remained upright, for much had been crushed by massive rockfall piled on top of it. For the first time, Vambran had a real sense of just how much debris must have rained down on top of the ruined city after it slid into the ocean.

Ahead of him, lining either side of the ancient street, Vambran could see two or three partially intact buildings. The architecture was scalloped and wavy, and everything must have once soared to great heights, for the design seemed to be all spindles and towers and flying bridges. The topmost portions of the buildings were destroyed, though, tumbled down as huge boulders had smashed them away. Only their bases remained, tilted and canted at strange angles as the overbearing weight of a million tons of rock, and the water of the ocean above, pressed down.

Perhaps most impressive, though, was the largest structure at the far end of the cavern, much below him. Mostly buried under rock, gravel, and broken paving stones, the building looked much as Vambran had imagined the great hall from Arbeenok's vision. All he could see was a façade, but it appeared round with many columns adorning the outside.

Before Vambran could discern any additional detail, though, his flare faded, leaving him blinking in the much dimmer light that his coin could provide. He considered firing another light into the air, but he decided against it, for he already knew he wanted to explore that building at the base of the hill.

He picked his way carefully down the slope of the ruined street, working somewhat sideways, switching back and forth at an angle to lessen the steepness of descent. The street had buckled and heaved out of alignment during the destruction of the city, so plenty of places had formed for Vambran to gain handholds and footholds.

At last he reached the bottom. Standing on a pile of loose rock that had partially covered the surface of the building's façade, Vambran surveyed the ruins of the doorway. The portal yawned open, a hole that was almost level with flat ground because of the way the building had come to rest on its back. The doors that might have once sealed the opening were nowhere to be seen. Beyond the frame, the lieutenant could see that a great circular hallway wrapped around the whole of the building, a concentric walkway that might once have surrounded the chamber in the center and been brightly lit with evenly spaced windows.

The way the building was canted, Vambran realized, he would be forced to drop down into the darkness and slide down the steep incline. At first, he wasn't sure how he was going to get out again.

He was beginning to wish the chamber was flooded, because swimming through the ruins would be much easier.

Fool! he chastised himself, remembering his climbing magic. He was especially thankful at that moment that he no longer needed to swallow things such as spiders and blobs of nasty stuff to bring his magic to life. The manifestation of his abilities suddenly were that much more useful.

Nodding in satisfaction, Vambran invoked the arcane force that allowed him to skitter across walls and ceilings, and he lowered himself down through the hole. Once on the underside of the wall, he scrambled down to the next level, the inner wall of the ancient building. He was on the verge of maneuvering toward another doorway farther in when something whizzed past his ear.

Vambran spun in place, searching for whatever had soared so close. He was painfully conscious of having lost his trident. Whatever had passed him had traveled so fast that he had barely caught a glimpse of motion—he didn't know if it was a flying beast or an object that had been hurled. He spotted nothing, even while holding his light high overhead to illuminate as large an area as possible.

Motion attracted his attention again, and he watched as something swished toward him a second time. It was a small blade, perhaps a short sword, and as it whisked by, nearly slicing into his ribs, he followed it visually. The sword stopped and hovered, turning in place and pointing at him once more.

What the—? Vambran wondered, watching the floating sword warily. When it shot toward the lieutenant a third time, he deftly stepped aside and swiped at the blade with his hand, trying to knock it from the air to the floor. He managed to strike the sword upon its hilt and redirect its flight slightly, but the sword recovered and zipped away, into the deeper darkness beyond the range of Vambran's coin.

The mercenary waited, listening. The sword did not appear again for several moments, and Vambran wondered if he had scared it off with his strike. Still, he wanted to be sure, so he turned his gaze all about, seeking some sign that the blade was coming again.

When the sword did strike, Vambran did not see it, for it attacked him from behind. It caught the lieutenant in the small of the back, but thankfully, it was a glancing blow and not a direct stab. Even so, Vambran staggered from the impact and felt burning pain erupt in the wound. The sword danced away into the darkness as Vambran staggered over to a wall and placed his back against it, watching for more attacks and speaking the words of a healing orison.

The mercenary had barely managed to complete the spell to soothe his wound when the sword slashed in again. Vambran ducked and the blade struck hard against the wall behind the mercenary. The collision did not seem to confound the weapon, which skittered sideways along the wall and disappeared once more.

How am I going to fight this thing? Vambran wondered. I don't even have a blade of my own. Then he had an idea.

Grasping his coin once more, Vambran visualized the magic he wanted to use, and with the words on the tip of his tongue, he waited patiently. Sure enough, the sword came swooping in again, trying to catch the mercenary off guard by dashing down from the ceiling. Vambran almost didn't notice in time, but he spotted the enchanted blade at the last moment, leaned out of the way, and cast the spell he had readied.

As his magic dampening prayer radiated out from his coin, Vambran watched the sword plummet to the floor, motionless. Before it could grow active again, Vambran leaped on top of the blade and pinned it to the stones. He reached down and gingerly grasped it by the hilt. When the sword didn't react, Vambran eased it out from under his foot and let it rest in his hand, testing its balance and weight. It was a fine blade, well crafted, and was still shiny and free of corrosion. He wondered what sorts of enchantments had been placed on it, or if it might suddenly animate and attack him again. He considered pinning it beneath a heavy rock, hoping to preclude the weapon from coming after him again, but he decided to hold onto it for a while instead, in the event of any other kinds of trouble.

Vambran turned his attention once more to the task of finding the center of the great building, feeling certain that an inner door inside the circular hallway would lead there. But because the building had tipped when it came to rest, the lieutenant had to walk on the inner, rounded wall. As he followed that wall around, the descent became steeper and steeper. Eventually, he was forced to return to his spidery wall-walking to keep from slipping right down the curved slope into the depths below.

When Vambran had traveled perhaps a quarter of the way around the path and it appeared to him that he was in a nearly vertical shaft, he discovered a broad double door leading deeper into the building. He clung to the wall next to the portal and tested it, but the door appeared to be warped in its frame and wouldn't budge. Vambran remembered his newest gift of arcane sorcery, and despite the terrifying results of its previous use, he decided to employ it once more. Backing up a few steps, he gestured and watched as the doors groaned and rumbled, forcing their way open. As the twin panels parted, Vambran peered inside.

The chamber beyond was magnificent. The soft glow of colored illumination was the first thing that caught the lieutenant's eye—points of light scattered in random locations around the periphery of the room. He wasn't sure what was creating the lights, but enough of them were present, giving off a soft glow, that he could see without difficulty. The chamber was huge and round, as he had suspected from traversing the outer hallway. It was capped by a domed ceiling, with columns throughout the hall, many of which still held it predominately intact. A number had broken away, their remains littering the lowest surface, what Vambran thought of as the back wall.

The floor itself was not flat but rather bowl shaped, with rows and rows of benches in concentric circles filling it at one time, all facing toward the center, a theater in the round. In the center, a dais stood high enough that all in attendance would have been able to see without hindrance. A large stone altar, built to be one continuous fixture together with the dais, still remained in place. The intricately carved cube jutted out almost horizontally from its base.

Vambran was mesmerized. Somehow, he knew that it was the chamber spoken of in the sea elves' histories, the same one Arbeenok had seen in his vision. He was standing in a place of history, wondrous history. The thought made him eager and sad at the same time.

All of this had been wrought to endure, he realized. It was built to withstand the test of time. And in a way, it has, though not as they would have wanted it. A shame.

Still using his magical climbing, Vambran stepped through the doorway and moved inside. He still held the sword he had subdued, afraid to release it lest it attack him, but thus far it had remained quiescent. Taking a deep breath to control his excitement, Vambran decided to investigate the sources of light first.

The glittering specks were clusters of gems, put together as flowers, and as best as Vambran could tell, they had been enchanted with minor magic that caused them to glow. Nothing more, he thought. And they function still, fifteen centuries later. The simple beauty of them made the lieutenant grin. He considered prying one loose from its mounting, a token to take back with him, but the idea appalled him for some reason.

I'm here for one thing only, Vambran told himself. And people on the surface are waiting.

Turning his back on the curious glowing gem blossoms, Vambran began to cross the vast floor toward the center, traversing it on hands and feet since it was nearly vertical. He was careful to avoid the benches that still clung to their mountings, fearful that he might dislodge one and send it crashing to the bottom of the room. Even with his caution, he dislodged a number of fragments of stone. The floor had buckled and shifted during its tumble to the bottom of the sea, leaving myriad cracks and fissures throughout the stonework.

At last, Vambran arrived at the dais. Clinging to the surface near it, he began to circle around the altar, wondering if it might not be protected by some mechanical or arcane traps. He wondered how he was going to open it. The etchings on the box were a mixture of runes and images. The pictures he recognized easily enough—stylized faces, creatures, and landscapes—but he had no idea what the runes said. He did not even recognize most of the symbols, though some of them were distantly similar to modern ones.

Vambran was just about to crawl onto the altar to make a closer examination of it when he felt a faint vibration in the stone beneath his hands and feet. A momentary surge of panic struck him, and he wondered if he were feeling some sort of earthquake. The vibration grew stronger and the lieutenant feared that chunks of the chamber would begin to loosen and fall, possibly right on top of him. As if to prove him a prophet, a column cracked and tumbled down, missing the altar by perhaps a sword length. It hit the lowest end of the room with a thundering concussion, jarring everything in the chamber, including the mercenary.

I don't want to be in here, Vambran decided, turning to scramble out of the chamber. I'll come back after the earth has finished growling.

He was perhaps halfway across the floor when the lowest surface of the chamber erupted in a spray of stone. The force of the burst nearly shook Vambran free of his perch and sprayed him with shards of rock, even at his considerable distance. As the dust billowed up, Vambran looked down.

A gargantuan worm-thing the color of amethysts reared up out of a newly formed hole, bobbing and swaying. Its mouth could easily swallow him whole and looked vaguely like an orchid, but four slimy tentacles snaking out of it and wriggling all about certainly dispelled any sense of beauty. The stench of it made the lieutenant gag.

The massive worm had no eyes as far as Vambran could see, but that didn't slow it down. With little hesitation, its tentacles writhing in a mad dance, the ponderous creature lurched forward, directly toward Vambran.

...

"You may begin," Grand Trabbar Perolin said, giving Pilos a warm smile. "Remember, we will know if you speak any falsehood," he warned.

Pilos nodded and began to tell the council his story. No fewer than three priests were arrayed about him, focused on the various spells that would aid them in determining if he was lying, exaggerating the slightest bit, or even conjecturing rather than providing facts. He left no part out, even admitting to sneaking through the hidden passages in the temple to spy on the meeting between the highest of the high priests. That brought about a few raised eyebrows.

"Are even our own private meetings not sacred?" Lavant blurted out, red-faced with anger.

"Be silent, Grand Syndar," Perolin warned. "You may sit on the high seat, but these proceedings will not be debased by your outbursts."

Lavant glowered but said nothing more.

Pilos told the high priests of his encounter with Mikolos, and the message the departed Grand Syndar had delivered to him. He expected Lavant to balk at the veracity of that as well, but when he looked over at the Grand Syndar, the pudgy man looked uncomfortable, perhaps even a bit pale.

Finally, the Abreeant confessed to infiltrating the Generon with Emriana, explaining how she had been captured in a magical mirror by Junce Roundface, an agent of Grozier Talricci's, and how Laithe the wizard had mentioned Lavant by name in a conversation with Junce. At that revelation, numerous gasps escaped from the high priests and Lavant began to fidget.

Pilos knew he might be punished in some way for revealing everything to the finest detail, but he believed that, in the end, it would help his cause to be thorough.

Once the young priest finished his part of the story, he was taken aside and flanked by temple guards. One by one, Horial, Adyan, Grolo, and even Edilus were brought before the council to tell their part of the tale. Each played his part well, explaining what had transpired, beginning with the voyage at sea and ending with their current situation, standing beside Pilos and under scrutiny. Their descriptions of the destruction of *Lady's Favor,* the subsequent flight through the Nunwood, and the capture of so many of their companions drew more than a few exclamations of surprise and dismay. Pilos then finished the testimony by explaining that Lobra Pharaboldi, who was currently in House Darowdryn custody, had already admitted to everything the men and dwarf had asserted. He offered the temple the opportunity to take her into its own custody to verify her involvement.

When Pilos finished, Grand Trabbar Perolin stood. "These are all very grave accusations," the high priest said, but he was looking at Lavant, not Pilos. During the entire proceeding, the three priests monitoring the truth of the testimony had given no signal that anything in the tales was amiss.

Lavant opened his mouth to retort, then must have thought better of it, for he snapped it shut again with a frown, his jowls bouncing.

After all of the confessions were finished, Pilos was granted his final statement. By temple law, he was allowed to present whatever speech he felt appropriate to sway the court's opinion.

He gave the speech of his life.

"Perhaps it is beyond my place as a mere Abreeant priest to question the activities of one so highly positioned as our Grand Syndar, but I could not in good conscience allow his actions to proceed unchecked. Because of my own lowly station, I knew I could not sway very many of you sitting on this council with my speculations alone. I did what I did, broke the laws that I broke, not out of disregard for the customs and respect of the temple and its clergy, but out of love for seeing it exalted. I could not bear to see one so bent on callous personal gain to remain in that position of power. So, whatever punishments are accorded me for violating temple law, I accept these as a necessary consequence to right many wrongs."

Pilos could see a number of high priests frowning, for his claim that the ends would justify the means did not sit well with them. He understood that even before he began, and he did not expect sympathy from them in that regard. Shrugging off their disapproval for the moment, he continued.

"This man, this leader among leaders," the Abreeant said, emphasizing his words with demonstrative pointing toward Lavant, "is guilty of the manipulation of many people, including the temple clergy itself. He has a powerful faction loyal to him, and I daresay he has the political clout to wriggle free

of these charges, but I say he does not deserve his
high seat!"

The chamber erupted in much shouting at those
words, some supporting Pilos's assertions and others
vehemently denouncing them. Lavant's face turned
a bright hue of purple as he gave Pilos the most malevolent stare the young priest had ever seen from
any man.

"Order! Order, I say!" Grand Trabbar Perolin
shouted. The chamber grew quiet once more. "Please
finish your remarks, Abreeant," he said, perhaps a
bit sternly.

Pilos swallowed and nodded, wondering if he had
pushed too far. For an Abreeant to call for abdication
of the Grand Syndar . . .

It was too late for second thoughts, Pilos knew. "I
conclude with this. The depth of this man's dishonesty
seems to know no limits. I would not put it past him
to be in some way responsible for the outbreak of the
plague in Reth!" Pilos knew that was far-fetched,
but in an unsettling way, it seemed to tie everything
together, explain why everything had happened the
way it did. He just hadn't yet figured out a motive. So
he threw it in, figuring he was already hip-deep in
trouble if the council didn't see things his way.

Might as well go all out, he had decided.

The chamber was a cacophony of shouting once
more as high priests debated with one another over
the absurdity or plausibility of Pilos's final state-
ments. Pilos stood still at last, waiting expectantly.
When the council chamber was silent once more, all
eyes turned to Lavant.

The obese priest looked decidedly uncomfortable,
but he stood to address the assembly with as smooth
and as stoic a face as ever. "Dignifying such outra-

geous claims as this whoreson has made is beneath me, but obviously, there is some truth in what he says, insofar as he believes it to be so. It is true that certain events have unfolded in a favorable way, both for me personally and for this temple, but to go so far as to say that I was deceptive in my endeavors is laughable. Many of the points he raises are pure conjecture, with no substantive proof to back them. To bring the woman Lobra Pharaboldi and submit her to further questioning would be useless, for I have met with her myself—as Pilos so vehemently has asserted—and I can assure you she is quite delusional. The things she has apparently claimed about my involvement with her House's affairs are simply false.

"However," he continued, raising his voice to be heard over the muttering that began anew in the gallery, "in light of the questions that have been raised, I will in good conscience remove myself from these deliberations and allow you to conduct them to their conclusion without me. If you see fit to accept this fool's words as an accurate portrayal of the truth, then find me guilty and charge me. If, however, you feel you can trust that everything I do is done for the glory of Waukeen, and that I would still make an able and energetic leader of her works, then I would humbly consider remaining as Grand Syndar."

With that, Lavant stepped down from the dais and strode purposefully across the room. All around him, the noise of debate rose again, until someone shouted for Lavant's arrest. Lavant refused to stop walking even after several guards blocked his path, and only when they forcibly restrained him, amidst ear-splitting chaos within the chamber, did he begin to break down and struggle, a look of genuine fright on his face.

As the guards who had been assigned to watch over the five companions on trial began to release them from their bonds, Pilos looked over at his companions. Horial nodded to him approvingly, and Edilus actually smiled.

"Well done, lad," Horial said, clapping the young priest on the shoulder. "Fine speechmaking. You should consider becoming an orator for the temple."

Pilos started to respond, but the noise of the chamber suddenly shifted, becoming more frantic, more desperate. Pilos looked up and saw that everyone was pointing where Lavant and his enforced escort had been standing.

Lavant had disappeared.

CHAPTER 14

Waukeen, Vambran pleaded, dazed by the enormity of the creature slithering toward him. *What in the bloody Nine Hells* is *that thing?* Shaking off the paralyzing fear that gripped him, the lieutenant went into action, scrambling upward, away from the ranging, reaching tentacles.

The sudden motion only seemed to spur on the monstrosity. Vambran scuttled to the very top of the chamber, thankful that his arcane ability still functioned. Once there, he turned to see if he was out of the thing's reach. To his dismay, the mercenary officer saw that the body of the worm reached halfway across the floor, its head near the altar, and it still hadn't completely cleared the hole from which it had emerged. The tentacles wriggled and quested for him, elongating to span the distance.

"Son of a whore!" Vambran swore, trying to figure a way to escape. He got an idea and pulled forth his holy coin. Uttering a familiar prayer, he conjured a swarming field of coins and sent it flying toward the behemoth below him.

The buzzing swarm of coins did not distract the giant worm as Vambran had hoped. He began to mentally command the glowing, ghostly weapons to attack the creature, and he was relieved to discover their effect on the worm. The coins did nothing against the worm's tough outer skin, but whenever they hit a tentacle, it spasmed and writhed, trying to get away from the source of the pain.

Changing tactics, the worm reared back, withdrawing its tentacles. Vambran got the uneasy feeling that the creature was on the verge of spitting something, and he feared whatever it disgorged could easily reach him. Sure enough, the worm's head darted up toward him and a great gout of liquid burst forth from its mouth, right at Vambran.

The lieutenant had no chance to duck or dodge, so he did the only thing he could—he let go.

He dropped fast, plummeting past the spot targeted by the gout of liquid, which Vambran realized at that moment was the source of the beast's foul odor. The spray of fluid spattered over the stone walls where Vambran had been. The rock surfaces sizzled and popped.

Acid, Vambran concluded. And powerful.

The mercenary's plan was to drop far enough to escape immediate threat and use his magic to slow himself to a stop farther down, but the worm had other ideas. As Vambran slid past, the worm's head darted in his direction, snaking out a tentacle. With deftness that surprised the man, the first tentacle grabbed him around the waist and slowed his descent.

The second one encircled his neck, choking him.

The lieutenant, his air cut off, began flailing. The life was being squeezed from his body. Spots darted in his vision. In his desperate efforts to free himself, Vambran dropped the enchanted sword he had subdued. He heard the blade slide away.

Fool, he cursed himself. Now you'll die with no weapon. A fine soldier you are.

As Vambran struggled to remove the ever-tightening tentacle from his neck, his sight grew dim. He tried to command the swarm of coins to attack the tentacle that ensnared him, but his concentration had been broken while leaping clear of the acid and the coins had dissipated. With his body gripped in the tentacles, he had no way to mouth the words to summon another spell.

The tentacle began pulling him toward the worm's maw. He punched it with his fists, but that resulted in two more tentacles wrapping around his wrists. Vambran's flailing grew panicked. He knew he was going to die there, at the bottom of the ocean, hidden away from all the world. It was a lonely thought.

Vambran? Em here. Horial and Adyan arrived. Rescued Xaphira, kicked Grozier out of the estate, going to unseat Lavant. Know about the plague. What news?

By the gods, Vambran thought, I'm sorry, Em. She'll never know, he realized. He wanted desperately to answer her, to let her know he loved her, but no words could come. It made him furious.

There was movement. He saw a flash of blade, slashing near his head.

The tentacle that held his neck jerked once, then loosened. Vambran yanked at it, working his fingers beneath it, making room for air. He managed to suck in half a lungful. The blade swung into view again, cutting and slashing at the tentacle again. It loosened a bit more.

Vambran could breathe. He tried to talk, to answer his sister, but he only managed to cough and splutter. Beside him, the blade worked, moving furiously, cutting and slashing over and over at the tentacle that held his neck. The thick, rubbery appendage withdrew.

"Em!" Vambran cried out. "I'm here! Can't talk!" He wasn't sure if the message got through.

The magical blade was still at work, hacking and sawing at the next tentacle. But the worm had pulled Vambran close to its mouth, close enough that the scent of its acid breath stung his eyes, made him choke on the fumes. And his arms were still trapped.

"Vambran!"

The shout from Arbeenok came from the side, near the door where the lieutenant had first entered the great round chamber. He managed to steal a quick glance in that direction. "Do something!" he shouted back. "Hurry!"

He could see that the elves were having a difficult time maneuvering into the chamber. They did not have the benefit of his magic. Just hurry, he thought.

The worm's head erupted in a column of flame. Vambran was so close to it that he swore he was being scorched. He turned his face away from the heat.

The worm thrashed madly, jerking Vambran about for a moment, and then suddenly the soldier was free.

And falling again.

He reached out and grabbed at a column on the way down, managed to snare it with his magically enhanced grip. He hung there, breathing hard, as the worm whipped about, crashing into the floor of the building and making the whole chamber shake and groan. Several large chunks of stone fell from above as part of the wall collapsed.

Vambran scrambled to pull himself up onto the top surface of the column, still trying to suck in a full lungful of air. A large block went tumbling past him, slamming into the next column and obliterating it.

Time to get out, the lieutenant decided. He lamented the further destruction of the ancient ruins. He looked to the stone altar, wondering if he still had a chance to open it. I have to try, he decided.

His spider climbing magic was still active, so he scrambled toward the dais as quickly as he could. In the meantime, the worm had recovered from its frantic writhing and was approaching the newcomers. It reared its head back in a familiar way.

"It spits acid!" Vambran shouted, motioning. "Get back!"

Serille nodded and shouted a curt order, and the sea elves tried to retreat back through the doorway.

Not all of them were fast enough.

Vambran turned away as their screams rose in pitch and went silent. He focused his full attention on the box. Make their lives count, he told himself. Get this accursed scepter! He still could see no way to open the box. But Serille said the elves believed the ruler of Naarkolyth had sealed the scepter inside! How?

The lieutenant slapped his forehead, feeling the fool. He focused his arcane energy on the stone, conjuring the magic of opening. There was a heavy click and the top of the box fell away, tumbling to crash into the debris below. Vambran peered over the edge of the huge stone container and looked inside.

A box, crafted of wood and perhaps very fine once, rested canted against one corner. It had broken open and the lid was twisted, one hinge snapped. A cudgel lay there, nestled in a form-fitting depression in the lining of the box. It was made of living things, grapevines and leaves and feathers all wrapped together. The head of the artifact held one of the largest emeralds Vambran had ever seen.

He reached inside, afraid to touch it, terrified it wasn't real, wasn't the right piece of history, would crumble if he disturbed it. He laid a single finger on it, felt its smooth hardness.

The worm loomed into view, its body blotting out all other light in the chamber. Its tentacles darted toward Vambran. The lieutenant grabbed the scepter and lunged away just as the enchanted blade shot past him, slicing into the flesh of the nearest probing appendage. He did not waste time looking back. He clambered across the stone surface of the floor as fast as he could, raced toward the doorway where the rest of his companions awaited him.

"Go!" he shouted. "I'll catch up!"

The elves began to vanish, retreating from the chamber. Arbeenok remained, waiting for Vambran to reach them. Behind him, Vambran could sense the worm moving toward him again, could almost feel the tentacles reaching out, grasping at him.

He scampered faster.

Vambran finally reached the alaghi and together, they departed the great chamber. As they moved, Vambran still climbing the stony surfaces and

Arbeenok using a length of kelp rope, Vambran said, "So, please tell me this was the place from your vision."

The alaghi chuckled. "Indeed. It was magnificent once, don't you think?"

A horrific thud on the underside of the stone wall bounced them both. Vambran could only guess what the worm was doing inside.

"What I think is, we'd better hurry."

Out beyond the great hall, the rest of the group was already climbing the canted street, working their way toward the top of the hill. Water was spilling down the slope, runoff from above. Vambran stared at it. "That wasn't happening before," he said.

"The worm's vibrations must have shifted some of the rock," Arbeenok said. "The chamber may be flooding now."

Vambran found himself thinking of the enchanted sword, wondering if it would still defend its home once it was submerged.

The return trip to the cave was uneventful, though Serille seemed pensive for most of the way. When pressed about her mood, she replied, "I lost three today."

Vambran nodded. "I'm sorry," he said. "Who were they?"

Serille looked at him with puzzlement. "Why does it matter to you?"

"I grieve for everyone who falls in battle. It helps me keep the cause of the fight in the forefront of my mind, making sure they never die in vain."

"Ah," the sea elf said. "Then you will be sad to know that Ishuliga was one of the three."

Vambran was surprised at the depth of his own sorrow.

At the cave, the mercenary and the druid gathered their belongings and with a smaller escort, departed for the surface. They were bestowed with the enchanted necklaces as farewell gifts. "For the next time you come to visit me," Serille said with a mischievous look in her eye.

After bidding farewell to Serille and the other sea elves, Vambran and Arbeenok walked up the beach toward the rocks. The last rays of the setting sun were fading in the western sky, and Vambran felt some remorse in parting ways with the elves. But he also felt a keen sense of urgency to return to Reth with the healing power of the scepter.

"Have you figured out what must be done with it?" he asked Arbeenok, who was fondling the object delicately.

"I am becoming attuned to it," the alaghi replied, "but I am also simply enjoying the history of it. Imagine—this was created over fifteen hundred years ago by elves who lived in a forest twice as large as what we know here now. And the landscape wasn't even remotely similar. This might have been uplands, low hills running along a ridge of mountains that no longer exist, for all we know."

Vambran regarded the druid. "You have a knack for seeing things in a grander way than most people. Nature made a good choice in granting you the ability of portents and visions."

When Arbeenok smiled, Vambran thought he could detect a glint in the druid's eye.

"We must hurry, though," the lieutenant said at last, breaking the moment. "People in Reth are dying even as we stand here."

"We will reach her in time," Arbeenok said, understanding Vambran's thoughts without the mercenary needing to voice them. "My slowing magic should still be effective."

"I hope so," Vambran remarked. "The only way we'll reach her in time is to travel into the city the same way we departed. Can you do that?"

Arbeenok nodded and stepped back from his companion in order to have room to transform. He shifted and twisted to become a giant hawk, then the druid lofted himself into the air, reaching out with his talons to grasp Vambran by the shoulders as he had before.

Together, they soared into the sky, gliding their way toward the city and the plague.

It was nightfall by the time they landed in the city street near the villa where they had left Elenthia that morning. As soon as they arrived, Vambran was running into the home, calling to the woman. "Elenthia! Elenthia, we've returned. We found a way to heal you!"

Elenthia was not where Vambran had left her.

Vambran called frantically for a few moments, running from room to room, but the woman was nowhere to be found. He raced back down to the garden, trying to guess what might have happened to her. He jogged through the gate and out into the street, calling to Arbeenok.

The druid was surrounded by mercenaries of the Order of the Silver Raven, many of them holding lanterns aloft. They held crossbows leveled at him.

When Vambran appeared, several more soldiers moved to surround him, though they stayed back far enough that they clearly showed their fear of contracting the plague from the two visitors.

"You will stand very still, or we will kill you on the spot," one of the Silver Ravens said.

"All right," Vambran answered, remaining motionless. "But may I speak?"

"Only to answer our questions," the leader replied. "First, what are you doing here?"

"We've brought a cure for the plague," Vambran said, "and we've returned to this spot because I left a woman here. She had magical healing placed upon her by my druid friend here so she would not get sicker and die."

"A druid? I think not," the man said. "The only thing druids are good for is dying."

Vambran had to clench his teeth to avoid an angry outburst. Instead, he simply said, "My men and yours have been at odds for the last several days, but if you give us a chance, we can show you that I speak the truth. If we can cure the plague, would you want to hinder us?"

The soldier considered Vambran for a moment, then shook his head. "I won't make this decision myself," he said. "We'll leave this up to Captain Havalla." He turned and ordered a runner to fetch the captain, and the young soldier sprinted off to find the officer.

"May I ask if you know what happened to the woman I left here this morning?" Vambran asked. "She was too sick to go very far on her own."

"Someone undoubtedly found her," the soldier said, "and rounded her up into the middle of the city, in the quarantine camp, with all the rest."

Vambran was aghast. "But the plague works so fast!" he said. "Anyone who has it is likely to die and rise as a zombie!"

The man nodded, looking grim. "It's the only way we could control it," he said. "No one has been able to figure out what else to do. We're waiting for healers from Arrabar to arrive, but that could take days."

"Then let us help," Vambran said, feeling desperate. "Let us go to the quarantine camp and see what we can do to cure those people!"

At just that moment, a commotion began behind the soldier who had been speaking with Vambran. A runner appeared and began whispering to the men. When the soldier in charge heard what the runner had to report, he paled.

"What is it?" Vambran asked. "What's happening?"

"Zombies have gotten free of the quarantine area," the man said. "They're moving through the sewers and coming up in other areas of the city. We didn't contain them after all."

Men who had been steady and confident a moment before began milling about in panic, eyeing the sewer openings in the middle of the streets. Others turned and ran, despite shouted orders from others half-heartedly demanding that they stand their ground. Vambran knew that the confusion might be the only chance to escape and employ the scepter, but something told him that their chances were better if they could win over the leader of the Silver Ravens. He stood his ground.

"There's something else," the soldier said, shaking his head in dismay. "Something seems to be controlling the zombies, coordinating their movements and actions. They're actually attacking our lines."

"There's no time to waste, then," Vambran said. "You must let us help these people and destroy this plague. Otherwise, the city will be overwhelmed and no one will remain alive inside its walls. We can't wait for your captain to make this decision. You have to let Arbeenok and me defeat this disease."

The soldier hesitated, obviously unpracticed at

making monumental decisions, but he nodded at last and ordered his men to lower their weapons. "What do you need us to do?" he asked.

Vambran sighed in relief. "Arbeenok?" he asked, hoping the druid understood the scepter's powers well enough to employ it. "Do you have it mastered?"

Arbeenok nodded. "I think so," he said. "I can wield it when I get close enough to see its effect. But Vambran," he said pointedly, "you must go to the palace."

Vambran looked at his companion, quizzical. "Why?" he asked.

"You must stop the source of this madness, and that source lies at the heart of seven great towers." The alaghi pointed. "There."

Vambran turned and looked at the highest structure in the city and saw but one tower—the tower of the Palace of the Seven.

"I'll never get there with the city blockaded and swarming with zombies," he said. "Can you become a hawk once more and take me there before you activate the scepter?"

"One time more," the druid said. "It will benefit us both." The alaghi shifted and took the shape of the dire hawk again, the emerald scepter safely tucked inside his form.

As Arbeenok pushed off and began to beat his powerful wings, Vambran gave a quick salute to the soldier who had been wise enough to let them go. "Don't worry," the lieutenant said, "you're doing the right thing. Tell Captain Havalla I want to meet with him once this is over."

The druid reached down and grabbed Vambran by the shoulders, as before. They launched into the air, soaring into the night sky and swooping

over the fires and the clashing forces of men and
undead below. After seeing firsthand the masses
fighting and the devastation they were leaving in
their wake, Vambran was even more thankful for
his companion's assistance. I'd never have gotten
through, he decided.

Arbeenok glided low toward a protected courtyard
along one side of the palace, one that was screened
off from the rest of the city by low walls. Vambran
wasn't sure if the druid could sense the same thing he
did, but a palpable feeling of malevolence hung in the
air, making the mercenary feel unclean. It seemed
to radiate from the palace and it was particularly
strong at some point below ground level, near the
plaza the druid had selected for landing.

Arbeenok drew up and released Vambran before
alighting on the stones beside him. The druid cocked
his avian head to one side, regarding the lieutenant.

"Good luck," the mercenary said to his companion.

Arbeenok replied with a single screech and a
nod, then he pushed off and began winging his way
toward the city's center.

Vambran turned in place, eyeing the courtyard.
The sick, evil sensation bubbled up from below him.
A door provided egress from the enclosed plaza, but
Vambran could sense that the most direct route to his
quarry was straight down, through the rain grate.
He yanked the heavy grille aside, muttered a quick
prayer to Waukeen in order to light his holy coin,
and dropped down into the darkness.

...

House Talricci seemed abandoned when Emriana
and her aunt approached.

They had decided to wait until nightfall to proceed, for they knew that barging onto the property, as they had done at their own home, would not work. Besides the issues of trespassing, Grozier and Bartimus undoubtedly expected the two women to hunt them down, and had most likely prepared a few magical surprises for them. Thus, Xaphira had unpacked a few additional scrolls from her collection, magic that she claimed would help her spy any dangerous traps or magical threats to the two of them.

"I don't want another case of ringing bells giving us away," she had said to Emriana.

While waiting for darkness, Emriana had at last made an effort to contact Vambran, to apprise him of the state of things in Arrabar. And to find out if he's still alive, she had thought, fearing the worst. Hearing the news from the Darowdryn House wizards that Vambran had encountered the plague in Reth had made the girl's stomach turn flip-flops.

Her brother had not answered.

"He can take care of himself," Xaphira had insisted, but Emriana had seen the hint of fear in the older woman's eyes. "And we can't do anything for him right now, anyway," her aunt had admonished. "Focus on Obiron and Quindy. They need us."

Once evening had arrived, they departed the Matrell estate by themselves, asking Steelfists Darowdryn to stay behind and protect their family, especially in case they didn't return. The huge man had agreed, though Emriana could tell by the look in the fellow's eyes that he was spoiling for a confrontation with Talricci and his wizard almost as much as she and her aunt were.

The two women climbed over a wall into one of the

gardens. Unlike the lush green places that filled most of the estates throughout Arrabar, the gardens of Talricci's abode were wild and overgrown, thick with weeds and swarming insects, and nearly impossible to pass through. In other circumstances, Emriana would not have cared much for the place, but because of the covert nature of their arrival, being able to slip over a wall behind a screen of impenetrable flora held a decided benefit.

"Stay close," Xaphira said, creeping through the thick vegetation, trying to keep from rustling the plants. Cattails around a pond ahead of them grew so tall that Emriana doubted she would be able to reach their tops even if she stood straight up on tiptoes and stretched her hands upward. She listened for telltale sounds of House guards nearby, the usual low laughter from a coarse joke or scuffing of boots on paving stones as they walked. But the grounds of the estate were eerily quiet.

The two women reached open lawn then, and Emriana peered over Xaphira's shoulder toward the back of the house at the top of the slope. There were no lights burning inside that she could see. "Where is everyone?" she whispered, peering intently to try to detect some movement, perhaps a darker shadow hiding at the base of a tree or in a window.

"I don't know," Xaphira said. "Maybe they took the twins and went somewhere else, hoping we wouldn't be able to follow."

"Well," Emriana replied, "we can't, can we?"

"Which is why we're going in anyway," Xaphira explained. "To make sure. I don't want to go back to Marga empty-handed."

Neither do I, Emriana thought. "Do you see anything?" she asked, wondering what Xaphira's magically enhanced senses were telling the older woman.

"No," Xaphira replied, sounding a bit surprised. "There's nothing. No spells, no traps, nothing." After a few moments more, she said, "Let's go in."

Together, the Matrell women darted across the lawn toward the house. When they reached the porch, Emriana scampered up the steps and went to one side of a large set of glassed double doors, pressing herself against the stone. As Xaphira moved to the opposite side, Emriana held her breath, listening for any sounds from within. There were no footfalls, no creaks of doors, no noises at all.

Tentatively, Xaphira reached over and tried the door. It was not locked. "It's almost like they want us to come inside," she said, hesitating.

"I don't care," Emriana said. "Quindy and Obiron could be ..." She left the thought hanging, but it seemed enough to convince Xaphira to keep to the plan.

Xaphira pulled the door open and Emriana waited a couple of silent counts, just to make sure no trap was sprung by the motion. Then she barely angled her head around the corner of the frame, trying to see if anyone stood within. When she was satisfied that the chamber beyond the doors was empty, she glided silently inside.

The girl found herself in a tall open hall, with stairs running up to the second floor of the estate along either wall, meeting again at the top where a balcony led to several other passages. On the ground floor, numerous doorways and halls led out from the central chamber. The house was dark and silent.

Xaphira moved in beside Emriana, breathing slowly. "Still no traps," she said, "and no magical emanations anywhere."

Emriana nodded. "If you were expecting uninvited guests," she said, "would you possibly hold back your defenses until they were deep inside, perhaps lulled into a false sense of security?"

"Perhaps," Xaphira answered.

"And where would you wait for those uninvited guests to arrive?"

Xaphira didn't say anything for a long moment, then she replied, "The basement."

"That's what I was thinking, too," Emriana said. "Let's see if we can find our way down."

"If we get separated for some reason," Xaphira said, pulling a glowing coin from a pouch at her waist and handing it to Emriana, "use your necklace to call to me." She removed a second lit coin, which she kept. "And if you think you hear something, slip that into a pocket and hide."

"I will," Emriana said. And with that, they started forward. The girl crept along, rolling the balls of her feet to be as silent as possible as she roamed toward the nearest doorway. Inside, she saw an open chamber with several dark figures standing still, waiting for her.

She nearly yelped out loud before she realized they were suits of armor, assembled on stands. It was something of a trophy room with numerous treasures displayed on shelves, in cases, and hanging from the walls. There weren't any other visible exits from the room, and she didn't see the point in checking for concealed passages until they had exhausted all the other possibilities.

The girl turned back to try a different doorway and saw motion from deeper in the house. She swallowed hard and slipped the coin into her pocket, dousing the illumination and peering into the darkness. It had not been Xaphira, for Emriana could easily see her across the way by the glow of her coin, moving about in a dining room. Whatever had moved, it had been hidden in the near-darkness on the edge of Emriana's vision.

I need the eyes of a dwarf, the girl thought, frustrated. They can creep around without any light at all and see just fine.

As Emriana stared at the blackness ahead of her, trying to spot whatever had caught her attention without being exposed herself, she heard the rustle of cloth and a single footstep brushing softly across a stone floor.

"Xaphira!" Emriana cried out, yanking the coin free of her pocket and throwing it in the direction of the sounds. "Hurry!"

The coin bounced and rolled into the hallway, lighting the passage enough as it traveled that Emriana could clearly see Bartimus standing in a doorway several paces away. Even her suspicion that someone was present didn't help Emriana contain her fear, and she shrieked slightly when the wizard's face came into view.

Bartimus seemed just as startled as the girl, for he jumped when the coin came at him, his eyes wide with apprehension. He took one look at Emriana, then turned and ran, his robes swishing behind him.

"Come back here," Emriana yelled just as Aunt Xaphira came running out of the dining room. Emriana took off after the wizard, determined not to let him get away.

"Em, wait!" Aunt Xaphira called, hustling to keep up with the girl. "Don't get foolish!"

Emriana stopped to pick up her coin before she continued, allowing her aunt to catch up to her. "It's the wizard," she said, charging through the doorway where Bartimus had disappeared. "He's escaping!"

Bartimus was no sneak and Emriana could easily hear him huffing and puffing as he tried to evade her and her aunt. He ducked around a corner and Emriana spotted him a moment later at the far end of a hall. He had stopped and was gesturing toward her. She froze on the spot, knowing he was about to launch some arcane force at her, and she couldn't make her legs move to get out of the way. Xaphira grabbed at the girl and jerked her sideways into a sitting room, just as a burst of flame came roaring down the hall. The blast of heat that cascaded over Emriana's face from the searing jets of flame was enough to help her regain her caution.

"All right," Xaphira said once the fiery blast faded away, "I've got something for him, now," and she stepped back into the hallway, holding her holy coin in front of her. "Come here, you little worm," she said, and went trotting down the hall, her light receding with her.

Emriana started out the door to follow her, but a sound caught her attention from the other direction. She paused, keeping her coin in her pocket for a moment, and just listened. Someone was in the next room over!

Quietly feeling her way with her hand on the wall, Emriana moved in the opposite direction her aunt had gone. Xaphira had vanished quickly, for when Emriana glanced back once, wondering if she should let her know what she had heard, the woman and her light were both already gone. For a moment, Emriana fingered her opal pendant.

No, she decided. Can't give away my presence even with a whisper.

Emriana bolstered her courage with a single deep breath and proceeded. The noises from the next room continued, and it sounded to Emriana as though someone were shifting crates around. She used the wall to guide herself, and when she found the frame of the door, she stopped, listening again.

Someone was definitely on the other side of the door. She felt for the handle and pulled the slightest bit, hoping to get a peek inside before anyone noticed she was there. It was dark in the room, but the sounds continued. Emriana listened for a moment longer, keeping the door open only a crack. It still sounded as if someone were stacking crates.

How odd, she thought, preparing to swing the door wide and toss the coin inside for a better view. Then she grew suspicious. Can wizards make magic that sounds like someone moving around? she wondered. Probably, she decided. Wants me to just walk in.

Instead, she took a length of rope that she carried—in case we need to do any serious climbing or tie someone up, she had told Xaphira—and very carefully tied one end of it to the pull handle of the door. She uncoiled the rope as she walked backward, away from the portal, perhaps ten paces. Then she yanked the door open.

An audible click sounded in the hall and a whoosh of air was released from inside the room. A blink of an eye later, something loud popped on the far side of the hall.

Despite her preparations, Emriana jumped at the sound. Then she stood stark still, waiting to see if anything else happened. When it did not, she carefully moved back to the wide-open door and listened. The sound of crates being stacked was still in evidence, and in fact, hadn't changed at all.

Knowing that such noises couldn't be natural, Emriana pulled her coin out of her pocket, blinking in its brightness. The room was no more than a storage closet, but mounted on a stand in the center, aimed right for the door, was a small ballista. A bit of twine ran from the trigger mechanism to the door. Turning, Emriana found the remains of the large bolt that had been fired. It was as long as her leg and as thick as her thumb.

It would have skewered me, she thought unhappily.

The sounds of crate-stacking continued, but Emriana realized they were merely a trick of magic, some sort of prestidigitation Bartimus likely conjured to draw her or her aunt into opening the door.

Aunt Xaphira!

Emriana turned around, ready to grab her pendant and call to her aunt when a face loomed into view just inside the girl's circle of light.

It was Denrick, smiling at her.

CHAPTER 15

Vambran moved down the smoky, torchlit hallway, sword in hand. The stink of sweat and fear clung to everything so many levels below the surface. The lieutenant knew he was near the dungeons of the Palace of the Seven, but his magic seemed to be leading him in a different direction. He had not encountered any guards, no one to stand in his way, though that was not a surprise. The city is in chaos, he thought. Why stay here and protect empty corridors?

The mercenary was close to the source of the malignancy, and he knew it. Malevolence radiated through the place, oozed from the walls, hung on him like a funereal shroud. It was a sense of evil so pervasive that he no longer needed divine guidance to track it. Whatever was causing the plague was in the bowels of the keep, and he was closing in on it.

He had to fight the urge to leap ahead, to charge forward and find that source. Whatever was down there was strong, and he could not afford to underestimate it. But he craved the hunt. He needed it the way he needed air. After everything he had endured over the last three days, the urge to vent his frustrations on the source of it all was like a bad taste in his mouth.

The pulsating evil led Vambran to a door at the end of the passage. The force he sought lay beyond that portal. It beckoned to him, taunting. He hesitated, listening. No sounds arose from the other side, but some presence lay beyond. Something that hated him. Adjusting his grip on his sword, he shoved the door open and peered inside.

The chamber beyond was out of a nightmare. Implements of torture filled much of the room, and the lieutenant could see a laboratory along one wall, jammed with alembics and decanters containing all sorts of vile things. Half of them turned his stomach when he recognized them and the other half—well, he didn't even want to guess at those.

A cloaked figure stood at a table in the laboratory, its back to Vambran, apparently working. Even when the door slammed open, the figure barely twitched. It wore a brown robe with a hood pulled up, completely hiding its head. It didn't stop in its work as it said in a masculine voice, "I wondered when you would get here."

Vambran paused with one foot inside the room. He stared at the figure, unsure what sort of trap he might be falling into. "How did you know I would

come?" he said, hoping to draw the man out, get him
to turn around. He looked around the room as he
spoke, searching for other threats. He saw nothing,
but there were so many items filling the chamber, so
many places to hide, that it seemed ridiculous *not* to
have allies hiding among it all. The lieutenant sensed
death everywhere, and not all of that palpable hatred
emanated from his counterpart. The whole chamber
was filled with it.

"I know a great many things," the figure said,
moving from a small apparatus over to a flask resting atop a ring stand and heated by a candle. "For
example, I know that you are here to stop me from
completing my quest, and that you have brought
great magic with you to do so."

Vambran swallowed, circling wide of the figure,
wary of having some caustic substance hurled in his
direction. "Then you must also know that I'm set on
staying around until I finish the job."

"Finish the job?" the figure in the brown robes said
with a hearty chuckle. "You aren't serious, are you?"
And he began to turn around, spinning slowly to face
Vambran. "After all," he said as his face came into
view, "you couldn't finish the job twelve years ago."

Vambran stared at the man whose features
remained partially hidden within the hood of the
robe. The cryptic comment baffled him. But when
his enemy reached up and pulled his hood back, fully
revealing his face, a memory came flooding back
to the mercenary. A memory of a man lying near a
pond, with a crossbow bolt protruding from his chest.
A dead man.

"You!" Vambran said, stunned. He reached out to
grab hold of a table to keep his balance. "But you're
dead! I saw your body!"

"As I said," Rodolpho Wianar replied, "you couldn't finish the job then, so how do you expect to do so now?"

Vambran reeled at the revelation. Still alive! How was it possible? Then another thought struck him. No, he realized, dismissing it. Xaphira would not have made such a mistake. He was dead, and brought back from the dead. But why?

Vambran's eyes narrowed. "Your death was a screen, a cover-up, wasn't it? Everyone was supposed to assume you had died, and I was set up for it."

"Right you are," Rodolpho Wianar said, looking pleased. "They said you were bright," he added, chuckling. "I just didn't believe them, seeing how you kept dragging your family into the middle of all this."

Vambran shook off the backhanded compliment. "But I wasn't the one who killed you before," he said. "And you know that."

"Too true."

"I bet you know who did, too."

"Yes, he does," came another voice from a corner of the room, one that Vambran recognized. He shot a glance over to confirm that Junce Roundface was standing there. "He knows very well I was the one who punctured his heart with one of your own bolts that night."

Vambran snorted in disgust. "Of course," he said sarcastically. "Speak of a devil, and he appears." The lieutenant moved slightly so he could keep both opponents in view. "Come to gloat over my shock and surprise?"

"Truthfully, no, though I'll take that as an added bonus," the assassin said, smirking. "I actually came to throttle Rodolpho here for not living up to his end of the bargain." He turned to the hooded man and asked, "Unless you'd like to reconsider giving up the cure?"

Vambran eyed the assassin with suspicion. "The cure?" he asked. "You have a cure?"

"No," Junce answered, still looking at Rodolpho. "This wretch of a man refuses to divulge it."

Rodolpho laughed. "What, and ruin everything just when I'm on the verge of marching an army to my cousin's gates and demanding his surrender? I think not. Now, why haven't you died yet? Surely you've been exposed to the plague by now." He spun and hurled a beaker of something viscous and yellow at Junce.

The assassin seemed to anticipate the attack, for he leaped out of the way, allowing the glassware to shatter against the wall behind him. But as soon as it did, a phlegm-colored cloud of vapors expanded outward, drifting to fill the room.

Junce backed away from it, stumbling as he bumped into a horrific torture rack. The cloud billowed up and outward, threatening to engulf them all.

"I'm sorry you won't be able to take that cure back to dear cousin Wianar," Rodolpho said, striding across the room to another door on the far side, "but you can let him know yourself, once you're part of my army." He opened the door as Junce and Vambran retreated from the cloud, backing into the same corner, trapped. "Just in case you manage to evade my recipe," Rodolpho added, swinging the door wide, "my seven apprentices are on hand to finish the job."

One by one, seven figures filed into the chamber, fanning out to stare at the two men pinned in the corner. Each man and woman might have been young and strong when they entered into Rodolpho's service, but no longer.

Vambran could see the beauty that might once have been part of each face, but that beauty was twisted and distorted in undeath. Pieces of flesh were missing, exposing bone beneath, and where the creatures' eyes should have been, red points of malevolent light glowed instead. Dressed in fine clothing and wearing cloaks of red and gold, the seven gruesome figures stood waiting and watching.

Rodolpho waved at the two men and disappeared through the door.

...

As memories of the previous night washed over Emriana, she felt her knees weaken, her hands tremble. Denrick was leaning against the wall, his hands folded across his chest, still wearing that smug grin that haunted her. She retreated a step, wanting to turn and run, fearing that she would never flee fast enough.

"Hello, Em," Denrick said, pushing away from the wall and following her, sauntering. "I was hoping you'd stop by for a visit. I enjoyed last evening so much, and I thought you might like to spend time with me again."

No! Emriana silently screamed, fighting the feelings of helplessness. Not again! "Get away from me," she said with as much cold hatred as she could muster. "I know you're not real."

"I'm not?" Denrick asked, looking wounded. "Last night sure felt real enough," he said, that smug smile returning. "And this is certainly real," he added, lunging forward and grabbing at the girl's wrist.

His grip was strong, so strong. He twisted her arm, bending her hand and elbow awkwardly out to her side. The pressure locked the joint and forced her to torque her body, to bow. She understood what he was doing, the mental edge he was gaining from making her bend to him. She wanted to fight it, but he kept twisting, forcing her down, down to one knee lest her arm pop free of her shoulder. His smile was gone, replaced by a grimace of effort. His eyes held a sparkling glint that radiated hatred.

"Ow!" she cried out as he continued to push, continued to angle her body to the floor. Her arm hurt and her mind told her she was not strong enough to fight him, to resist him. He would have what he wanted, again.

No, she thought, more firmly. Not again. Never again.

And in that one moment of clarity, Emriana remembered that she was strong, too. She could fight Denrick in ways that he could not defend. She could turn the tables, gain the upper hand. She stopped giving in to her fear and started feeding off it, garnering strength from it.

She reminded herself that it was not really Denrick. Oh, last night was real enough, she told herself. Accept it. But it was not Denrick. The thing in front of her needed to pretend to be Denrick in order to cow her. And she would not be cowed.

She would not succumb to it.

With a kick, Emriana lunged upward, flipping her body completely over in a single, fluid motion. As she spun, she rotated herself half a twist so that her opposite shoulder was nearest the shapeshifter, and the arm it gripped was draped across the front of her body. The look on its face was mild surprise, but

Emriana did not wait for it to recover. Her free elbow came up hard beneath its chin, snapping its head up and back. A second strike with her elbow into its gut made it grunt. At the same time, Emriana yanked hard, thrusting her hip out and using leverage to hoist the shapeshifter off the floor. She pivoted on her foot, rotating her shoulders, and sent the Denrick lookalike tumbling away from her.

The thing landed in a heap a pace or so away, glowering at the girl. She ignored the stare, made a quick run forward, and snapped her foot out at its face, as Xaphira had taught her.

"I said," she growled, kicking again, "that you're not real!" A third kick. "You're just a pathetic forgery. And I'm done messing around." A final kick, then Emriana retreated a step, crouching. She drew one of the two daggers that Xaphira had given her, hidden at the small of her back. She was ready to finish the fight once and for all.

Denrick's face looked at her, a wounded expression on it. "I thought you loved me," the thing said.

"Drop the act," Emriana replied, raising her dagger, ready to snap her wrist and flick it right between its eyes. "I'm done being afraid of you."

"Please," it said, shifting its form. "Don't hurt me," it added, its voice changing, softening, rising in pitch.

Emriana gaped, her intention to deliver a death blow with her dagger forgotten for a moment. She stared at an exact image of herself, as though she were gazing into a mirror.

In her amazement, the girl let her guard down and that was all the shapeshifter needed. In a sudden burst of speed, it shot up from the floor and rammed its shoulder into Emriana's stomach. She felt the

wind knocked from her lungs, and the feeble attempt
she made to stab at the creature caught only air. She
stumbled back, her balance lost, as her duplicate
stepped back from her, light on its feet, grinning.

"So what do you think?" Emriana's reflection
asked. "Good enough to fool your aunt?" And before
the girl could catch her breath enough to answer or
react, the shapeshifter was gone, sprinting off deeper
into the house.

· · ·

Arbeenok wished that it were day, to make it
easier for him to see. You cannot force the pattern of
the butterfly's flight or the pictures the stars make,
he reminded himself. They simply are. Day or night
didn't change the fact that he had a task ahead of him.
He considered where to start the healing. The center
of the city, he decided. That is where the fighting will
be the worst.

Aloft, even at night, the alaghi saw the destruction, for many fires burned again. He could see that
the mercenaries had done a credible job of erecting
barricades, for those were what burned. An effective
deterrent, he thought. If only they'd remembered
the sewers.

In one neighborhood, Arbeenok witnessed a shambling horde of zombies moving down a street, while a
contingent of soldiers tried to keep them at bay with
crossbows. The soldiers had no burning barricades
to huddle behind and the fight was not going well
for them. More zombies were appearing in an alley,
crawling out of the sewer. From the height at which
Arbeenok observed them, they appeared as sluggish
beetles.

Unlike before, when Vambran and the druid had last battled the zombies in the city, the ones below seemed more persistent, focused.

They had a purpose.

Arbeenok wondered what was stirring them, driving them to such destruction. He felt a pang of anger shoot through him. He thought of Vambran and hoped the mercenary would succeed. The city very well depended on both their efforts to overcome the virulent death.

Alighting in the midst of the skirmish below was not easy, for zombies came after him without regard for his form, and the soldiers gawked in awe and fright. One even raised his weapon, ready to fire at the enormous bird, but Arbeenok changed into his true shape quickly, before the soldier got the nerve to pull the trigger. It was not often that a dire hawk appeared in Reth, but Arbeenok doubted an alaghi had, either.

"I'm here to help," he said, letting his voice carry across the lane. "Please don't shoot at me."

The soldiers did not respond, but neither did they fire at him.

Turning his back on the mercenaries, Arbeenok hoisted the scepter in his hands and looked at the zombies. The scepter could not save them, the druid knew, but it could destroy them, wipe the taint of the plague from their undead bodies.

The were getting close, shambling forward relentlessly. Arbeenok ignored their approach and instead closed his eyes, filling his mind with the power of the scepter. The gem pulsed and began to glow, its greenish light penetrating the druid's eyelids. When he felt attuned to the device, Arbeenok opened his eyes again and held the scepter aloft.

He began to sing.

The zombies approached and Arbeenok focused the power of the scepter at the nearest one. A flash of brilliant emerald shot out from the tip of the scepter, a ray of green that disintegrated the zombie and turned it to dust. Behind him, the druid heard a gasp from one of the soldiers. Ignoring the man's reaction, Arbeenok turned on the next zombie. Like the first one, it was obliterated, vanishing in a puff of dust. The druid continued, disintegrating one and another, sending forth bolts of green energy over and over, vanquishing the undead.

When the street was cleared of the gruesome things, the alaghi turned back toward the soldiers. He could see that many were suffering the effects of the plague, that men who had been strong and healthy moments before were down on their knees, coughing and choking, their skin blistered and discolored.

I must hurry, he thought. Every moment that goes by is another victim.

Arbeenok held aloft the scepter and began to sing again, funneling his own essence into the artifact and drawing out its healing touch. A shimmering curtain of pale green sprang forth from the gem, a soothing wave of light that radiated out in all directions and cascaded over the sick soldiers. As the curtain of magic reached them, men who had been crying out in pain and terror suddenly changed their demeanor, sighing or crying in relief.

A few of the soldiers still watched the alaghi with uncertainty. He understood that to them, he would always remain the enemy, a druid against whom they fought. He could never change their perceptions. But at least on that night, as the healing power of the scepter became evident, those suspicious soldiers would acquiesce to his company, accept his magic. On that night, Arbeenok's presence would mean relief.

After healing the soldiers guarding the street, Arbeenok set off to find more people to aid. He knew that he had a long night ahead of him.

...

"I'm sorry, Grand Trabbar," the temple guard said, looking forlorn. "We've searched the entire grounds and every level of the temple, and he's not here."

"Well, start again," Grand Trabbar Perolin snapped. "Wherever Lavant is hiding, sooner or later he'll try to move, and we'll catch him." The guard saluted and jogged off to relay the order to his superiors.

Pilos sat with the Grand Trabbar, not participating in the hunt for the renegade priest, but privy to all the high priests' efforts to bring Lavant to justice. Some of the high priests of the council gave Pilos scathing stares from time to time. They were, no doubt, part of the faction that had been loyal to Lavant, had supported his cause to ascend the high seat after Mikolos had died. Pilos's revelations about the Grand Syndar had not only deprived them of their leader, it had crippled their political power within the temple. The thought warmed the Abreeant's heart.

"They will just shift alliances, you know," Grand Trabbar Perolin said, drawing Pilos out of his thoughts. "That is the way of things here, as with every temple. Power begets power struggles."

Pilos nodded, frowning. "I find that I do not have much of a taste for politics," he told the older man. "It leaves a foul taste in my mouth. What happened to just serving the glory of Waukeen?"

Perolin laughed. "What happened, indeed? Serving
the Merchant's Friend purely for the sake of devotion
is an admirable quality, young Abreeant, but sooner
or later, you will find that you cannot escape the
machinations of those who would utilize that devotion
for their own ends. The two are inextricably inter-
twined." When Pilos felt his frown deepen, Perolin
added, "Even the gods themselves play at politics, and
we mortals are simply the pawns in their game."

That thought did little to placate Pilos. "I don't
think Grand Syndar Midelli was such a player of
these games," he asserted. "I've never known a more
pious, straightforward leader. I will miss him."

Perolin chuckled. "You saw what you wanted to
see," he said. "Mikolos Midelli was a good leader, Pilos,
and you were right to ally yourself with him. But he
was not just the kind, generous man you believe you
knew. He was also a shrewd negotiator, and ruthless
in his schemes against his enemies, both within the
temple and beyond. Did you know that when he was
first named Grand Syndar, Lavant was his personal
attendant?"

Pilos started. "Before me?" he asked, shocked. "He
served Mikolos?"

Perolin nodded. "Actually, two before you," he
said. "And Lavant was as devoted to Mikolos as you
were."

Pilos tried to wrap his mind around the notion of
Lavant being a devoted ally of the Grand Syndar. It
was nearly impossible. "What happened?" he asked,
not sure he wanted to hear the answer.

"Mikolos championed a business deal that was
beneficial to the temple but hurt Lavant's own
House. I don't even remember what it involved," Perolin said, stroking his chin in thought. "Something

to do with grain shipments from Estagund or Var the Golden, far to the south and east of here." The older man shrugged. "Whatever the case, Lavant wanted Mikolos to look at another deal, something that would hurt his own family businesses far less, but Mikolos would not. He had already promised three other high priests to set it up a particular way, because it was in their personal interests, and he needed those high priests' support for a pet project of his own. Something to do with granting land and titles to a mercenary outfit his brother was part of." He shrugged again. "Lavant never forgave him and began building his own faction within the temple to thwart everything Mikolos did after that."

Pilos sagged in his seat. "I never knew," he said. "I always disliked Lavant, but I thought it was because he seemed so manipulative. I wonder now how much of that was Mikolos's subtle manipulations?"

"It was probably a bit of both," Perolin replied. "I'm sure Mikolos recognized your pure but some-what naïve piety and took advantage of it to turn you against a conniving man like Lavant. I tell you, he was very good at it, better than Lavant, because he kept it all under the table. No one had much cause to feel slighted by Mikolos Midelli, not often, anyway."

Pilos looked up at Grand Trabbar Perolin. "And how much are you manipulating me now, telling me these things?" Perolin looked at the young priest, but there was no anger in his expression. More like appreciation, Pilos thought.

"You say you don't have a taste for politics," the older man said, "but you are shrewd to them." He paused for a moment, as if trying to find the right words to use. "There will be a new Grand Syndar," he said, "and the high priest who claims the high seat will need many allies backing him or her. I could use the hero of Lavant's ousting, and the power of House Darowdryn, on my side." When Pilos didn't answer right away, Perolin continued. "After the damage Lavant has done, the temple will need to rebuild some relationships. If I succeed to the high seat, I will need able young priests to serve as diplomats to other power groups, like the Houses of Arrabar and the Emerald Enclave. How does the thought of becoming one of my envoys sound to you, Trabbar Pilos?"

It took Pilos a moment to register the new appellation Perolin used to address him. A bribe for his loyalty. "I will think about it," he told the Grand Trabbar.

"There will be others who seek you out," Perolin warned. "Now that you have made a name for yourself, you wield power within the temple, whether you like it or not."

Pilos swallowed, nodding in understanding. Inextricably linked, he thought. Can I stomach it?

CHAPTER 16

Emriana could not breathe. She wanted to stand, to chase after the dreadful duplicate of herself, but she could only gasp for air. Precious time slipped away before the girl could right herself and rise to her feet. Fearing for the safety of her aunt, she somehow found the strength to begin walking, moving deeper into the house, chasing after the shapeshifter. As she stumbled along, Emriana reached for her opal pendant, ready to call to Xaphira and warn her of the double.

The necklace was not there.

No! Emriana thought, realizing she had lost it. She stopped for a moment, thinking to turn back and find it in the hallway where she had fought with the shapeshifter. Then

her eyes narrowed. It took it, she realized, understanding. When it hit me, it must have snapped it
free. It knew I could use it to warn her. Damn!

"Xaphira," Emriana called out, desperate to find
the woman before harm came to her. "Xaphira, it's
me! You're in danger!"

There was no answer.

Near to panic, Emriana roamed the house, calling
to her aunt. In the kitchen, she found a stairwell leading down. Remembering the earlier discussion with
her aunt, the girl began to descend, listening. She
thought she heard a conversation, low and indistinct.
Conflicted between running blindly into danger and
the need to reach her aunt and prove that she was
the true Emriana, the girl galloped down the steps
two at a time. At the bottom, she found a partially
open door with light streaming from behind it. She
threw herself at the door and went into a roll as she
passed through the portal. She came up on one knee,
her two throwing daggers in her hands, surveying
the room.

Grozier Talricci stood with his back to a pantry
shelf, his arm wrapped around Obiron, a knife in
his other hand. Bartimus stood next to his employer,
looking as befuddled as ever, with that embarrassed
smile he always seemed to be wearing. He held
Quindy by her shoulders, though his grip was less
constrictive than Grozier's, and the wizard was not
holding a blade. Xaphira had her back to the two men,
no weapons in her hands, a dagger at her feet. Her
arms were out to her sides, as if she were showing the
pair that she was not a threat.

Behind Xaphira, out of the older woman's field
of vision, Emriana's double was standing as though
her aunt were protecting her. The thing held a

dagger, poised to strike at Xaphira's back.

When Emriana burst through the door, everyone in the room turned in surprise to see her. Even as Xaphira's eyes grew wide, the shapeshifter smiled and raised the dagger for a killing blow.

Emriana never hesitated, though time slowed to a crawl as she reacted. Cocking both arms back, she snapped her elbows and flicked her wrists just as Xaphira had taught her. Two blades sailed from her hands, tumbling as they crossed the room. The girl watched them both, praying to Tymora, to Waukeen, to any god she thought would listen. Everyone else in the pantry stood rooted to the floor, watching the spinning blades.

And the two weapons reached their startled targets.

One struck Grozier Talricci in the face.

One struck the false Emriana in the face.

Only then did Emriana let out a breath.

The changeling staggered back, shrieking and clawing at its eye where the dagger had embedded itself, destroying the orb. The creature fell to the floor, still looking like Emriana. It thrashed and screamed, making a horrible sound that echoed through the entire room.

Grozier died much more peacefully. He stood for a moment, his knife hand going limp at his side, and tried to focus his eyes on the hilt of the weapon that protruded from his forehead. Then he twitched, dropping the knife from his grasp, and sagged to his knees. Obiron, feeling the grip around his chest loosen, squirmed free. Grozier toppled over, sprawled on the hard stone floor.

Obiron, startled by Grozier's fall, threw his arms around Xaphira's waist. He clung for a few moments, then his mouth opened and he began to sob vigorously. A glance down at the dead man who had recently held him captive brought terror to the frightened boy's sobs.

Xaphira turned and stared at Emriana for a moment, then looked down at her false neice, watching it transform into a gray humanoid with a large, bulbous head as it stopped twitching and screaming and lay still. The room was silent except for Obiron's sobbing.

Sympathetic to her twin, Quindy screamed, and Emriana regretted not having another dagger to throw at Bartimus. Lucky for him, the girl was unharmed. Quindy kicked backward with the heel of her boot, catching Bartimus on the shin.

The wizard yelped and released the young girl, crouching down and grabbing at his leg. Quindy scrambled free of the man, running to Emriana with tears running down her face.

Emriana hugged her niece even as she saw Bartimus straighten and begin to mutter. "Xaphira, he's bolting!" she cried out. Her aunt bent down to pick up her own dagger, but Bartimus was too fast. He finished his arcane phrase, conjuring one of his blue doorways, and just as Xaphira cocked her arm for a throw, the wizard stepped through and was gone.

"Damn," Xaphira said, watching the blue outline of the magical portal fade away. Then she looked at Obiron, who was again staring at Grozier's body. "Don't look," she told the boy gently. He turned his face up to her with big, round eyes.

"He's, he's . . ." Obiron was trying to say, but he couldn't make the words come out. His head turned toward the body again.

"I know," Xaphira said, squatting next to the boy

to hug him more closely. "Look away from it, Obiron." When the boy didn't comply, Xaphira took his chin in her hands and forced him to look at her instead. "It's all right," she said in soothing tones. "He can't hurt you."

Obiron buried his face in her shoulder then, and Emriana saw him shudder.

When the two children had settled themselves, Xaphira stood. "Let's get out of here," she suggested. "I think someone would like to see her children."

Emriana nodded, pausing just long enough to retrieve both of her throwing daggers. She also removed the opal pendant from around the doppelganger's neck. As she stood, she regarded the creature for a moment, studying its pallid gray skin and its revolting head. She remembered the previous night, in Lobra's bedroom.

She gave the body one severe kick, snapping several ribs, then turned around and followed her aunt up the stairs.

...

Vambran knew what he needed to do. It came to him unbidden, an innate understanding of arcane forces that he could control and manipulate. The sudden insight was no longer as jarring as it once was.

One moment, Vambran was trapped, standing next to Junce as the noxious gas from the broken beaker billowed ever closer. The next instant, he was conjuring a force, a wall of wind, setting it to push the vapors and drive them away. He didn't understand how he knew what to do, but he was thankful for the gift.

The lieutenant looked at Junce, trying to decide if he should kill the man right there. The assassin was still watching the fumes from Rodolpho's attack, not yet understanding that he was safe from them for the moment. Vambran wanted to strike. He truly did. All of the hatred, the sorrow for losing those who had died, could be directed at the man in black easily enough.

But other problems demanded to be dealt with.

The seven apprentices, their red pinprick eyes smoldering with unabashed malevolence, approached, clawed hands outstretched. They tried to push Vambran and Junce into a retreat, to drive them toward the noxious fumes.

Vambran decided that Junce could wait.

"The plague can't reach us," he said. "I blocked it. But the only way we'll survive is if we fight them," he said to the assassin. He left unspoken the word "together," unable to stomach it, but he hoped that Junce understood.

Junce regarded Vambran for a moment, his eyes wide with concern. Vambran could tell the man didn't trust him. "Rodolpho's getting away," Vambran said pointedly.

Junce grinned then, a slight smile, not overly warm or friendly, but a smile nonetheless. He turned and lunged at the first apprentice, driving his blade through its chest. The creature staggered back, swaying on its feet, but two others snarled and rushed in, trying to take down the assassin.

Vambran slashed at the closest of the undead, deflecting its first blow. The mercenary parried another strike, then kicked at the foe, sending it stumbling into a spike-lined post. One of the many spikes protruded from the creature's abdomen,

sending a trickle of pus running down its robes, but
it did not seem harmed by the wound and struggled
to extract itself from its own impalement.

Three more of Rodolpho's pets came at Vambran,
their red eyes blazing in hatred. The trio lunged and
feinted frequently, testing the lieutenant. They didn't
seem to want to strike him so much as keep him at
bay, and Vambran realized their primary task was
to prevent him from getting past them and going
after Rodolpho.

"They want to keep us cornered," Junce said, echoing Vambran's own thoughts as he battled his own
adversaries. "Makes it harder to fight."

"But harder for them to surround us," Vambran
rebutted. "Which do you prefer?"

Junce didn't answer.

Since the undead weren't keen on taking the fight
to him, Vambran decided to call on his faith. Grasping
his holy coin with his free hand, he drew in divine
energy, drawing himself up to his full imposing
height. He held out the coin at the three apprentices
fighting him. "I condemn you, abominations!" he
shouted, focusing Waukeen's glory at the corpses. "I
defy and condemn you. Go now! Harry me no more!"

The closest one cringed and fell back, throwing
an arm up across its face, but the others ignored
Vambran's command and closed ranks. The mercenary swore softly.

"That was cute," Junce said. "Very effective."

"I'm not seeing you doing any better," Vambran
retorted.

One of the undead things was sidling down the
wall to Vambran's right, trying to get on his flank.
With a growl, Vambran sliced at it, drawing a deep
gash across its shoulder, cutting almost all the way

through the limb. The thing halted, staring at its arm, which hung limply by a few strands of desiccated tissue and fabric. But Vambran didn't have a chance to finish it off, for the other two monsters were taking advantage of his momentary distraction and closing in.

The first went in low, trying to grab for his legs, while the second one raked at his face with its claws. Vambran parried the high attacks, lopping off a few fingers in the process, but the move allowed the other corpse to encircle his leg, dragging its claws down the flesh above his boot. The mercenary yelped in pain and stabbed downward, driving his blade through the creature's back. The thing jerked, let out an unnatural keening wail, and released Vambran, jerking its arms back over its head, trying to reach the blade that pinned it to the floor.

Vambran used the opportunity to move, yanking his blade up only when he had stepped out of the apprentice's reach. He was breathing hard and the wounds on his leg throbbed, but he could do nothing but ignore them—the fingerless adversary was coming at him again. He stabbed at it, but it anticipated the attack and shifted out of the way. It lunged toward the lieutenant's unprotected side, its teeth bared, and Vambran had to retreat from the bite, causing him to bump against Junce.

"Watch it," the assassin growled as he shifted his weight, knocking a clawed hand to the side. "You're messing me up."

"Happy to help," Vambran retorted, but he discovered—almost to his chagrin—that he could move well with his counterpart, feel the assassin's motions and react accordingly. They began fighting as a team, back to back, keeping the undead things at bay. As they worked, they gradually moved toward the center of the room. Vambran could sense that Junce was guiding them both there, and he had to choose between going with the assassin's intentions or breaking off the teamwork and dueling his undead foes on his own. He chose to stick with Junce.

He's an excellent fighter, Vambran grudgingly admitted, working to keep up with the other man's blazing quickness and sure footwork. *Just makes killing him later more satisfying,* the mercenary told himself.

The pair continued to battle, working their foes, watching both flanks. Vambran was growing tired and they still faced five of the seven undead, though all were missing limbs and stumbling with noticeable limps. *Can't do this much longer,* the lieutenant thought. *And they don't seem to get tired.* But he refused to give up. The people of Reth were counting on him, whether they understood that or not. Behind him, Junce battled just as fiercely, moving in unison with Vambran. Each man guarded the other as they fought, flicking a sword strike out from time to time to deflect a blow meant for the other. They moved well together, battling the undead beasts.

At long last, only two of the creatures remained standing, and Vambran saw his chance. He feinted a cut toward the one battling him, and when it reacted, he kicked out hard, shoving the undead brute away from himself. Before it had a chance to recover, Vambran took off, running for the door that Rodolpho had used to escape.

"Hey!" Junce called out from behind the lieutenant, but Vambran ignored the man. Flinging open the door, the mercenary raced through the portal and found a set of steps leading up. They were narrow and spiraled tightly, but he never hesitated. He took them two at a time, using the wall for support. His arms and legs were weary, but he refused to stop. Rodolpho was up there.

Farther up, Vambran was forced to stop skipping over steps, but he fought through the burning pain in his thighs and kept going, up and up, his breath ragged. He knew he was climbing to the top of the tower, the highest feature of all of Reth. That made the task more daunting. To spur himself on, Vambran reminded himself of all the people who had died because of Rodolpho's terrible creation. He reminded himself of Elenthia, not knowing what had become of her, and the responsibility he felt for her.

After what seemed like an ascent into the heavens themselves, Vambran reached another door. He threw it open and found himself on the top of the tower of the Palace of the Seven, an open platform surrounded by waist-high battlements. Rodolpho was there, staring down at the city below. As Vambran stood in the doorway, gasping, the man spun around to face him. The look on his face was one of dismay and horror.

"What did you do?" Rodolpho demanded, pointing down past the edge of the wall. "My plague! You're destroying my plague!"

Vambran would have chuckled if he hadn't been so weary. "So it goes," he said, taking a step, closing the distance. "What will Wianar do about you now?" he asked.

"No!" Rodolpho shouted, darting to try to escape from Vambran. "I'll put a stop to it! I'll destroy that scepter!"

As he tried to evade Vambran, the lieutenant struck. He swung his sword and just caught the fleeing man across the shoulder. The strike wasn't deadly, but in his attempt to avoid it, Rodolpho stumbled sideways and lost his balance. Tripping, he fell to the stones, very near the edge of the tower. He struggled to regain his feet as Vambran stepped near.

"It's over," he said. "You're finished."

Rodolpho glared at Vambran. The look in his eyes told the mercenary that he knew Vambran was right, but he wasn't yet willing to give up. Vambran planted his sword against the man's chest. "Did you hear me?" he asked softly. "I said, you're done."

"Perhaps," Rodolpho said, squaring his shoulders. "But I won't go with you. So can you kill me? Can you do willingly what you thought you did unwittingly twelve years ago?"

Vambran paused, staring at the man. He remembered all those times when he had grieved, feeling the weight of it, saddened by what he had imagined Rodolpho's friends and family had felt. He remembered how he suffered for what he'd done. Despite the change in circumstances, despite the knowledge that Rodolpho Wianar was responsible for the deaths of so many people down below, the little boy inside Vambran who had suffered so much guilt could not deliver the killing blow.

"You see?" Rodolpho said. "I told you you couldn't finish the job."

"Do it," Junce said from behind Vambran. "Do it, or you'll live with your weakness forever."

Vambran never took his eyes from Rodolpho, but he directed his question to the assassin. "What would you know about it? All you do is kill."

There was a long pause. Then Junce said, "I know about it because I watched my father kill my mother when he grew tired of her, and I have never lifted a hand to do anything about it." Vambran glanced at the man, then, only for a moment. But he saw Junce's face, and he knew the man was speaking the truth. "Do it," Junce whispered. "Or become like me." And with that, he muttered a magical phrase and vanished from the tower.

Vambran returned his gaze to Rodolpho. "Does he speak the truth? About his father?"

"Yes," Rodolpho replied. "Eles Wianar has a habit of doing away with the mistresses he grows tired of. But he took a liking to Darvin there, or Junce, as you know him. I never understood why."

Vambran's eyes widened. "Wianar! Eles Wianar is his father?"

Rodolpho nodded. "Yes, but don't let that story get you down. Killing me won't change who you are. There's no nobility in it, and as I'm sure you've figured out by now, revenge is never satisfying." Then he cocked his head as if considering something. "Funny, isn't it?" he said. "The Shining Lord of Arrabar had such a heavy hand in the shaping of both your lives. He took someone away from both of you, someone you cared for deeply, but you each turned out quite different. Makes me wonder if he considered that at the time. But then Eles was always a bastard like that. I mean, look what he did to me," he added, then he shoved himself forward, pushing away from the wall, driving Vambran's blade into his chest.

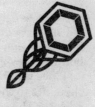

CHAPTER 17

In the chapel of House Matrell, Vambran stared at the two sarcophagi before him. He thought about Rodolpho Wianar's final words as he watched the memorial ceremony. Each of us shapes those around us, he realized. Either by our absence or our presence, we affect those we are close to. He glanced over at Xaphira, sitting next to Ladara, who was crying softly. And when that changes, when people in our lives are gone, or when they return unexpectedly, we feel unbalanced, unsure. We don't know how it will make a difference, but we know it will. He glanced over at Quindy and Obiron, sitting next to their mother. It always has an effect.

The mercenary felt Emriana squeeze his hand. He looked at her sitting next to him and saw her smiling at him, though a few tears were running down her face. His heart was heavy, and he felt his eyes grow moist, too. It's hard, saying good-bye to someone. Not just because they are gone, but because they made a difference in your life.

I love you, Hetta, Kovrim, he thought, sending his thoughts to the sarcophagi. Rest well.

After the ceremony, members of the family and their guests drifted to different parts of the house. Vambran decided to wander out to the yard, to spend more time thinking, but Emriana followed him.

"I think she knew it was time to go," the girl said, sounding very different than Vambran remembered. All grown up. "She was too long out of her body to go back, and she didn't want to stay in that ring forever. But I think she knew that it was all right, that she was leaving the family in good hands."

"I know," Vambran said, strolling down to the pond.

"I'm sorry you had to see Kovrim the way you did," she told him, taking his hand again. "I can't imagine what that must have been like."

I pray to Waukeen you never do, Vambran thought. "I'm going to miss them."

"Me, too."

They stood at the bank of the water, and Vambran watched the reflection of the high white clouds drifting overhead. It was going to be a hot day, the lieutenant realized. Spring was turning into summer. The height of trade season. And of campaigning.

"Are you going back?" Emriana asked suddenly. "To the Crescents, I mean."

Vambran looked at his sister. "How did you know that I was thinking about resigning? I hadn't said anything to anyone in the family yet."

"I can tell," she said. "It's in your eyes."

Just like I can tell that someone hurt you, Vambran thought. Badly. He shrugged. "I love it, but there's a part of me that feels like I should stay here now, help run the businesses. Dregaul is gone, so there's no reason to stay away, and I feel like you, Xaphira, and Marga need me."

"Don't be a meazel-face," Emriana said. "We can run things just fine. And it's in your blood. You have to do it."

Vambran chuckled. "Maybe, but shouldn't I start being a little more responsible?"

"I can't think of anything more responsible than maintaining our relationships with business partners abroad," the girl said. "On this last campaign alone, you managed to arrange good alliances with the Emerald Crescent, the Senator of Trade in Reth, and the sea elves. I call that a good tenday's work."

Vambran had to laugh at that. It was true. House Matrell was in the process of negotiating a fair and sensitive deal with the druids to lumber part of the Nunwood without stripping the forest bare. Part of the negotiations required regular face-to-face meetings. Shinthala had insisted on that. The family already had strong trade in place with the sea elves, but things had improved on that front, as well. Serille had seen to that. And Elenthia's father, so thankful that Vambran and Arbeenok had done so much to save the city—not to mention rescuing his daughter from a certain horrible death—was eager to generate business between his city and House Matrell.

"Let's just hope I don't have to stop a war every time," Vambran quipped. "Though Captain Havalla made me a pretty generous offer to serve as his second in the Order of the Silver Raven."

"You turned him down, right?" Emriana asked, and when Vambran looked at her, he saw that she was serious.

He nodded. "I offered him thanks, but I told him it was the Crescents or nothing for me. We still agreed to coordinate our efforts in the region from this point forward. No more fighting both sides of the battle at once."

"So is it the Crescents, or nothing?" Emriana asked.

"I haven't decided. Horial and Adyan don't want me to leave, either." He thought it was time to change the subject. "How about you? What are you going to do? And how serious is it between you and Pilos?"

Emriana blushed slightly. "Don't make it bigger than it is," she said, but the smile on her face told Vambran she was hoping her relationship with the priest would turn into something more.

"He seems like a fine fellow," Vambran said. "And having a more formal relationship with House Darowdryn would be beneficial."

"Oh, gods, you're turning into Uncle Dregaul, trying to marry me off!" she said, punching her brother in the shoulder.

"At least I let you pick him," Vambran said, laughing.

At that moment, a shout came from up the hill, near the house. The siblings turned to see Quindy and Obiron bounding down the hill toward the pond. The boy had his crossbow in hand, and his sister was lugging the quiver of bolts beside him. Behind the pair of boisterous children, other members of the family and several guests were strolling toward the pond. Xaphira and Marga were talking, and Vambran could see Pilos, Adyan, Horial, Grolo,

Edilus, and Arbeenok with them. The alaghi had come to the city of Arrabar, his first visit there, along with Edilus and Shinthala, to represent the druids at Hetta's memorial. Shinthala was in the rear, engaged in a deep conversation with both Elenthia and Serille, who had thankfully donned some clothing for her visit to land.

"It looks like all of your ladies are getting to know each other," Emriana teased.

Vambran groaned. "I liked it so much better when they were in separate places," he said. "I need to go on campaign."

"Maybe I'll go join in the conversation," the mercenary's sister taunted. "I have a few interesting stories they'd like to hear."

"Do it, and I'll make sure you can never show your face to Pilos again," Vambran warned.

Emriana gave him one scathing look before the crowd reached them. "Don't you dare," she muttered. "Or I'll sneak into your room at night and pour scorpions in your bed."

"I love you, too," Vambran said, and he meant it.

"All the women are going riding," Xaphira announced. "At the country estate. Do you want to join us, Em?" she asked.

The lieutenant raised his eyebrow in question. "All of you?" he asked, looking at Serille, Elenthia, and Shinthala with trepidation.

"Everyone but Shinthala," Xaphira answered. "She has to get back to the forest."

Vambran's gaze turned to the sea elf. "You, too?"

Serille nodded. "I would like to see what a horse is," she said, smiling sweetly.

Vambran resisted the urge to groan.

After the others had departed for the country

estate, Vambran was left standing with the other mercenaries and the druids.

"I just learned that Perolin was named Grand Syndar this morning," Pilos said. "I think the temple is in good hands."

"As good as when Mikolos Midelli sat on the high seat?" Vambran asked.

The young priest nodded. "I think so," he said. "There's a lot of work to be done, repairing the damage Lavant created, but I find Perolin the most forthright of the high priests. I've given him my support."

"And he's named you ambassador," Vambran pointed out.

Pilos nodded, looking slightly chagrined. "I can't avoid the politics altogether," he explained, "but I can at least try to make sure they always work to put the best side of the temple forward. We'll see if I'm successful."

"Still no sign of Lavant?" the lieutenant asked.

Pilos frowned. "None," he replied. "And none of our divinations are giving us anything, either. It's very strange."

There was an uncomfortable silence as everyone contemplated what that might mean. "So, what's happening to Lobra?" Vambran asked, steering the conversation in another direction.

"Ah," Pilos said, nodding. "Perolin doesn't want to make a civil issue out of her crimes, because the temple wants to distance itself from any link that might exist with the Generon. Ariskrit agrees, so long as Lobra is punished for her transgressions against the temple. She's going to be washing laundry in the bowels of the temple for a long while, I think."

"And Falagh?"

Pilos shook his head. "No one has seen or heard from him since the night of Sammardach. House Mestel isn't speaking of it, and Perolin believes they are dealing with it internally."

"I've heard how they 'deal' with that sort of problem," Vambran said. "We'll never hear about him again."

"We are returning to the forest," Edilus announced to no one in particular. "Finally," he added, sounding gruff.

"That's a good thing to hear," Horial replied. "I was beginning to worry you liked the city so much that you'd never leave, and your stench was starting to get to me."

Edilus glared at the mercenary for a moment, and Vambran tensed, wondering where that outburst had come from, but then he saw Horial's mouth twitch in the beginning of a smile, and next he noticed the humorous twinkle in the druid's eyes. As one, the two burst out laughing, clapping each other on the shoulders.

Vambran sighed and turned to Shinthala and Arbeenok. "It's too bad they hate each other so much," he quipped, "otherwise we might all be friends."

Shinthala chuckled, then gave Vambran a warm hug. "Be well," she said. "And come to the Nunwood soon."

"I will," he promised.

Arbeenok took Vambran's hand and grasped it tightly. "You are a good friend," he said. "We will see one another again soon."

Vambran cocked his head and asked, "Is that just hopeful thinking, or have you had a vision?" The alaghi smiled and stepped back. "Sooner than you think," he said.

When the druids departed, taking Pilos with them to begin establishing a relationship with the Waukeenar, Vambran was left alone with Adyan, Horial, and Grolo.

"So, have you made up your mind yet?" Adyan drawled.

Vambran sighed. "Everyone keeps asking me that."

Horial shrugged. "I won't follow another, Lieutenant," he said. "I can't imagine campaigning under anyone else."

Vambran eyed his three sergeants, all of whom were nodding in agreement. "All right," he said at last. "I'll stay in."

Horial whooped and Adyan just grinned, his scar pale in the sunlight. Grolo smacked Vambran on the back. "That's what I want to hear," the dwarf said. "Now, what do you boys say we go over to the Crying Claw and have ourselves a cool one?"

Vambran liked the sound of that.

...

Out in the Reach, aboard *Spinner*, a trade ship bound for Turmish, a paunchy wizard pushed his spectacles up on his nose and tried without success to keep the papers he was scrutinizing from fluttering in the sea breezes. After the third attempt to read a paragraph in a treatise on the magical uses of yuan-ti scales, he gave up in exasperation and stuffed the sheaf of parchment into a leather binder. He stood up from the coil of rope he had been using as a seat and glanced over the stern. The coastline of Chondath was receding in the distance.

About that time, another figure strolled onto

the deck of the ship. Darvin Blackcrown spotted the wizard and smiled to himself. He made his way over to the bespectacled fellow peering across the bow at the wave-tossed horizon and said, "Hello, Bartimus."

The wizard jumped, startled, and whirled around to face the assassin. "Where did you come from?" he stammered, fear plain in his eyes.

Darvin chuckled. "From Arrabar, the same as you," he said. "Don't worry, I'm not here to cause you trouble. I'm just on my way to Hlondeth to conduct some business on behalf of ... my employer." He wasn't sure Bartimus would want to know that Eles Wianar was sending him. "Where are you headed?"

"Away," Bartimus answered. "To someplace where I can conduct my research undisturbed. I don't ever want to see a House insignia again."

Darvin had to chuckle. "I don't blame you," he said. Then an idea hit him. "Perhaps you'd like to travel with me? Where I'm going, I could use your help. And if it works out, I can make it worth your while. Think about it—a fully stocked laboratory, all the research time you want, no one bothering you to scry on folks when you are busy. Sound good?"

"Maybe," Bartimus said. "What would you want in return?"

Darvin smiled. "Let's just get to Turmish and see how things go. If you are interested, we can talk details later."

The wizard nodded. "All right," he said.

"Good," Darvin said, smiling. Perhaps he could get back into his father's good graces more quickly than he had thought.

...

In a scrying chamber in the deepest recesses of the Generon, Eles Wianar stared at a stack of notes, piles of parchment with information on them that he had been carefully scribing for twelve years. In a burst of fury, he took hold of one of the piles and tossed it into a brazier, then sat and watched the corners curl up from the heat before the pile burst into flame.

Twelve years! What a waste, he thought.

There were so many people to blame. The Matrells, of course, had earned his enmity for all of their meddling. He would have to do something about that. He was certain of it. But that could wait. Let the fire burn down to embers, he thought. Then the time will be right.

But there were others, as well—incompetent fools to single out. He was not happy with Darvin. Sending him away, insisting that the boy visit Turmish, was a good thing for both of them. Kept apart, Darvin would learn the lesson of humility and redouble his efforts at accomplishing the goals Eles set before him. And Eles would be less tempted to disintegrate him in a fit of rage.

Grozier Talricci and Falagh Mestel weren't really at fault. If anything, they were only guilty of figuring out their roles in the whole affair a tad too soon. But that hadn't really affected the outcome. No, even with all of that, Rodolpho was the one most responsible for the breakdown in the plan. It couldn't have been helped, of course; Eles had hoped he could trust his cousin, but it was not something he could control. Not for twelve years, at any rate.

That just left Lavant. Fool priest, Eles thought. Got a little too power-hungry for his own good. And see what it cost him?

Eles turned toward a large mirror leaning against

a wall of his scrying chamber, one mirror among several. He spoke a command word, watched as the surface of the mirror rippled and glowed, and smiled as a fat, pale face appeared. "Hello, Lavant," the Shining Lord said.

"By Waukeen's mercy, please let me out of here!" the naked, obese priest pleaded. "I am at your service, ready to do anything you need! You know my powers are formidable, and they are at your command. Just please, please release me!"

Eles smiled. "In good time, Lavant, in good time," he said. "I'm formulating some new ideas, a new possibility for bringing Reth back into the fold of Chondath, where it belongs. I think you might be able to help me with my plans."

"Yes, oh, absolutely, my lord," Lavant said, looking hopeful. "Whatever I can do."

"Excellent," Wianar replied. "I'm so happy to see your enthusiasm. I should be ready for your services in about twelve years."

As Lavant screamed, Eles Wianar uttered the command that closed the window on the priest's cell, sending him back to the darkness.

ED GREENWOOD

THE CREATOR OF THE FORGOTTEN REALMS WORLD

BRINGS YOU THE STORY OF
SHANDRIL OF HIGHMOON

SHANDRIL'S SAGA

SPELLFIRE
Book I

Powerful enough to lay low a dragon or heal a wounded warrior, spellfire is the most sought after power in all of Faerûn. And it is in the reluctant hand of Shandril of Highmoon, a young, orphaned kitchen-lass.

CROWN OF FIRE
Book II

Shandril has grown to become one of the most powerful magic-users in the land. The powerful Cult of the Dragon and the evil Zhentarim want her spellfire, and they will kill whoever they must to possess it.

HAND OF FIRE
Book III

Shandril has spellfire, a weapon capable of destroying the world, and now she's fleeing for her life across Faerûn, searching for somewhere to hide. Her last desperate hope is to take refuge in the sheltered city of Silverymoon. If she can make it.

www.wizards.com

NEW YORK TIMES BESTSELLING SERIES

R.A. SALVATORE'S
WAR OF THE SPIDER QUEEN

The epic saga of the dark elves concludes!

EXTINCTION
Book IV

LISA SMEDMAN

For even a small group of drow, trust is the rarest commodity of all.
When the expedition prepares for a return to the Abyss, what little
trust there is crumbles under a rival goddess's hand.

ANNIHILATION
Book V

PHILIP ATHANS

Old alliances have been broken, and new bonds have been formed.
While some finally embark for the Abyss itself, other stay behind to
serve a new mistress—a goddess with plans of her own.

RESURRECTION
Book VI

PAUL S. KEMP

The Spider Queen has been asleep for a long time, leaving the
Underdark to suffer war and ruin. But if she finally returns, will
things get better...or worse?

www.wizards.com

NEW TALES FROM FORGOTTEN REALMS CREATOR
ED GREENWOOD

THE BEST OF THE REALMS
Book II

This new anthology of short stories by Ed Greenwood, creator of the
FORGOTTEN REALMS Campaign Setting, features many old and well-loved
classics as well as three brand new stories of high-spirited adventure.

CITY OF SPLENDORS
A Waterdeep Novel

ED GREENWOOD AND ELAINE CUNNINGHAM

In the streets of Waterdeep, conspiracies run like water through the
gutters, bubbling beneath the seeming calm of the city's life. As a band of
young, foppish lords discovers there is a dark side to the city they all love,
a sinister mage and his son seek to create perverted creatures to further
their twisted ends. And across it all sprawls the great city itself: brawling,
drinking, laughing, living life to the fullest. Even in the face of death.

SILVERFALL
Stories of the Seven Sisters

This paperback edition of *Silverfall: Stories of the Seven Sisters*, by the creator
of the FORGOTTEN REALMS Campaign Setting, features seven stories of
seven sisters illustrated by seven beautiful pages of interior art by John Foster.

ELMINSTER'S DAUGHTER
The Elminster Series

All her life, Narnra of Waterdeep has wondered who her father is. Now
she has discovered that it is no less a person than Elminster of Shadowdale,
mightiest mage in all Faerûn. And her anger is as boundless as his power.

www.wizards.com